NO WOMAN LEFT BEHIND

Previously published Worldwide Mystery titles by
JULIE MOFFETT

NO ONE LIVES TWICE
NO TEST FOR THE WICKED

NO WOMAN LEFT BEHIND

JULIE MOFFETT

W❖RLDWIDE®

TORONTO • NEW YORK • LONDON
AMSTERDAM • PARIS • SYDNEY • HAMBURG
STOCKHOLM • ATHENS • TOKYO • MILAN
MADRID • WARSAW • BUDAPEST • AUCKLAND

Recycling programs
for this product may
not exist in your area.

No Woman Left Behind

A Worldwide Mystery/May 2016

First published by Carina Press.

ISBN-13: 978-0-373-26992-1

Copyright © 2015 by Julie Moffett

Printed in U.S.A.

Acknowledgments

One of my favorite parts of writing about Lexi and the gang is working with my fantabulous Carina Press editor, Alissa Davis. She has remarkable talent and knows just how to motivate me to push even harder to make the story just right. I greatly value her thoughts and insight on the story arcs and character development. Her understanding of all that is Lexi is especially unique and valued because she's been with me since *No One Lives Twice*, the first book in the series. Her efforts on this book, and the series in general, cannot be understated. I'm so glad we're a team, Alissa!

I would also be remiss if I did not mention the extraordinary assistance given to me on this book by my older brother Brad. He brainstormed, helped me plan the military missions, and reviewed the text and dialogue to make sure I got every detail just right. He was not only extremely supportive and gracious in sharing his knowledge, but brilliant with his critiques and observations as an excellent writer himself.

My father, Colonel William F. Moffett (Lexi's biggest fan!), also read the manuscript, offering suggestions to make the action tighter and more exciting. My mother, Donna B. Moffett, and sister, Sandy Parks, gave me additional emotional insights from a military family perspective (to add to my own experiences as a military brat), and also reviewed the novel for consistency and plot threads. They are absolutely the best beta readers EVER!

As much as I appreciate their assistance, any mistakes in the novel are on me alone. Hope you enjoy the story!

~Julie

"Heroes are ordinary people who make themselves
extraordinary."

~Unknown

*No Woman Left Behind is dedicated to my family, nearly
all of which are part of the US military. May your sac-
rifices, and those of your families, never be forgotten.
Much love to all of you.*

Colonel William F. Moffett (Ret.)
Major Willie B. Craig (Ret.)
Lt. Colonel Bradley L. Moffett (Ret.)
Colonel Scott E. Parks (Ret.)
Captain William Parks
Captain Christopher Parks
Captain Katy Moffett

ONE

FOR A GEEK girl like me, having a boyfriend is a lot like texting. They both require precise input and appropriate response. Unfortunately, I'm not good at properly expressing my feelings in person, let alone in a text message. Emoticons scare me. I mean, what exactly is a pig in high heels or a smiling cactus supposed to signify? It's totally outside the scope of a geek girl's knowledge. Plus, no matter how hard I try, it all seems to go south anyway because I usually end up in autocorrect hell.

Not that I've ever had to worry about texting, or a boyfriend, or texting a boyfriend, until now. My name is Lexi Carmichael and my teen crush was a comic book figure. Computer genius and circuit engineer Ace Argento (aka Code Man) was the absolute best. He didn't count on guns or bombs to save the day, but relied on his superior intellect to outwit Byte Bandit and stop his fictional computer virus from infecting the internet. Given that Ace was perpetually unavailable, not to mention fictional, I figured I'd never have to worry about navigating relationship dynamics. So, instead of hanging out at the mall with girlfriends and talking about guys, I hung out in chat rooms and discussed the latest SDN controllers and bypass protocols. My social life was completely virtual, and I preferred it that way.

Then, somehow, at the age of twenty-five, I stumbled into my first real relationship. In a series of events that surprised everyone—but especially me—I finally graduated from a comic book crush to a flesh-and-blood boyfriend. It turns out there are significant perks to having a real boyfriend, including delicious home-cooked Italian food, a guy who doesn't fall asleep when I start talking about enterprise-level security metrics and some totally excellent I-didn't-know-you-could-do-that-on-the-dining-room-table sex. Yep, being a girlfriend does have its rewards. Except now that my parents have caught wind of the fact I'm no longer single, they're pressuring me to bring said boyfriend over for an evening of dinner and conversation.

That's worrisome because my father is an attorney for an exclusive, high-priced firm in Georgetown. His masterful interrogation skills could make the leader of North Korea confess to wearing woman's underwear…even if he didn't. My mother is a former Virginia beauty queen who sits on the boards of several national charities. She has long despaired at my lack of social skills and, to my dismay, has appointed herself the task of finding me a husband. They're pretty good parents, and they're both proud of my position as the Director of Information Security at a cyberintelligence firm, but they haven't ever been quite sure how to handle me.

My childhood love of Code Man and disdain for dolls and the color pink might not have been that big of a deal, except I'm the only girl in our family. I have two older brothers—Rock, who is an investigative reporter for the *Washington Post*, and Beau, who is a detective with the Baltimore PD. As a result, my mom somewhat desperately pinned all her girly hopes and dreams on me. It didn't happen the way she envisioned, but we're trying to work things out.

Naturally all of that worried me in terms of bringing

home my very first boyfriend. In addition to the statistically high chance my parents would make embarrassing comments and drag out pictures of me sitting naked in front of a keyboard when I was two, I worried my mother might start planning the wedding right away. For ten years or so she has despaired over my lack of male attention. Now that I actually *have* a boyfriend, she has spent the last couple of weeks in a full-court press to meet him. I know what she wants—she wants to get to know him really well. Problem is, *I'm* still getting to know him, and I haven't made much progress.

See, Slash, my boyfriend, is not an ordinary guy. He's a hacker, a super-secret agent for the NSA, and a possible member of the Vatican's secret service, which technically doesn't even exist. He's Italian-American, speaks multiple languages, and, in addition to his gig with the NSA, has a business on the side running simulation-based training for the government. There are lots of things I don't know about him, including how *he* will react to my parents, but at least he has made it abundantly clear how he feels about me.

After careful consultation with Slash, a date for a dinner meeting at my parents' house was agreed upon. Although I'd had several days to prepare, I was still a mental wreck by the time Slash knocked on my door.

I opened it, and Slash stood there, looking amazing and smiling at me like there was nothing in the world he'd rather be doing than picking me up to go meet my parents. He was dressed in a light blue dress shirt, a gray sports coat and black slacks and shoes. His dark shoulder-length hair had been slicked behind his ears. I predicted Dad would approve of the clothes, but loathe the long hair. I just hoped he wouldn't say so aloud.

Before I could greet Slash, he'd swept me into his arms, kissing me lightly on the mouth.

"You look beautiful, *cara*. Royal blue is a lovely color on you."

I pulled away, then tucked a strand of loose brown hair behind my ear. "I wasn't sure about the color. Basia sent me a photo of the dress and I ordered it online."

Basia is my best friend and, in my opinion, an expert on all things to do with social interaction and fashion. She was currently in Hollywood taking my place on a reality TV show I'd gotten involved with while on another case, but she was never too busy to help me pick out any piece of clothing that wasn't a T-shirt.

"It's perfect. Are you ready?"

Was that a trick question? Of course I wasn't ready. I'd never be ready.

"Actually, I think I might throw up."

He stepped into my apartment and leaned against the wall, watching me with amused brown eyes.

He thought this was funny, but he had no idea what he was up against. "Look, Slash, I don't know if I can go through with this."

He reached out and touched my cheek. "There is absolutely nothing they can say or do that will change my feelings for you."

"You say that now, but you haven't met my parents."

"I'm pretty sure I can handle whatever happens. Trust me, I've survived a lot of dangerous situations. I feel like I can make it through dinner without spilling soup on your mother."

He smiled, waiting for me to share in the joke. When I couldn't muster a smile, he drew me into his arms and held me close, stroking my hair. "You're truly worried about this evening—even more so than I'd anticipated. Can you tell me what's wrong?"

"It's just that you meeting my parents…it seems so significant."

He released me, searching my expression. "How?"

"Well, it makes us official."

"You wish for our relationship to remain unofficial?"

"No. That's not what I mean. It's just that introducing you to my parents is scarier than I expected. Once my mother meets you and confirms you're real, the whole world will know."

He spread his hands. "So?"

"So, there will be a hundred questions. Relatives will call to congratulate me. My brothers will bug me. My grandparents will want to fly out to meet you. It will be a national Carmichael holiday because Lexi brought a boyfriend home, and I'm not sure I'm ready for that. I don't even know what to tell my parents about you. They'll want actual details. What can I tell them?"

"Just keep it simple."

"*Simple* is not in my parents' vocabulary."

"You can tell them I work at the NSA."

"I already told them that."

"I was born in Italy."

"Not helpful. What if my father makes a Godfather connection?"

He laughed. "Relax, *cara*. Every nuance doesn't have to be explored."

"You don't know my family."

He reached out and touched my shoulder, and I could feel the heat of his hand through my dress. "We can cancel if you want. I don't want you to feel rushed."

I appreciated that he cared enough to say it. "No, it's not that. I don't feel rushed. It's just another big emotional step for me, dealing with all the inevitable questions from family and friends. I've been taking a lot of steps in that direction lately and it's all shaky ground for me."

"Are you sure it's not something else?"

"Well, okay." I fidgeted anxiously. "I wasn't going to say it, but you have a right to know. There's something else that's worrying me."

"And that might be?" He kept his eyes on me as he leaned against the wall again and crossed his arms over his chest.

I hesitated, then blurted it out. "Sex."

TWO

HE BLINKED. "SEX?"

"Yes. My dad is going to take one look at us and know we're having sex."

I'd never seen Slash go pale like that before. Guess he hadn't seen that one coming.

"And he will know this exactly how?"

He looked like he needed comforting, so I patted his shoulder. "I know you've probably had significant training in withstanding interrogation, but my dad is the best lawyer in DC. He's going to take one look at us and know everything, including that innovative maneuver you did to me on the kitchen table last Thursday. Then he'll do his famous stare, and we'll both be struck by this insane desire to confess every secret we've ever had. I've run a statistical analysis attempting to predict his response after hearing about the kitchen table thing, and a vast majority of the scenarios did not end well."

I waited for him to say something, but he didn't. "Well, what do you think?" I prodded.

"I'm speechless at the moment."

I played with the folds of my dress. "See, I've been reading up on human socio-somatic interplay during a first meeting of a male suitor and the father of the female in question. I decided it would be best to come at this gathering from a purely scientific angle."

"You didn't."

Did he know me at all? "Of course, I did. What I've discovered is that bringing a male suitor home can be a dangerous interaction on many levels."

Slash paused. "Define *dangerous*."

"Maybe we should sit down for a moment." I waved toward the couch.

"Maybe we should."

I perched as carefully as possible on the edge of the cushion in my new dress. Slash took a seat next to me, brushing his knee against mine.

"Well, technically my dad is the alpha male of the Carmichael pack," I continued. "While he might seem all polite and agreeable on the outside, beneath his expensive shirt and tie he could be bristling. By wooing his daughter, you're openly threatening his alpha status. After all, his only female offspring, who has relied on him for protection and guidance, intends to leave him to run around with a younger, virile alpha male."

He grinned. "Virile?"

"Yes. Don't distract me. Your scent is on me."

He opened his mouth and then shut it without saying a word.

"Anyway, our scents are co-mingled because we've had sexual relations. That's an important development because, until you came along, my father has been the main male figure in my life. Theoretically I listen to him and look to him for guidance and security. Now you, a young and unknown element, have come into the picture. It's going to be a rough transition for him. I'm nearly certain he's going to dislike you. A lot."

Suddenly Slash wasn't looking so confident, and I still hadn't finished. This didn't bode well for the dinner. Regardless, I owed it to him to make sure he fully understood the situation.

"My mother, on the other hand, will spend at least five minutes studying your butt. She won't be checking you out—she's attempting to guess what size tuxedo pants you'll need for our wedding. We could end up engaged by the time we finish the second course. *This* is what you're getting into when you meet my parents. *That's* why I'm panicking."

I gave him a moment to digest that. When he still didn't speak, I sighed.

"Okay, my first instinct was correct. We should definitely call and cancel. I'll tell them one of us is experiencing gastrointestinal distress. Do you want it to be you or me?"

He leaned forward, resting a hand on my back. "I appreciate the warning, *cara*. Nonetheless, I intend to risk it. I'll try to handle things with your parents delicately."

"Easy for you to say, Mr. I-Never-Get-Ruffled."

"Why do you say that? I get ruffled all the time, especially around you. In fact, I'm completely ruffled right now."

"Really?"

"Really. It's a big step for me, too, but I'm willing to accept your dad's posturing *and* your mother's review of my posterior if it means we can stay together."

I searched his face. "I feel a lot better knowing you're so calm about this."

"After that thoroughly scientific, not to mention daunting, explanation, I'd better not bring your attention to my now-sweaty palms."

I looked down at our joined hands. "You're nervous?"

"A little. I'm not above admitting I want to make a

good impression on your parents. You're important to me, so by extension, they're important as well."

"Wow. For some reason, knowing you're nervous actually makes me feel better. That makes no logical sense."

He squeezed my hand. "So, do you want to do this or not?"

I did a mental checklist of the pros and cons of having him meet my parents, and then put the list away. For once in my life, I had a feeling I'd make a better decision if I relied on emotion than prediction.

"Yes, I do, Slash. I really want you to meet my parents. If you're game, I'm game. Let's do this."

Slash stood and helped me put on my coat. We held hands as we walked to his SUV. The chilly January air froze my ears. I shivered, wishing I'd thought to wear a hat.

Slash opened the car door for me. Before climbing in, I looked up and down the street. "Where's the FBI?"

Slash was considered a national asset because of his extensive knowledge of the nation's most sensitive computer systems, including the president's. He was followed 24/7 by the FBI as part of a special security protocol not that different from the Secret Service. We sometimes joked about it, but I knew it wasn't easy for him to be followed all the time.

He pointed to a dark sedan beneath a streetlight. It had its lights out, but the engine was running. A plume of smoke rose from the exhaust pipe.

"I've instructed them to keep a low profile so the car won't be visible from your parents' house."

Good. I totally didn't want to freak out my parents. I'd told them Slash worked on computers at the NSA. Given that I'd worked there before I moved into my new position at X-Corp, my parents would understand that. Maybe they wouldn't ask how we'd met. There was no way I could tell them I'd woken up in the middle of the night to find Slash in my bedroom after he'd broken in to discover what I knew about a case he'd been working on.

Slash pulled out of the parking lot and I started talking to take my mind off the impending meeting.

"Basia called me today. She finally had time to catch me up on her vacation in Greece. She said she had an amazing time at the villa with Xavier."

Basia had recently started dating Xavier Zimmerman, who was one half of the genius Zimmerman twins and brother to my other best friend, legendary cyber wizard Elvis Zimmerman. The twins had rented a villa for three weeks. She'd flown to Greece for a weeklong Christmas vacation with Xavier. Elvis had waited until she left before flying over to join his brother.

Slash kept his eyes on the road. "I'm glad."

"Me, too, I guess. Seems like they're going strong."

Secretly I was worried Basia might dump Xavier. Although I adored my best friend, she was a bit of a free spirit whereas Xavier's social skills were about on par with mine. Poor guy, if it happened he would never see it coming. He was crazy about her.

"Did Elvis leave for Greece yet?" Slash asked.

Just hearing his name made me tense up. Elvis and I were going through a sort of…friendship evolution. Now that we were both in relationships, things had begun to change between us, though I'd stupidly thought we could maintain the status quo. As I understand more about human social relationships and experience them for myself, I'm beginning to see that people and relationships can't ever stay the same. But our evolving friendship was still tender ground for me. I was terrified of losing Elvis as a friend, but I wasn't sure how to keep him as one.

"Yeah, he left a few days ago," I said. "He loves the beach, so he's probably having a great time."

Elvis and I had met on a beach when I'd been slammed into him by a giant wave. He'd tried to help me up, but I'd stumbled and accidentally yanked his bathing suit down to his ankles. It hadn't been funny then, but thinking about it now made me smile.

My silence caused Slash to pick up the conversation. He began talking about a new security protocol he'd been working on. He was trying to help me relax, and I appreciated it.

Finding a parking spot near my parents' townhouse in Georgetown was always a pain, but by some miracle Slash found curb space big enough for his SUV. No room for the FBI sedan, so they kept circling.

After he'd parked, Slash pulled some flowers and wine from the back seat. Arm-in-arm, we approached the front door. Anxiety swept through me. It wasn't too late to pretend I'd gotten food poisoning, was it?

I opened my mouth to suggest it, but it was too late. Slash had already pressed the doorbell.

My mom threw open the door before the first chime ended. She looked lovely as always, dressed in a soft green wrap dress and a diamond necklace that nearly blinded me. She immediately enveloped me in a hug, and I got a whiff of her expensive perfume.

"Oh, Lexi, darling, it's so good to see you. I've missed you."

She let go of me and turned to Slash, holding out her hand. "Hello. I'm Clarissa Carmichael. You must be Slash. It's delightful to meet you at last."

"It's a pleasure to meet you, too." He took her hand

and kissed it. My mom beamed as he handed her the flowers and wine.

"Oh, they are lovely. Thank you so much. Please do come in."

As Slash stepped across the threshold, my mom smiled at me and then fanned herself behind his back before giving me an enthusiastic thumbs-up.

Alarm bells clanged in my head. Slash was already making too good of an impression. I needed to find a way to let him know he needed to dial back the charm before my mother started suggesting baby names.

I followed Slash inside, and it felt nice to be out of the cold air. He helped me out of my jacket and I showed him where to hang our coats.

My mom disappeared into the dining room, calling out, "What can I get you to drink?"

The dining room was ablaze with the light from the chandelier and several candles placed in crystal candelabras on the table. My mom had brought out her finest china and crystal, the stuff she only used when we were entertaining US senators or any of Washington's top power couples. She was at the sidebar buffet, fussing with the flowers Slash had given her and placing them into one of her vases.

"Water for me," I said, following her. I wanted to keep a perfectly clear head tonight so I could stay on my guard.

"You will not have water. Your father bought some perfectly lovely wine. I've already poured a glass for you."

Figures. She would take every advantage she could. Get me tipsy and then press her advantage to get details about my love life when my thinking was muddled. She motioned with her head to my usual spot at the table.

Sighing, I picked up my wineglass from the table and looked over at Slash. "Do you want some, too?"

"I do. Thank you."

Before I could pour it, he leaned over the table and picked up the open wine bottle, pouring some into an empty glass. He lifted his glass to me. We clinked them, taking a sip at the same time. He looked into my eyes and smiled, which immediately calmed me. So far, he was taking this whole meet-the-parents thing a lot better than I was.

My mother set the pretty purple orchids in the center of the table, then stepped back to admire them. "Perfect. You have a good eye for flowers, Slash."

"I'm glad you like them."

She turned to give me a closer perusal. "What a lovely dress, darling. It looks like a Miraka Chan design. Did you pick that out by yourself?"

"Of course not. Basia sent me a link and I ordered it online."

"Oh." Her disappointment was visible.

Guilt reared its ugly head. Mom had always hoped I'd learn to love shopping so that we could go on mother-daughter shopping excursions to her favorite, expensive boutiques. Unfortunately, I couldn't tell a Miraka Chan dress from a sewed-in-my-basement special. In fact, the thought of learning how to do so filled me with such dread that I actually shuddered.

"Well, it still looks very nice."

"Thanks, Mom." I glanced around, hoping to change the topic, and quick. "Where's Dad?"

She motioned to the living room. "He's in there. Tell him dinner is just about ready. I need to check with Sasha about our first course."

I headed for the living room with Slash following.

My dad sat in his favorite oversized chair, facing the fire blazing in the hearth. He was bent over the coffee table, working on something.

"Dad?" My eyes widened when I saw what he was doing.

He looked up at me. "Oh, hello, Lexi. Good to see you, sweetheart."

Things were way worse than I expected.

"Dad…is that a gun?"

THREE

My DAD SNAPPED the chamber shut and stood, still holding it. "It sure is."

He turned toward us, a flash of surprise crossing his face when he saw Slash. It occurred to me when I told Dad Slash worked with computers, he might have pictured a pale, bespectacled scrawny kid. I tried to suppress a giggle, but one slipped out anyway.

Dad turned his laser gaze on me. I pressed my lips together, straightened my posture and tried desperately not to think about the kitchen table thing lest it show on my face.

"Lexi, introduce me to the young man there."

"Ah, Dad, this is Slash. Slash, this is my father, Winston Carmichael."

Slash held out a hand. "It's a pleasure to meet you, sir."

My dad took Slash's hand and shook it. Hard. For a moment we all stared at each other awkwardly.

I spoke first. "Dad, what are you doing with a gun? I didn't even know you owned one."

"Of course I own a gun. I know how to use it, too."

Before I could reply, my mother called out for Slash, asking him if he could reach something for her on the top shelf of the buffet. Slash excused himself and left to help her.

When he was gone, I glared at my dad, lowering my voice to a whisper. "What are you doing? A gun? That is so cliché, not to mention sexist and insulting. I can take care of myself."

My dad glared back. "I know you can. But there's no harm in letting the boy know we've got your back."

"He's not a boy. He's a man. Stop it already. You'd better be on your best behavior tonight."

"Your insinuations wound me."

"There's no insinuation. You're holding a loaded gun! Promise me you'll keep the dinner conversation light, friendly and relaxing. No more guns. And no verbal bullets either."

"Agreed, but I reserve my fatherly rights of getting to know him better. If I sense deception, all bets are off."

"There is no deception."

"Excellent. Then there won't be a problem, will there?"

Mom called out to us. "Lexi, Winston, come to the dining room, please. Sasha is getting ready to serve the first course."

Dad set the gun on the coffee table, straightened his tie and offered me his arm. Nerves jangling, I took it and we walked to the dining room. My dad's assurances only made me more anxious. I took a series of shallow breaths and began to calculate how much time we had to stay before we would be able to leave without insulting my parents too much.

I slid into the seat next to Slash and had just put the napkin on my lap when Sasha came out of the kitchen holding two bowls of steaming soup.

"Lexi," he said with delight when he saw me. He carefully placed one of the bowls in front of my mother and then me. He kissed the top of my head as he bent over me.

"Hey, Sasha. It's good to see you. Can't wait to taste whatever you made."

"It's corn chowder, one of your favorites. Wild salmon with asparagus is the main course."

I'd always liked his Russian accent. He'd been a nuclear scientist in the Soviet Union, but now he was living his dream life as a private chef. In high school, I used to sit at the marble counter in the kitchen and he'd help me with my physics homework while he whipped up Beef Borscht.

"It's been too long since you came to dinner," he scolded me. "By the way, I watched every episode of you on that geeky television show. Who knew you'd be a star?"

My cheeks heated. "Well, I'm just glad my television stint is over. Hollywood is not for me."

He turned to Slash. "So, this is the boy you've brought home?"

Slash stood and shook hands. "Pleasure to meet you. Lexi has spoken often of you."

Sasha narrowed his eyes. "Lexi says you know computers and math. Is that true?"

"More or less. I understand you were a nuclear physicist in Russia."

"It was the Soviet Union back then," I interjected. "Sasha studied the quark-gluon plasma of nuclear matter."

My mother pressed her napkin to her lips. "Really? Can we speak English, please?"

Slash grinned. "Ah, quark soup—the immediate phase of quantum chromodynamics or the state the universe is believed to be in shortly after the Big Bang. It's a pretty exciting field."

Sasha raised an eyebrow. "So, you do know physics."

"A bit."

"Good enough. Well, you be careful with our girl, okay?"

"Okay."

Sasha leaned over close to me and whispered, "He's smart *and* manly. Nice catch."

I rolled my eyes as he disappeared back into the kitchen. "You passed the test," I told Slash. "Be prepared to listen to the latest developments in quantum theory while watching him make his specialty, Chicken Kiev."

"I look forward to it."

Sasha returned with bowls for Slash and my dad. We all started to eat in silence, then my mom asked her first question.

"So, Slash, what do you do for a living? Lexi said something about computers at the NSA, but she wasn't very specific."

Slash set his spoon down. "It's pretty routine stuff. Networks, firewalls, software. The usual."

What Slash did was so far from routine I almost laughed. Instead, I watched my mother's expression. Not being a tech head, she wasn't sure how to probe for more information after that. But I could tell she was still curious.

Fortunately for her, my dad picked up the slack. "You make a decent living at that computer stuff?"

Slash nodded. "I do, but it doesn't mean I'm not on the lookout for new investments."

"Investments?" My dad lifted his napkin and wiped a corner of his mouth. "Do you gamble?"

"Dad!"

Slash put a hand on my arm. "No, sir. No gambling. Not my style."

My dad leaned over his soup. "So what *is* your style?"

"Honest, hard work. Smart investments."

"What kind of investments?"

"Mostly technological ones. I feel the most comfortable with them."

"Because you're into computers."

"That's part of it."

Whether it was the weird exchange of testosterone or my extreme nervousness, I'd started to sweat. I held up the basket of bread. "Bread, anyone?"

Slash declined, but my dad took a piece of bread and tore it apart in his hands, chewing slowly. "So, I take it that Slash is a nickname?"

"It is. For reasons connected to my current position, I'm unable to provide my birth name at this time. I could give you a false one, but I'd rather not. Most people who know me well call me Slash."

My father studied him. "You do realize that not knowing your real name doesn't sit well with me, young man."

"I agree it's out of the ordinary, sir. Unfortunately, I'm bound by the rules of my employer."

I shifted nervously in my chair. "Forget it, Dad. He works at the NSA. You know how that goes."

"You worked at the NSA and you could tell people your real name."

"I didn't work in the same position as Slash. It's only because I worked there that he even feels comfortable telling you it's his place of employment. The secrecy thing is all in the name of national security. Can we stop the interrogation?"

"It's not an interrogation. I'm just getting to know him better."

"It's okay," Slash said. "I don't mind."

I *really* wished he wouldn't have said that. My dad— now feeling he was completely within his rights—pressed on after another spoonful of chowder.

"Where did you go to school, Slash?"

"Undergraduate or graduate?"

I interrupted. "Slash is from Italy."

"You're a foreigner?" my mom asked, looking up from her soup in surprise. "I mean, you don't have an accent."

"I was born in Italy and attended the Sapienza University of Rome for both of my degrees. I'm an American citizen now."

Wow. I hadn't known that Slash had two degrees. I didn't even know what the degrees were in. Jeez. Serious girlfriend fail.

"I guess that means you speak Italian." My mom seemed delighted with the prospect.

"*Si.*" He took a sip of his wine.

"He can cook, too," I offered. "I think all Italians must be born with the cooking gene."

My father's eyebrows shot up. Uh oh. I'd definitely said something wrong.

"He cooks for you? Does that mean you're already living together?"

"Dad!"

"Winston!"

My dad pushed his bowl aside. "It's a legitimate question, so we might as well get it off the table. I admit I'm being a bit overprotective, but Lexi has never brought anyone home before. She's one of the smartest people I know, but she's inexperienced. I don't want you to take advantage of that. Therefore, I'd like to know up-front—man-to-man—what are your intentions toward my daughter?"

"Wait—what?" I leaped to my feet, nearly spilling my wine. "Oh my God. Did you really just ask that?"

He didn't have time to answer, because two things happened almost simultaneously: something flew past my ear and thudded into the wall behind my dad, just as the lights in the house went out.

Before I could even register what had happened, Slash shouted, "Get down!" and tackled me with the force of a football lineman.

FOUR

I WENT DOWN HARD, my arm tangling in the tablecloth. As I fell, the contents of the table came with me—china, crystal, flowers and food. I hit the floor with a jarring thud. Mom screamed and my dad shouted something I couldn't understand.

"Stay down," Slash ordered. "Someone is shooting at us from outside." He rolled off me and came to a crouch. "Everyone keep still."

I shook off my daze and pushed up on my elbow. I could see Slash illuminated by the glow of the streetlight outside. He was making his way toward the front door in a low crouch, a gun in his hand. He must have had his shoulder holster on under his jacket.

There was a noise at the kitchen door and Sasha walked into the dining room. "What's happening? Who turned off the lights?"

"Get down," we all shouted at the same time.

Without a word of protest, Sasha dropped. Good reflexes born from the old Soviet era, I guess.

"What's going on?" my dad hissed at me.

My mom's favorite glass vase exploded in one corner of the room. "I don't know. Someone is shooting at us. Just stay down, okay, Dad?"

"What? Why?"

"I have no idea."

"What's Slash doing?"

"Saving us, I hope."

Slash murmured something into a cell phone. He was by the front door in a protective crouch. Where the heck were the FBI agents who were supposed to be watching him? I hoped they weren't on a bathroom break or something.

I could hear my mom's sobs, so I got up on my knees and began crawling. As I moved toward her, I glanced at the kitchen and saw the door move slightly.

"Slash!" I screamed, just as a man dressed in black opened the door and fired, strangely, at the chandelier.

I rolled under the table. Crystal shards rained down on me, but I barely felt them because I was already covered in all the food and crap from the table. Slash must have returned fire because I heard a thud and the intruder ducked back into the kitchen. My mom started shrieking. Slash dashed across the room.

"Get them out of here," Slash shouted at me as he kicked open the kitchen door and went in low, disappearing from sight.

I scrambled out from under the table, shaking something wet and gooey from my cheek. I'd lost a shoe and my heart was pounding so hard I thought I might pass out. My eyes had adjusted to the dim light and I saw the shape of my mom huddled against the wall. My dad was sitting in front of her protectively. Sasha still lay motionless on the floor.

"Come on," I said, grabbing my mom's hand. "Sasha, get up. Now. Everyone follow me."

Sasha crawled forward and stood in a crouch, bracing himself against the wall.

"Stay low," I warned them.

To their credit, my mom and dad came to their feet without a protest. I debated taking them into the living room where I could retrieve Dad's gun, but I wasn't sure it was actually loaded and the area was way too open and dangerous with multiple hiding places. Instead I led them down the opposing hallway toward Dad's study.

The house remained ominously quiet and dark. I couldn't hear the intruder or Slash. I carefully opened the study door. After a quick peek into the room, I ushered them in, hoping no one was in there. I couldn't see a darn thing.

"Get in the closet," I whispered, closing the study door behind me. No lock, so I couldn't secure it.

Everyone crowded in the closet except me. I started to close the closet door without getting in.

"What are you doing?" my dad said, grabbing my hand.

"I'm staying out here. I'll hide behind the chair. If the intruder goes for the closet first, I can take him from behind."

My dad's mouth fell open. "What?"

"Just get in and be quiet. I'll be okay." I pushed him in, still protesting, and clicked the door shut. Snatching the heavy crystal paperweight off his desk, I crouched behind one of the stuffed chairs perpendicular to his desk with a full view of both the study and closet doors.

I heard sirens in the distance and nearly cried in relief. It was about freaking time.

I hoped I was doing the right thing. My initial instinct was to go look for Slash to see if I could help, but intellectually I knew that was a dumb thing to do. First, I had no idea if Slash and the intruder were even still in the house. I hadn't heard a door open or slam, but that didn't mean anything certain. They could still be out there stalking each other. I didn't need to get in the middle of that.

Second, if they *were* still in the house somewhere, the odds were high of me getting shot by either the intruder or Slash if I went creeping around the house trying to find them.

Third, there wasn't much I could do to help Slash anyway without a weapon. I could retrieve my dad's gun, but if my dad saw me with it, he'd try to wrestle it away from me. All I needed was for my dad to shoot himself trying to protect me.

No, I had to use the paperweight as a weapon. If the intruder entered and went for the closet—a statistically high probability given that I could hear my mom sniffling from out here—I could draw attention away from my folks.

The sirens became louder and I figured we were minutes, if not seconds, from rescue.

Suddenly, the door to the study opened. Quietly, silently. My breath froze in my throat. I could see the silhouette of a man creeping through the doorway. He had a gun at the ready. It definitely wasn't Slash. He was thicker and his shape was different. I pushed my fear aside. I had to focus.

The man paused and then, hearing the soft noises from the closet, headed toward it.

I clenched my fist around the paperweight. It seemed pathetically small now in comparison to a gun, but I wasn't going to stand by and watch him shoot my family. The man stood to the side of the closet door, reached forward and put his hand on the door handle.

I spent a precious two seconds calculating the weight of the paperweight, the speed at which I would throw it, and the distance before leaping up and hurling it directly at his head.

I missed. By a mile. So much for two-second calculations under extreme duress.

The paperweight crashed into the closet door and fell

harmlessly to the floor. I was *so* not going to be hired by the National Baseball League any time soon.

The intruder turned to shoot at me. Thankfully, two things happened to disturb his aim: first, I was already in mid-jump over the chair toward the desk, and second, my dad flung open the closet door at that exact moment, hitting the arm holding the gun. The bullet hit the ceiling as I landed hard on the other side of the chair, rolling quickly to my feet. My dad and Sasha were already struggling with the intruder. Grunts filled the room as I jumped into the fray, fists swinging. I had no idea where the gun had gone or whether the intruder still had it.

"Hey, hey. Stop. Stop it."

The voice was familiar. We all froze. My dad and Sasha immediately slid off him. My mom took a step out of the closet.

The intruder sat up, rubbing his jaw. "What the hell is going on here?"

I sat back on my heels, staring at him in disbelief.

It was my brother Beau.

FIVE

"Beau?" I couldn't believe my eyes.

Beau is the middle child, sandwiched between our brother Rock and me. I stared at him. "What are *you* doing here?"

"I was on my way over to visit Mom and Dad when I heard a call on my car scanner that shots were fired at this address. I hightailed my ass those last two blocks with my heart in my throat. I came in through the side door with my key. I heard voices in the study, so that's where I started."

Before I could say anything, two shadowy figures appeared in the doorway. "Police. Everyone on the floor with your hands locked behind your heads. Now."

We all complied instantly. The policeman had pulled out a flashlight was pointing it at us. My dad started talking.

"My name is Winston Carmichael. I'm an attorney. This is my home. The individuals in this room are my wife, children and house staff. Someone was shooting at us."

More police entered the room, waving flashlights around and making me dizzy. "The house is clear."

My brother lifted his head from the floor. "I'm Detective Beau Carmichael with the city-wide robbery unit at the BPD. My service weapon is on the floor next to the chair. It's been discharged. My badge is in my pocket."

A policeman discovered Beau's gun in front of one of

the bookshelves. He slipped on a pair of rubber gloves and bagged the weapon.

"I understand, Detective. But you know I have to cuff you until we can get this sorted this out. Is everyone okay?"

"I think so," Beau answered. "Lexi, are you good?"

"*Good* is a relative term. But thankfully I'm uninjured."

My mom, dad and Sasha confirmed they were all fine.

"Okay, everyone be calm and cooperate," Beau instructed. "This will be over shortly."

I felt cool plastic slide around my wrists and then one of the policemen helped me stand up. Another policeman assisted Beau to his feet and then wrestled his detective badge out of his pocket. He handed it to the first officer who had entered the room.

"It's legit."

I was scared to ask, but I had to.

"Did you find anyone else in the house?" My voice wavered.

"Not yet. Why? Is there someone missing?"

"Yes, my boyfriend. He was here with us, but he went after the intruder. The last time I saw him, he was headed into the kitchen."

"Whoa. Wait. *You* have a boyfriend?" Beau interrupted.

My dad harrumphed. "His name is Slash."

"What? Slash is your boyfriend?" Beau and Slash sort of knew each other from a case I had recently wrapped up.

Before I could reply, another figure stepped into the room. "There's no one else here. But the back door leading out from the kitchen is open and there's blood in the kitchen."

My heart skipped a beat. Blood? Where was Slash? Was he okay?

The policeman in the doorway shined the flashlight at Beau. "So, Detective Carmichael, can you tell us what's going on here?"

"I have no idea. I came late to the party. I was on my way here to visit my parents when I heard on the scanner there were shots fired at this address. Came in a side door and found my family hiding here. My sister, Lexi, wasn't in the closet with the others and jumped out at me, hurling something at me and startling me. I discharged my weapon, but missed her. You'll have to ask her for an accounting of what happened before that."

The policeman shined his flashlight at me. "You're Lexi?"

"Yes."

"Are you okay?"

"I'm fine."

"What's that in your hair?"

I shook my head and something plopped to the floor. "Chowder, I think."

"So, what happened?"

"Someone shot at us through the dining room window while we were having dinner. The first shot…it almost hit me. About the same time, we lost electricity. Slash called the police from his cell, I think. A minute or two later someone entered the house through the kitchen—I don't know if it was the same person who shot at us or someone else—and starting shooting again. My boyfriend returned fire and chased the intruder. While he did that, we ran back here to hide in the study. Then Beau, my brother, came in. I thought he was the intruder, so I attacked him. In turn, he shot at me, thinking I was the intruder, but missed. We all jumped on him until we realized who it was."

My brother narrowed his eyes at me. "I'm damn lucky you've got bad aim. You almost brained me with that paperweight."

"Well, you almost *shot* me."

My mother wailed and collapsed into the chair I'd been hiding behind.

The officer let out a loud sigh. "So, Lexi, is your boyfriend in law enforcement?"

"Not exactly."

"Not exactly?" The officer paused, considered. "But he was carrying a weapon?"

"Yes. He usually does."

"Wait. I thought he was a computer geek," my dad interjected.

"He's that, too."

Beau frowned. "Um, I thought he was a federal agent."

"He's definitely a federal agent."

"So, which is he?" the policeman asked. "A geek, a police officer or a federal agent?"

"A mixture of all three, I guess."

"I thought he looked manly," Sasha offered.

The policeman held up a hand. "Stop, everyone. Let me get this straight. An unknown assailant shot through the window from outside the premises, followed by an armed intruder actually entering the house and continuing to discharge a weapon. However, no one is clear if the intruder in the house is the same individual who shot at you through the window. So, technically we could have two perpetrators. Then your boyfriend, who was also armed, returned fire on the intruder in the house and chased after him. You'd all run in here to hide when Detective Carmichael arrived and discharged his weapon at you, his sister, after you attacked him, thinking he was the intruder."

"That's it in a nutshell," I said.

"Right. At this point, no one knows where your boyfriend Slash—who is either a member of law enforcement, a federal agent, or a simply a poser—is located."

"He's not a poser," I said. "In fact, there should have been an FBI tail on him. You should check that out, too."

The policeman sighed, punched some numbers on his phone, strode to the doorway and began talking rapidly.

I let out a big breath and leaned back against my dad's desk.

Beau walked over and joined me, scooting closer until we were touching shoulders. "So, sis, when did this love connection with Slash happen?"

"There'd better not be any love connection," my dad growled. "We're going to have to have a serious talk about this man."

My left shoulder ached where I'd hit it during my duck-and-roll. "It's complicated, Beau."

"I'll bet. But for you to call him your boyfriend is pretty significant. It must be serious if you brought him home to meet Mom and Dad."

"Nothing is serious." My dad's voice was hard. "She just started dating him. How is it that you knew about this Slash guy and didn't tell me?"

"Hey, don't get mad at me. I didn't know he was Lexi's boyfriend."

I closed my eyes. Was there a do-over button for this evening?

The officer in the hallway stepped back into the study. "Take the cuffs off. They all check out. You, Lexi. I need you to tell me more about your boyfriend."

"She can't," my dad said. "Apparently she doesn't know his name or what he does for a living."

One of the policemen tugged on my cuffs and my arms were released. I rubbed them.

"What do you mean she doesn't know his name?" The policeman walked over to me. "You're dating some guy and you don't know his name?"

"Not exactly. He goes by Slash."

"Like the famous guitarist from Guns N' Roses?"

"No, as in short for Backslash. It's hacker lingo."

"Okay." He wrote something down. "You got an address for this Slash?"

I thought about it. "Actually, I don't. He usually comes to my place."

"A phone number?"

I rubbed my hands over my forehead. "He has several. He usually calls me from different numbers. Security and all, you know."

"Hold on. You're dating a guy and you don't know his name, what he does for a living, or where he lives?"

"It does sound pretty bad when you put it that way."

"And he's supposedly followed by the FBI?"

"It's for his own protection."

The officer shook his head but didn't ask any further questions.

Jeez. Welcome to Meet the Parents Night From Hell.

Beau helped my mom up from the chair so the policeman could get her cuffs off. "Look, this Slash guy is legit as far as I know," he told the police officer, making me feel better. "He was tight with the feds and helped run that recent terrorist situation at the high school Lexi was trapped inside. I saw him in action. He's definitely got some kind of law enforcement or military training.

He seems like a good guy. My gut instinct says he's the real deal. Lexi, why would someone be shooting at him?"

"Slash was the target?" my dad asked.

I hadn't even had time to think about who might have been the target. "I have no idea. Maybe it was random. A house invasion or something."

If that were it, we were all damn lucky Slash had been with us. But thinking about Slash reminded me of the blood in my parents' kitchen. My stomach churned. I knew he could take care of himself, but what if he'd been shot? And why hadn't he come back? What if he were lying somewhere bleeding to death?

I started to hyperventilate. Beau must have noticed, because he put an arm around me. "It's okay, Lexi. The officers are already doing a sweep of the neighborhood, looking for Slash and the perps. It's standard procedure. Plus, if someone's bleeding, they should be able to track it. Don't worry. Slash can take care of himself."

I swallowed, feeling dizzy and light-headed. The adrenaline rush had faded and I tried to calm my breathing and get my focus back. But I was scared. More scared than I ever thought I would be.

"I know. He's…he's good like that."

Suddenly the lights came on and we all blinked. I shielded my eyes until my sight adjusted. And just like that, I saw him standing in the doorway, flanked by two officers.

Slash.

SIX

I RAN ACROSS the room and threw myself in his arms, almost knocking him over. His arms went around me.

"Are you alright? Are you bleeding?" I asked.

He held me for a moment before stepping back and studying my face. "I'm fine. Are you okay? Is everyone okay?"

I nodded. "We're good. No one is injured. What happened?"

"He got away. I hit him with return fire. How badly, I'm not sure. I tracked him, but he was good. Highly experienced, whoever he was. I didn't want to spend more time on finding him in case he was circling back here or serving as a distraction to whatever was going on here."

The officer who had been questioning me stepped forward. "You're Slash?"

"I am."

"What happened here?"

Before he could reply, another uniformed cop ran into the room. "I'm sorry, sir, but we've discovered the bodies of two federal agents in a car parked a little way down the street. Got the CSI unit on the way."

The officer looked at Slash, who closed his eyes. "My tail."

My stomach lurched.

"We've been instructed to bring this man to headquarters immediately." He pointed at Slash. "Apparently the chief is coming in to handle this one personally."

The officer looked between Slash and me for a long moment, then nodded. "That's highly unusual, but what the chief says is gold. Do it."

APPARENTLY THE CHIEF wanted only Slash at that time, so my parents, Beau and I were released from further questioning and permitted to check into a local hotel. The house was a crime scene and we would have people coming and going all night long. I wanted to go home, but Slash had warned me against going anywhere alone until they figured out the purpose of the attack. To make matters worse, reporters arrived just as we were heading out. The police cleared them out so we could get out of the driveway, then escorted us to the hotel, but it wasn't pretty.

We were all exhausted by the time we got to our rooms. After borrowing a toothbrush from the front desk, I showered, put my T-shirt and undies back on, and immediately climbed in bed. I thought I'd never fall asleep, but I must have been out the second my head hit the pillow.

I didn't remember anything until I rolled over and realized Slash was passed out next to me, lying on top of the covers fully clothed. His gun lay on the nightstand and his sports coat and shoulder holster had been draped over a chair. Light was peeking in through the curtains. I squinted at the clock. Seven forty-two in the morning. I had no idea when he'd come in, how he'd found me or how he'd got into my room—that was just who Slash was. Master hacker, master of disguise and all-around talented guy.

He made a little noise in his sleep and twitched. I wondered if he was still chasing the bad guy. His face was smashed in the pillow and his mouth was slightly open. He needed a shave.

I reached out and gently pushed back a strand of black hair that had fallen across his forehead. A tenderness, an affection for him, swept through me.

His eyes opened, and he looked at me and smiled. He rolled over on his back, one hand resting on his forehead.

"Hey." His voice still sounded sleepy.

"Hey back."

His hand snaked out, catching my wrist and pulling me down on top of him. He rolled me over, kissing me with a warm, lazy heat as if he were still dreaming and wanted to wake slowly.

After a bit, he lifted his head. "Now that's what I call a good morning."

I smiled. "Where were you?"

He started nibbling the sensitive skin along my chin, moving toward my ear. "Police station. There was a little party with the DHS, NSA and FBI. Might have had a CIA agent there, too. It was a busy night."

I struggled to sit up. "What happened?"

He sighed and pushed himself up on his elbows. "The two federal agents who were following me are dead. Executed. As I was directly involved in the incident, I was questioned repeatedly by all the different agencies. They want to see both of us downtown at a CIA satellite office at nine o'clock for more questioning."

"But I don't know anything."

"I know. Something unusual is up. They generally leave questioning like this for local law enforcement."

I took his hand, pressed it against my cheek. "I'm sorry. I guess dinner at my parents' house wasn't a good idea. Except if you hadn't been there, who knows what might have happened?"

He reached behind my head, pulling me in for another kiss. "You could have been hit," he murmured. "My worst nightmare."

"I guess it was my lucky day."

He cupped my cheek so I was looking directly at him. "And mine. There can't ever be enough time for me to get my fill of you."

Before I could say anything, his phone rang.

He swore, but didn't answer it.

"Get it. It could be important."

Sighing, he rolled off the bed and snatched his phone from the bedside table. "Hello."

He listened for a minute, then his gaze raised to meet mine. "Yes, she's with me." Frowning, he listened for a bit more. "Twenty minutes."

Without even saying goodbye, he hung up and set the phone down.

"What was that all about?"

He sat on the bed and rubbed his cheek. "I'm not sure. They want to see me now. Alone. They asked for your whereabouts."

"They know about us?"

"Of course. They know everything about me, remember?" His voice held a trace of bitterness.

"Right. I'm sorry."

He leaned in for another kiss, but I could feel the tension in him. "No, I'm the one who's sorry. I have to go."

"Do they still want to question me at nine o'clock?"

"I don't know. I'll find out, okay?"

"Okay."

"You're safe here for now. There's an officer stationed outside in the hallway for you and your family's protection. Stay put until I figure out what's going on. But you'd better give your boss a call and let him know you won't be in today." He pointed at a black duffle in the corner. "I stopped by your place last night and picked up some of your clothes, a toilet kit and your laptop. Order room service and relax. I'll be back soon."

He picked up his briefcase and kissed me on the nose. "Don't worry. We'll get this sorted out."

After he left, I took his advice and ordered room service. I hadn't eaten last night, so I was famished. While I was waiting for the food, I booted up my laptop and called Finn. He wasn't in yet, so I left a message, giving him the details on my situation. After about twenty minutes, pancakes, scrambled eggs, sausages, pastries, orange juice and coffee were delivered. I dug into the food while surfing the net and tried to return to my happy place, but I had a hard time concentrating.

Someone knocked on my door. I crossed the room, peeked out of the peephole, then opened the door. Rock and Beau strolled in.

"Hey, sis, do I smell coffee?" Beau asked.

"And food," Rock added, lifting the lid on one plate and checking out the tray. "You didn't invite us."

"I didn't even know you were here," I said to Rock. "And I thought Beau was still asleep."

Beau picked up a sausage and ate it. "Nope. Most cops are early risers unless on the night shift."

Rock grinned. "Yeah, and didn't you know the early reporter catches the story?" He picked up a mug from the top of the hotel refrigerator and poured himself a cup of coffee. "Speaking of story, what's going on?"

I returned to the desk, sat, then picked up my own cold coffee. "I don't know, Rock. Someone shot at us at Mom and Dad's house last night. I have no idea why. I have to get questioned some more this morning."

Beau's eyes narrowed. "How come no one wants to

question me or mom and dad? We were there, too. It seems odd."

It did seem odd, but I wasn't sure what was going on. I shrugged. "You guys might be next on the list. Slash is with them now."

Rock perched on the edge of my bed. "So, what's this I hear about you having a boyfriend? Has the world stopped spinning on its axis?"

"Ha, ha. We just started dating, okay?"

"And he's already chasing masked intruders through our house?"

"We're really lucky he was there."

Rock sobered. "True. Look, something strange is happening. Both Beau and I checked our sources this morning. The incident at Mom and Dad's isn't being classified as a burglary or a home invasion. It's serious, though. Two federal agents were executed. From what Beau tells me, they were following your boyfriend as part of some kind of protection detail."

"Slash holds a critical position in the US government and is apparently not expendable. Even I'm not sure exactly what he does."

Beau joined Rock on the edge of the bed. "Well, I thought you might want to know that as of one hour ago, the police reports have been closed out. The incident has been now been classified."

"Classified? Why?"

"I don't know, but it's troubling. Speaking of trouble, how did Mom and Dad like Slash?"

"I don't have a clue. Dad was cleaning his gun when—"

"Whoa." Beau held up a hand. "Stop right there. Dad has a gun?"

"Exactly. After brandishing it and informing us he knew how to use it, he interrogated Slash with his finest lawyerly skills before demanding to know about his intentions toward me."

Rock winced. "Ouch."

"No kidding. Then all hell broke loose. So, the whole meet-the-parents thing didn't go as planned."

Before my brothers could comment there was a knock on the door. Rock looked through the peephole, then opened it. Slash stood there.

"Hey, Slash." He'd returned sooner than I expected.

"Come on in and join the party." Rock held out a hand. "Nice to finally meet you. I'm Rock, Lexi's oldest brother."

Slash shook hands, then walked in. Beau leaned forward and gave him an open-handed, sideways palm slap that apparently served the same purpose as a handshake.

"Good to see you again, Slash. Can you update us on the situation?"

Something was wrong with Slash. He wouldn't even look at me, and he *always* looked at me as if I were the only person in a room.

"Not much," he said to my brother. "But I'm afraid Lexi and I have to leave now for further questioning."

Even his voice sounded funny. Tense, coiled and worried.

"Can we go with you?" Beau asked.

"I'm sorry. Not this time. They want to see only Lexi for now. But you are all free to go home or to work. I should advise you, however, you'll have a police detail for the foreseeable future until we get this sorted out."

"What exactly is *this*?" Rock asked.

He shook his head. "I don't know yet."

After another minute more of chatter, my brothers filed out while I shut down my laptop and grabbed my coat.

"What happened?" I asked Slash.

"You'll find out. We can't talk about it until we get to our destination, okay?"

"Slash? What's wrong? You're scaring me."

He stopped, gripped both my shoulders and kissed me hard. "Just let me say that I love you and it's going to be fine. Trust me, okay?"

I stared at him for a moment and then nodded. "Okay."

SEVEN

WE TOOK THE elevator in silence to the hotel garage, then climbed into his SUV and headed out. I glanced over my shoulder and saw a black sedan on our tail. A new FBI team had apparently been assigned.

He drove to a non-descript building in Rosslyn, Virginia, not too far from my office at X-Corp. Slash flashed a badge and I had to produce my ID to the guy monitoring the parking garage. He checked his electronic tablet for our names, then waved us in. Once Slash parked, we took the elevator to the lobby. We both had to show our identification again, and this time Slash had to check in his gun. We both had to turn over our cell phones and endure a pat-down followed by a full-body scan. Only after that were we permitted to pass.

"I'm surprised they didn't do a rectal exam," I joked. Slash looked straight ahead, pressing his badge to the elevator pad and not even cracking a smile.

We went to the ninth floor and I followed him down a hallway to a conference room. I counted six men in suits sitting at a long, rectangular table. They had laptops and papers spread out in front of them and were talking animatedly when we walked in. As soon as they saw us, they fell silent. After a moment, a large man with brown hair and glasses, wearing a black suit, stood up and came to greet us.

"Hello, Ms. Carmichael. I'm Dex Woodward, Director of Cybersecurity Operations at the CIA. It's a pleasure to meet you."

I didn't know what was so pleasurable about meeting me under these circumstances, but he stuck out a hand, so I shook it. No one else in the room made a move to introduce themselves, so I sat without saying a word in the chair Woodward pulled out for me. For some reason, Slash didn't sit next to me, but moved to stand in the back of the room, still not meeting my gaze. He knew something I didn't, and whatever it was, I had a feeling I wasn't going to like it.

"We appreciate your cooperation in coming," Woodward said. "We have identified the man who shot at you from the blood sample we were able to obtain at your parents' house."

"Who is he?"

"His name is Abri Pentz." Woodward paused. He and everyone else in the room stared at me.

I looked around the room and then back at Woodward. "Okay. Is that name supposed to mean something to me?"

"I don't know. That's why I asked."

"I've never heard of him."

"You're sure?"

"I have a photographic memory. I'm sure."

"Well, Abri Pentz is one of the world's best snipers. He had one hundred and seventy-seven official confirmed kills in various Middle Eastern conflicts while serving in the British army. But the number is probably higher."

"Snipers keep count of their kills?" It seemed a bit gruesome, but what did I know about the military?

"They do. I assure you, he is a sniper of extraordinary skill. However, at some point during his military service, he lost it. Mowed down a bunch of innocents and was served with a dishonorable discharge. Now he kills for hire. He's currently a suspect in twelve high-profile political assassinations around the world."

"He sounds like bad news."

"He is."

Woodward stopped talking and just looked at me. I glanced over at Slash, who had started pacing and hadn't stopped the entire time Woodward was talking.

I folded my hands on the table. "I think it's painfully clear I don't have a clue who this guy is or why he was shooting up my parents' house. But for one of the world's best snipers, he has pretty lousy aim. If he were aiming at me, he would have had a perfectly clear target. The house was lit up like a Christmas tree and the drapes were wide open. But he missed. Now that I think about it, when he came inside the house, instead of shooting at any of us, he shot at the chandelier. How odd is that?"

"Not odd at all. He didn't miss. He didn't hit you on purpose."

"You're implying I was the intended target."

It was a statement, not a question, but Woodward glanced at a man who sat two chairs down. The man nodded and Woodward looked back at me. "Yes. You were the intended target."

"Me? Why? If this guy is an experienced sniper, why even shoot at me in the first place if he never intended to hit me? You aren't making sense. None of this is making sense."

Slash spoke for the first time since we'd entered the room. "He wanted you alive."

"Why would he even want me dead? I don't know who he is."

Woodward leaned forward. "He wants you alive for a game of cat and mouse."

"What game of cat and mouse? Look, I've never even heard of Abri Pentz. What is going on? Slash?"

Slash walked over to Woodward and slammed his palm on the table. "I told you she doesn't know him. Damn it. Move on."

Woodward jumped at the vehemence in Slash's voice. "Fine. We can move on. Why don't you assist me."

Slash pulled a chair over next to me. He sat down. "This isn't about Pentz, *cara*. He's secondary in all of this. His job was to send you a message, which is exactly what he did."

"Me? A message? Who would want to send me a message via a high profile assassin?"

"That's a very good question," Woodward said. "It might have taken us a long time to figure that out except apparently part of Pentz's assignment was to personally hand-deliver a message. If it hadn't been for Slash at your parent's house, he might have figured a more macabre way to do it."

Slash frowned and shook his head slightly, stopping Woodward from whatever he might have said next.

I shivered. "Can we just cut to the bottom line, please?"

Woodward took a drink of his coffee, regarding me thoughtfully. "The bottom line is that once we realized we were dealing with Pentz, our agents were able to piece together his activities for the past three days."

"And?"

"He's been travelling under the alias of Roman Krusky. Five days ago, he spent twenty-four hours in Tanzania, in the city of Mwanza, where we think he met his client."

"The client? The one who hired him to send me the so-called message?"

"Yes. Roman Krusky entered the US via Miami two days ago."

"Okay, so what's the message? Why is he so interested in me?"

Woodward held up a plain white thumb drive. "We found this in your parents' kitchen."

"He left a thumb drive in their kitchen?"

"Yes. It's addressed to you."

My stomach clenched. "What's on it?"

Slash put a hand on my back and began rubbing in small circles. "You need to steel yourself, *cara*. I don't... I don't know how to prepare you."

I felt his hand actually tremble through my sweater. He was scaring me way more than whatever was on that drive.

"Slash, just tell me." My voice wavered.

He closed his eyes and then let out a breath. His hand tightened on my shoulder. "It's Broodryk."

I blinked in surprise. "Broodryk?"

Johannes Broodryk was a cyber mercenary from South Africa. He had his fingers in a wide range of cybercrimes for hire including human trafficking, drugs, money laundering and assassinations. He'd work for the highest bidder regardless of politics or ideology. We'd had an exchange of wits on my last case and I'd come out the victor. While he hadn't been caught, I'd put a huge crimp in his worldwide cybercrime operations. I'd exposed him and now he was the number-one target of most intelligence and cyber agents all over the world. He had a big bone to chew and apparently wasn't going to let me have the last word.

Fear changed to anger. "What's his deal? He put a hit on me with some bigwig assassin and then had the guy miss? On purpose? Help me out here, because I totally don't get what he's after."

Slash reached forward and pulled a laptop close to him. He opened it, typed in a password, then plugged the thumb drive in.

The message was a video.

He pushed play and a roaring sound filled my ears. I couldn't breathe. I couldn't think.

The first image that filled the screen was one of a brown-haired man gagged and bound to a chair.

It was Elvis Zimmerman.

EIGHT

A LONG TIME AGO, when I was still a neophyte on the computer, I had dreams of controlling the world from my keyboard. I would be able to reach anyone, anywhere. Although I know better about my cyber capabilities and limitations now, at this moment, I wanted nothing more than to have the capacity to reach through the computer screen and bring Elvis to safety.

I don't know how long I sat there staring at the video. Someone on the screen was talking—Broodryk, maybe—but I couldn't hear a word. I could only see Elvis strapped to that chair.

Slash was saying something as well, but I couldn't hear him either. I couldn't hear or feel anything, only stare at the video flashing in front of me, tears pooling in my eyes and dripping down my cheeks.

Finally, mercifully, Slash closed the laptop. He turned my chair toward him, gathered me in his arms and held me. I sat stiff as a board. He kept saying something, but I still couldn't hear him.

At some point, he cupped my cheeks, made me look at him. I tried to focus on his brown eyes to bring myself back to the room, to the ugly reality I had to face. I couldn't help Elvis if I were a basket case. I had to gain control, to think. Elvis needed me to be logical right now, and crying wasn't going to do either of us any good.

"Slash?"

My voice sounded strange, like it was coming from a

great distance. I blinked once and tried again. "Slash." Now it sounded more like a croak than a word.

He nodded, brushed a tear from my cheek. "I'm here, *cara*. Just breathe, okay?"

I took a breath, blinked and looked around the room. It was empty.

"Where did everyone go?" I asked.

"I told them to give us a minute."

"Broodryk…it's him? He has Elvis? Where's Xavier?"

Slash swallowed. "Xavier is in the hospital in Greece. They were attacked and Elvis was taken. Xavier's alive, but he's been badly injured."

"Oh my God." My voice couldn't seem to go above a whisper. "Why?"

Slash kneaded the back of his neck, stood and started pacing again. "Broodryk wanted Elvis. Just like he wants you. I presume it's revenge for how you stopped him at the high school on your last case. His entire cyber operation is in serious jeopardy now. He's an internationally hunted man, and he's looking for payback."

"Elvis…" I could barely say his name without a shaft of pain spearing through my stomach. "Is he…still alive?"

"As far as we know. Do you want me to play Broodryk's message again?"

I blinked back more tears. "No. Please. I can't, Slash. Not yet. Can you just tell me what it says? I couldn't hear him. Sum it up, okay?"

He sat down again, fixed the chairs so we were face-to-face. He took both of my hands in his and held them tightly. His expression was so strained I could see new lines near the corners of his eyes.

"Bottom line is Broodryk thinks he can get you to come after Elvis."

I pressed a hand to my heart, as if trying to hold the

pieces of it together. After a moment I asked, "Will he keep Elvis alive until I decide what to do?"

"There's no decision to be made. You can't possibly go after Elvis. It would be a suicide mission. He'd kill you both—most likely in some horrible fashion—as soon as you were out of the States. Then he'd use you as some kind of grotesque example of what he does to people who cross him."

He muttered something in Italian, rose to his feet and started pacing again. I'd never seen him so upset.

I watched him, tried to get my mind around the situation. "What are my options?"

Slash stopped in front of me. "There are no options yet. We have a digital forensics team going over every inch of the video. Broodryk makes a brief appearance, but he's masked. We'll likely be able to match his voice characteristics to the ones we captured from the school incident. It worries me that Broodryk didn't make an effort to change his voice. He wants you and everyone else in the world to be sure it's him."

"What's the significance of that?"

"It means he wants the world to witness his game."

"Are you certain it's Elvis on the video? Maybe it's just someone who looks like him." I knew I was grasping at straws, but I had to ask.

He sighed. "It's him, *cara*. Elvis spoke on the video, so I was able to personally identify the voice match. I assure you, I reviewed the video multiple times."

"Okay." My head hurt and I had started to shake uncontrollably.

Slash sat beside me and put an arm around me. "We'll think of a way to extract Elvis."

"D-does Basia know?"

"Not yet. We've already alerted the police in Hollywood and she's got a covert detail on her, but she doesn't know yet. I'm trying to figure the best way to tell her and keep her safe."

"Thank you."

"Also, I have a friend who's a doctor in Rome. He's on his way to Greece now to personally keep tabs on Xavier. He'll check on his medical progress and report directly to me. I've arranged for a private room at the hospital and a couple of specialists who are willing to consult. All I know at this point is that Xavier is stable, but not out of the woods yet. You do understand we can't let Basia go see him? It's too dangerous for her to travel abroad. She'd be at risk, too. We'll get him home as soon as he's stable enough to travel. Until then, he's under police guard."

I nodded, my teeth chattering. "I understand. My parents, brothers, grandparents—are they in danger?"

"I won't lie to you. It's possible. Your parents have been permitted to leave the hotel and go home, but they remain under police protection. Your brothers are both there now with them. Both sets of your grandparents and your aunts, uncles and other assorted family have been made aware of the events."

"Oh my God. What about Wally, Piper and Brandon?" They were the kids at the high school who had helped Elvis and me defeat Broodryk.

"For now, all of them, including Bonnie, will have a police presence around the clock."

Bonnie was the headmistress of the high school Broodryk and the terrorists had attacked. Elvis had just started dating her a few weeks ago.

"There is a bit of good news, *cara*. We're pretty sure Abri Pentz has left the States."

"What? How can you be sure?"

"We've had dozens of international agencies all over

this, trying to piece together his activities. Pentz is nearly as hunted as Broodryk. We got lucky and found a match with one of Pentz's known aliases going out of Jean Lesage International Airport in Quebec about twelve hours ago."

I thought about it a moment. My head still hurt, but I had to focus, so I pushed aside the pain.

"You said Elvis spoke on the video. What did he say?"

He brushed a strand of hair from my shoulder. "Why don't you take some time to think over what we've already talked about and then we'll go over the video together in more detail. Okay? You need a breather. You're in shock."

"No." My voice firmed. "No, Slash. I don't want to wait. Elvis needs us. I want to know. What did he say?"

"I don't think—"

"I can handle it. Please, just tell me."

Slash caught my hand in his and squeezed. "Elvis told you not to come for him. He told you not to do what Broodryk wants. And then…" He closed his eyes.

"And then what?"

"And then Broodryk beat him."

NINE

I BOLTED FROM the chair and ran to the door, wrenching it open. I barely made it to the ladies room before I threw up, heaving until there was nothing left in my stomach.

I don't know when he came in, but at some point Slash was there with me, holding my hair back, whispering soothing words, pressing a paper towel to my forehead. When I finished, he helped me wash up, then led me out. I saw Woodward and a few of the others in the hallway, watching. Slash said something to them, led me down the hallway, picked up our things at the lobby and then went to his car.

He drove me back to the hotel and tucked me in bed like I was a little girl.

"Close your eyes, *cara*. Rest. I'm here. I won't leave you."

He stepped away for a moment and returned, handing me a glass of water and a pill. "Take it," he said. "Trust me."

Without a word, I took the pill and swallowed it. He sat with me, holding my hand and murmuring words in Italian until I drifted off. When I woke, Slash was sitting in a chair he'd pulled next to the bed, watching me.

I sat up. "How long was I out?"

He sat on the bed next to me, taking my hand and offering human comfort. "An hour, maybe fifty minutes. Not nearly long enough."

"What did you give me?"

"A mild tranquilizer. Apparently it wasn't strong enough. You were on overload."

"I shut down. I'm sorry."

He stroked my hand. "It's understandable."

"I shouldn't have. You didn't have to stay with me. You could have been figuring things out, doing something else."

"Honestly, I don't know what to do. I'm in a bit of shock myself. And, I feel guilty."

"Why?"

"I should have anticipated that Broodryk might do something like this. That he might seek revenge. Elvis and Xavier, they were out of the country, unprotected."

"I don't understand. Broodryk didn't even know about Elvis, that he was there at the school, too, working against him."

"He found out somehow. He knows you, so by extension everyone you know is at risk. Think about it. I found you through the Zimmermans. Broodryk could have easily found them through you. That's on me. I made an error in judgment. I thought Broodryk would go deep underground and lay low. Instead, he did exactly the opposite. He went big, flashy and obvious. He's thinking with his ego because you humiliated him. It's stupid and damn risky for him. The problem is that Elvis is the unknown variable in this. I can't see any way, yet, that this can play out where we get Elvis out safely."

"We have to think of something."

"I'm working on it."

"I want to see the video. All of it this time."

He shook his head. "Not yet."

He held up a hand when I started to argue. "There are many reasons for that, the most important being that I no longer have access to a copy right now. It's being tightly controlled at CIA headquarters where multiple teams, including some of the best network and digital forensic teams in the nation, are pouring over it."

He stood and joined me on the bed, putting an arm around me. I leaned my head against his shoulder. "I'm working on getting you a transcript. That way you can focus on the message without being distracted or distressed by the images."

I nodded. "Okay."

He was right. I needed time to get emotionally prepared and I couldn't do that if I kept imagining Elvis strapped to a chair. "I'm going to have to see the video soon."

"I know." He kissed my hair. "We'll figure something out, *cara*."

I'm not sure whether it was the biological byproduct of extreme stress or a desire to rid myself of the numbness in my mind and heart, but I slid out from beneath the covers and straddled Slash, wrapping my arms around his neck.

He looked at me with a question in his eyes.

I was emotionally and intellectually adrift, scared beyond anything I'd ever known. I was desperate to regain my focus, but first I needed the comfort and release I knew Slash could offer. Without a word, I kissed him. Fast, hard, needy.

He hesitated, then kissed me back. His hands slid into my hair, his mouth slanting over mine. Before I knew it, my sweater and T-shirt were off and his hands were everywhere. I reached for his shirt when his hands closed over mine.

His brown eyes shone with a predatory glow. But there was something else in them—concern. "Are you sure, *cara*?"

I didn't know what he was thinking, but I knew the

physical and emotional connection we shared would give me both the steadiness and relief I sought.

I lifted his hands to my lips and kissed them. "I'm sure. I'm not very good at expressing myself, but the truth is, before I met you, I didn't understand the cost of solitude. Now that you're here, I don't have to pay that price anymore. I'm never alone with you. You…anchor me."

He took one of my hands and pressed it to his chest. "No, you're not alone."

I cupped his face in my hands and lowered my head to his, letting my tongue taste the fullness of his mouth. He yanked me against him, rolling me over and pinning me to the bed. He crushed his mouth against mine, a heady onslaught of pleasure and torment. His body burned so hot beneath my roving fingers, it seemed fevered. Or maybe it was me. At this point, I wasn't sure where I ended and he began.

"*Cara*, I love you."

I opened my eyes. He watched me intently. How was it I'd never noticed how symmetrically perfect his features were? A mathematical masterpiece created by a random collision of genes and DNA.

He loved me.

Slash's eyes burned with a fierce light. "You're mine. Understood?"

I acquiesced. There was no submission here, only a joining of like minds and a promise of more to come.

"Understood."

TEN

WE STOOD SIDE-BY-SIDE in the hotel room, getting dressed. Slash passed me while retrieving his jeans from the floor and leaned over to kiss my bare shoulder. I didn't even shy away at the unexpected gesture. I was becoming less and less self-conscious around him.

I fastened my bra, then tugged my T-shirt over my head. "What now?"

He shoved his feet into a pair of black boots. "We have a meeting with Woodward in about an hour to review options and go over all the intelligence we've accumulated to this point."

"And until then?"

"You go to your parents' house. I need to figure out the best way to tell Basia about Xavier."

"I should be the one to tell her about Xavier."

"We both know she'll call you soon enough. Let me take first crack at it. I can give her the facts and fill her in on Xavier's condition minus the highly charged emotional component that will likely be present between the two of you. You're going to have your hands full with your parents for the next forty minutes anyway."

I wanted to argue, but he was right. My parents would be out of their minds with worry and I was the only one who could handle them.

"Fine." Sighing, I pulled on my jeans and laced up my tennis shoes. "I guess I'd better tell Bonnie, too, unless someone else already has."

Slash shrugged. "I think that's doubtful at this point. She'd probably appreciate hearing it from you."

I sat next to him on the bed and he gave me a kiss on the cheek. I liked that—his spontaneous show of affection.

"You better?" he asked.

"Yes." I paused for a moment. "It was more than the sex. You know that, right?"

"I know."

Impulsively, I pressed a cool hand against his cheek. "You're a pretty good guy."

He captured my hand, brought it to his lips and turned it over, pressing a lingering kiss to the inside of my wrist. "You're not so bad yourself."

He stood, reaching into his jacket pocket and pulling out a half-eaten power bar. "Want a bite?"

"Ugh. No thanks."

"Such disdain from a girl who eats processed peanut butter crackers from the vending machine."

I gave him a small smile. "I figure if I keep offering them to you, one day you'll learn to appreciate the processed goodness."

He looked so appalled, I laughed. "Don't worry. I'll catch something to eat at my parents'."

"An even better idea. Let's go."

We grabbed our coats and drove to my parents' house. I checked the house as we pulled up out front. The bay window had already been boarded up. The February wind was cold as I exited the car and I shivered, pulling my coat tighter as we walked up the sidewalk. Two policemen were standing guard at the front door. Slash and I stopped to chat with them. I learned there were more two more officers around the back and felt better for knowing it.

Slash gave me a quick kiss on the porch, then left.

I went into the house alone and found my family in the living room. Rock and Beau pounced on me immediately, asking questions, but my mom shooed them away. She ushered me to the couch, where I sat sipping a hot cup of tea and giving them a diluted version of everything I knew to this point.

My mom covered her mouth when I explained how the gunman was shooting at me. "Someone wanted to kill you?"

"Not exactly. He never intended to hit me. It was supposed to be some kind of threat or warning."

"A warning? What the *hell*?" My brother Rock slammed his fist against the table. "Let me get this straight. This South African psychopath, Johannes Broodryk, hired a trained assassin named Abri Pentz to shoot, but not hit you, and then kidnapped one of your friends?"

"Not just any friend," I corrected. "Elvis was with me in the school when it all went down. He was as instrumental as I was in putting a stop to that operation. Broodryk kidnapped Elvis first and is now trying to engage me."

"Engage you? Why? What exactly does this nut job want?" Beau asked.

I wrapped my fingers around my teacup. "I don't know what game he's playing yet."

My dad shot up from his chair. "This is some kind of game?"

My mom started crying, so I scooted closer to her on the couch and put an arm around her. "Mom, it's okay. Really. Please don't cry."

She swiped at her eyes. "If only you would have taken those ballet lessons when I begged you."

I smiled a little at that. "Sure, Mom. Go ahead and pull

the guilt card on me now. Yes, Dad, this whole situation is some kind of a game to Broodryk. He wants me to play."

My dad frowned. "You will not."

"Agreed," said Beau.

"We're all in agreement on that." Rock snatched his laptop and opened it. "We will not sit around here and do nothing. We have to research this guy. Figure out where he is, what he might do next."

At that moment, I had never loved my family so much. Their support, love and indignation meant more than I could ever express. Despite our—okay, mostly *my*— eccentricities, we were a family, a united front. Team Carmichael. Why hadn't I ever appreciated it properly before?

"Knock yourself out, Rock," I said. "But the best minds in the international community are already on it. They are piecing together his activities, and the movements of the shooter, over the past sixty-two hours or so. Still, I've learned never to underestimate the prowess of an investigative reporter, especially when he works at the *Post* and is my brother."

"Damn right."

My dad stretched out a hand to me. I looked at it and then put my hand in his. He pulled me to my feet and into a bear hug. I wrapped my arms around him and tried not to cry. I didn't want to worry my parents more than they already were. We were all at the breaking point.

"Okay, what next, pumpkin?" he asked, his face against my hair. "What do we do?"

"I don't know. I have to meet with the agents in less than an hour. Slash is coming to get me. This time, I have to actually watch the video. Broodryk's message is for me. There may be something he says or does that only I will understand. Earlier today, I wasn't prepared to see the video. Now that I am, I have to figure out the best way to help Elvis. Falling apart won't solve anything."

"We're here to help. Just tell us what to do." My dad hugged me tighter.

I felt a lump in my throat. "I don't know yet, Dad. Just be careful. All of you. Slash told me everyone will have a security detail until we get a handle on this."

"Agent Woodward urged us to take off a few days and stay together here at the house," Rock said. "I've been told I have to sit on the story until further notice. National security and all that crap."

"It's a good idea. We can't risk him doing anything more to Elvis in retribution."

"Well, I'm not just going to sit around doing nothing," Beau said. "I'm a law enforcement officer. I don't subscribe to running scared of criminals nor of sitting around doing nothing."

"You're not being idle. Help Rock research. I'll be reviewing the video and the intelligence on the whereabouts of both Broodryk and Pentz shortly. We all can do something."

"What's Slash doing?" my dad asked. "Where is he right now?"

"He's talking to Basia for me because I needed to come here to see you first. I'm glad I did. But I still need to call, uh, Elvis's girlfriend." The words stuck in my throat. "Then I have to see the video. It may help us pinpoint Broodryk's general location if we get lucky."

"And if we don't?" Beau asked.

"Then the ball is in Broodryk's court."

ELEVEN

THE CALL CAME sooner than I expected. Not thirty seconds after I hung up from talking with Bonnie, Basia called me.

"Slash said Xavier is in critical condition. He said I can't go to see him in Greece."

I hated the way her voice shook as if she were barely holding it together. I wondered how I sounded. I sat down at my parents' kitchen counter and looked out the window at the gray sky.

"I'm sorry, Basia. Slash is right. It's not safe. But Xavier is receiving the very best care possible. Slash has hired some Italian medical specialists to fly out there and consult. They'll report back. Xavier is safely under guard and receiving excellent services. You're fortunate you weren't there during the attack."

She spoke in barely a whisper. "Do we know what happened?"

"No. Xavier hasn't regained consciousness. He needs time to heal. He probably tried to fight back or help Elvis when they came for him. He's lucky to be alive."

"What are you going to do?"

"I'm going to figure out a way to save Elvis. I have to start with the video. I couldn't…" My voice caught and I cleared my throat. "I haven't been able to watch it yet."

"He's going to kill Elvis, isn't he?"

Anxiety shot through me. "I can't even begin to think about that."

She started to cry. "Why is that horrible man doing this?"

I knew why. Payback. Revenge. Retribution.

"I'm going to think of something. Okay? I promise. Don't worry about Xavier and Elvis. They're both smart and strong. Xavier will pull through and come home to you. Elvis will hang on. We have to believe that."

"God, how can you do this? How can you be so focused and calm?"

"I'm holding it together the best I can. You have to be strong, too. Show up for work, keep engaged and do the best you can. We have to stay resilient for them."

"Oh, God. Oh, God." She cried harder. "How are you able to think?"

I closed my eyes. "Okay, I'll tell you the truth. When I saw Elvis on that video a while ago, I totally lost it. But I'm done with that. I've got to get my head in the game."

"I don't know how to do this, Lexi. I'm too scared to think clearly."

"We rely on each other. That's how we do it. We'll make it if we stand together." I suddenly realized what a significant statement that was, coming from a loner like me.

"I'm glad you have Slash there to help you."

"Me, too."

We talked for another minute and I hung up. I lay my head on the counter. I wasn't sure I could speak to one more person about the situation. In fact, I was done talking. I had to pull myself together and *do* something.

I lifted my head when I heard a footstep. Slash stepped into my parent's kitchen, carrying his briefcase. I guess the officer outside had let him in.

"Basia?" he asked, motioning to the cell phone still in my hand.

I nodded and set it down. "I spoke to Bonnie before that. I'm totally wiped."

He walked over and rubbed my back. "It's hard. They look to you to make things right."

"It's a lot of pressure."

"*Si.* But remember we're in this together, okay? You aren't carrying this alone."

"Thanks, Slash. I needed to hear that."

He'd found time to shower, shave and change into blue jeans and a black sweater. His face was drawn and his eyes looked tired, but other than that, he didn't seem any worse for wear. I'm sure I looked like death warmed over. Twice.

He put down his briefcase and held me in a long hug. "How'd it go with your parents?" He rested his chin on top of my head.

"As well as can be expected, considering I told them one of the world's top assassins was taking a potshot at me on behalf of a crazed cyber terrorist and one of my best friends had been kidnapped."

"No easy way to explain something like that." He touched my cheek. "You ready for this?"

"No. I don't think I could ever be ready for what I'm about to see. But I'm going to do it anyway."

"I hope this will help."

He returned to his briefcase, punched in a code and popped it open. He took some papers right off the top and handed them to me.

"It's a transcript of the video. Word for word. I thought it might help."

"It will. Thanks. I'll read it on the way."

He drove in silence as I read the transcript, once, twice

and then three times. My stomach heaved, but I kept control. I was grateful Slash didn't interrupt or ask questions because I needed time to process.

Slash pulled up to the guard gate at the underground garage. We completed the same security song and dance we'd done before, finally taking the elevator to the ninth floor. Everyone in the conference room fell quiet as soon as we entered. All seats at the conference table were taken except for two. I counted at least seven others standing. A large SMART board stood in the corner with what appeared to be the video cued and ready to go. I was the only woman.

Looking around the table, I recognized one of the FBI agents from the cybercrimes unit. He'd debriefed me in the hospital after the school incident. The two open seats were at the head of the table next to Dex Woodward and across from a guy in full military uniform. Slash and I were ushered to the two open chairs and instructed to sit.

The table groaned under an impressive array of expensive tech equipment. I recognized most of it, but there were items even I hadn't seen before. Elvis would have known what they were. I wanted to ask about them, but Woodward was in a hurry to get started.

"How are you, Ms. Carmichael?"

I looked around. Everyone was staring at me.

I cleared my throat. "I've been better. But I'm okay for now."

"Good. We need to get started. I don't need to tell you that time is of the essence. If we want to keep the hostage alive—"

"His name is Elvis. Elvis Zimmerman."

Woodward dipped his head. "Of course. If we want to keep Elvis Zimmerman alive, we need to act imme-

diately. Our first concern is figuring out what Broodryk
wants us to do next."

I swallowed hard. "I don't think he wants *you* to do
anything. This is about me."

"Which is exactly why we need your thoughts on the
video. You're the only person we know who has had direct contact with Broodryk. You not only saw him, but
you interacted with him. Recently. That's important."

"Our interaction was virtual."

"Doesn't matter that it was virtual. You saw him, con-
versed with him. You know him in a way that none of
us in the room do."

I called to memory Broodryk's face. He presented as
albino with translucent skin and blue eyes so light and
cold they were almost colorless. I'd nicknamed him Ice
Eyes.

"I already provided extensive details on him during
my previous debriefing with the FBI." I glanced at the
agent I'd spoken with in the hospital after Broodryk's
rampage on the high school. He nodded.

Woodward pulled a file from the stack of papers in
front of him. "Everyone in this room has reviewed the
details of that debrief. What we need now is your take
on this latest event. We've already come up with some
interesting theories, so we want your thoughts on them,
too. Are you ready to view the video in its entirety?"

I wasn't, but I had to see it. "Yes. But first I want to
know why you're so interested in this case. Kidnappings
happen every day. Granted, some are more high profile
than others. However, it looks like we've got representa-
tives of the CIA, NSA, US military and FBI in this room.
Even though he's now in the private sector, everyone
here is still that invested in saving Elvis Zimmerman?"

Woodward folded his hands on the table. "He and his

brother have built many of our most sensitive computer networks. Although neither of them has been with the government for about two years now, they still have a lot of important information stored in their heads. So, yes, we want to rescue the hostage—" he paused and corrected himself "—Elvis. It's important for us to secure his safety. But I'm not going to sugarcoat it. Our paramount concern remains catching Johannes Broodryk."

"Because of his attack on the high school?"

"Not only." He exchanged a glance with a guy who sat three seats down and was dressed in a navy blue suit and red tie. "Broodryk has masterminded more than two-dozen high profile cyberattacks against our government and those of our allies. He is a murderer, drug trafficker, human trafficker and notorious cyber criminal. He's eluded a team of our best minds for more than six years. No one has ever been able to trace him, find him, or even encounter him directly, except for you. Then, not only did you come face-to-face with him, you shut him down. Pretty much single-handedly."

I shook my head. "No. It wasn't single-handedly. Elvis was there and Slash, too."

Woodward nodded. "I know. But right now his focus is you. The fact that we were able to shut down a huge operation like the one masterminded by Broodryk at the high school is big for us. But we shouldn't forget that he made that a two-pronged attack—cyber and physical. He has the capability to do that again."

"Tell me something I don't know."

"Okay, what you don't know is our intelligence has been intercepting a lot of chatter over the past two weeks. Something big is ready to go down and all indications are that it's cyber. We think Broodryk is involved. He's smart and savvy and hires himself out to the highest bidder. You put a stop to his last operation, so he wants to salvage his reputation and his ego. We believe this cyber operation has been in the works for some time, but Broodryk may be deviating from the plan in order to involve you and make this a worldwide show for his clients."

"Cut to the chase, please. You want me to act as some kind of bait so you can catch Broodryk, right?"

Woodward narrowed his eyes. "*We* didn't involve you. Broodryk did. But you are exactly what we need to get inside the operation and trace it back to him. If we can find him and shut him down, we've done the entire world an enormous service."

I didn't disagree, but there was something else they weren't telling me. I shook my head. "I'm missing a critical piece here. I can't help you if I'm in the dark. I need to know more about this cyber event you think Broodryk is plotting."

The room remained silent.

Slash leaned forward. "I suggest you read her in. Don't be stupid. She'll understand, and she's the best lead you've got."

Woodward and the guy in the navy blue suit exchanged glances again. The guy stared at me for a long moment, as if assessing my intelligence and worth, and then gave a slight nod of his head.

Woodward sighed. "Fine. It's a computer virus called Pruxrat. Slash has been working on a potential antidote for some time. It specifically attacks the programmable logic controllers, or PLCs. You know what those are, right?"

"Yes."

"Right. Sorry. Anyway, from what we can tell, Pruxrat is being designed as a platform for attacking the SCDA and PLC systems. It's unusual because, instead of having a typical triangular module, this one is quadrangular. Its four parts are a worm that will infect the system; a link file that will replicate the worm; a rootkit that will hide evidence of its existence on the system; and a new, innovative network probe that can penetrate weak or unguarded routes into new systems."

I digested that for a minute. "What else do we know?"

"Nothing much, except it's supposed to be released soon. Intelligence believes the first level of attack will be two-pronged, focusing on the dual assets of the US transportation system and our power grids, especially those serving military installations and dams."

Critical infrastructure. Any of which, if successfully penetrated, could lead to widespread disaster and confusion throughout the US on an unprecedented level.

I glanced at Slash. "It's not like we haven't been preparing for something like this for some time. We're lucky we have Slash, one of the best cyber minds on our side."

Slash acknowledged the compliment with a brief nod of his head, but I saw a smile touch his lips.

"This virus is different." Slash looked around the table. "Most viruses get their start as a hard attack. That means the first insertion of the virus has to be manual, put directly into a system by a USB port, or a flash drive." He turned back to me. "Pruxrat is a network penetration virus, which is far more dangerous, as well as much harder to prevent and contain. It will start off targeting whatever Broodryk wants, but it can spread unchecked to other systems as well."

I felt a chill. Cyber warfare, the new frontier. Most viruses and malware were specific to a system with a designated target. Pruxrat sounded more like a poison; it would bring down anything it touched. A virus of this magnitude would affect a lot more than just the United States. We were talking billions of people.

"Broodryk is the only one with the antidote," I said.

"Presumably, yes."

I considered the implication and then wondered how Elvis's extraction played into it. I turned to Woodward.

"So, you want me to play Broodryk's game and lead you to him. That's your priority. My priority is Elvis. How do you intend to reconcile those two goals?"

"They're not mutually exclusive. We'll try to get him out safely and we're willing to invest the full power of the US government to do it."

A cold calm had fallen upon me. A brief analysis of all the data up to this point indicated the situation was polarizing into two camps with different priorities. The problem was, we needed each other. Also, I couldn't ignore the fact that I had a moral, professional and patriotic responsibility to protect my country from a computer virus that could destroy millions of lives and put our national security at risk.

How would I balance that?

I hadn't started this war, but I was about to become the central player—the first to take a step into an ugly new battlefield. It wasn't a choice after all. I would do what they told me because I would go into the depths of hell to save Elvis.

I lifted my chin and met Woodward's gaze full on. "Show me the video."

TWELVE

SOMEONE TURNED OFF the lights. The video started playing on the SMART board set up in the corner.

Slash held my hand and I clutched his hard when that first image of Elvis strapped to the chair appeared. I needed to put my photographic memory into play and burn every movement, every pixel, into my brain. If there was a clue in this video, I'd find it.

Broodryk spoke and I flinched. He'd made no attempt to disguise or digitally alter his voice. Slash had been right. Broodryk wanted me to be sure it was him.

"Well, hello there. We meet again, Lexi Carmichael. Surprised? You couldn't possibly think that our relationship would come to an end just because you put a temporary crimp in my plan. Oh, no. I couldn't have that. I'm beyond confident that soon we'll be good friends. Maybe more."

Elvis wiggled, trying to free himself from the chair. A lock of his brown hair fell across his forehead, just like it always did. Only, this time he couldn't push it out of his face. My eyes filled with tears.

Focus.

I have to focus.

Broodryk was still talking, his voice cold, deliberate. "If you want him to stay alive, you will do exactly as I say. I do not care who helps you. You may involve the whole *fokken* US Army if you want. But you must come to me or your friend will die a very painful death. I assure you, I will take exceptional pleasure in doing it myself."

My hands were shaking uncontrollably, a sure sign of my anxiety, but I never stopped scanning the video.

Elvis sat in a non-descript room with white walls. No furniture except for his plain wooden chair. A painting or picture of some kind hung on the wall to the right-hand side of the video, but it was mostly obscured. The flooring was light-colored wood. That was it in terms of visual cues. The digital forensic team would have little to go on.

"There will be some who tell you not to engage," Broodryk continued. "I would suggest not taking their advice. I do believe that you, of all people, will best understand what I can do to you, your family, your place of business and your friends. I've plenty of time—my time is entirely my own. Rest assured, I will make it my mission to destroy you if you do not come. *No one* you care about is safe from me."

A whip came out of nowhere, lashing Elvis across the cheek. I jerked, biting the inside of my cheek and tasting blood. Slash squeezed my hand so hard I winced.

"You do what I say and we will deal. I'll let him go, no questions asked. I am a man of my word. So, are you ready to play, my dear? Will you come to me like a lover in the night? We will be good together, yes?"

I ignored the taunt and kept my focus on Elvis. He wore jeans and a white T-shirt spattered with blood. His feet were bare and looked dirty or bruised. His arms were tied behind his back and presumably to the chair. I swallowed hard and made myself examine his face. A blue cloth gag had been secured around his mouth and chin. His left eye had swollen shut. I couldn't tell how badly hurt the rest of his face was because it was mostly smeared with blood. But he held his head up and the expression in his one good eye spoke murder. The tears I'd been holding back threatened to fall. I blinked harder.

"You have until Friday at noon EST, to make contact after receiving your instructions from me. This video is your first clue. If you fail to find the method of contacting me, I'll kill him and move on to the next victim until you get it right. I wonder who shall it be next time? A friend, a parent? Your new lover? No one you care about is safe from me. I sincerely wish you luck as I look forward to matching wits with you once again."

There was a pause and then a man dressed in black pants, a dark long-sleeved shirt and black ski mask walked into the video, his back to the camera. He approached Elvis and yanked the gag out of his mouth.

"Say it," he instructed Elvis.

Elvis opened and closed his mouth for a moment. Then he spat on Broodryk's shoe, glaring at him. "*Jou bliskem!* Don't do it, Lexi."

Broodryk's fist hit Elvis's jaw so hard, it knocked the chair over with Elvis still tied to it. As I watched in horror, Broodryk strode across the floor and kicked Elvis several more times while he was down.

I pushed my fist against my mouth to keep from screaming. I had never felt such hatred for anyone in my life. I wanted to rip Broodryk's face to shreds with my fingernails. I wanted to shoot him a dozen times in the head. I wanted to drop to the floor and curl into a ball and erase these images from my mind forever.

I could do none of them.

"Let that be a warning to you, Lexi Carmichael," Broodryk said, breathing hard. He turned to face the camera, his ski mask still in place. "Don't be late, or else."

Mercifully, the screen went blank. Someone turned on the light. I blinked, then swiped at my wet cheeks with the back of my free hand. Despite my intention to remain stoic, it hadn't happened. Slash gently squeezed my hand.

I took a moment to compose myself before I spoke. "What did Elvis say at the end? It sounded like a foreign language. I couldn't hear it clearly."

One of the men with glasses, a white shirt and green tie, spoke up. "He said 'You bastard' in Afrikaans."

Leave it to Elvis to be in a dire situation and yet have enough brains to curse the bastard in his own language.

I waited until my heartbeat slowed, then tried to think past my fear for my family, Elvis and Slash.

Focus, Carmichael.

The room was silent. Everyone was waiting for me to say something, do something.

I withdrew my hand from Slash's and took a piece of paper and a pen from Woodward.

"According to my calculations, we only have about forty-eight hours left to find the clue. Why didn't you tell me this earlier? We've wasted time."

"We wasted nothing," Woodward said dismissively. "You were in shock. You needed time to process and recover. We haven't been idle and have had the best minds on this while you recovered. We wanted you in top form and now you are. In fact, I think you're going to be surprised at what we've already found."

In other words, he wanted to show all the important people in this room that he and his team could solve this part without me—a reminder of who was in charge. I wasn't a fan of his smug attitude, but I wasn't going to waste time arguing.

"Fine. What do we know so far?"

Woodward waved at the guy in the green tie. "Mark, you go first."

The guy shuffled through some papers and looked up

at me. "Hey, ah, my name is Mark Cohen and I'm an analyst on the CIA's International Digital Forensics Team. My team and I have gone over the video with a fine-tooth comb and gathered the following data so far. First, the video is four minutes and thirty-two seconds in length. A digital analysis of the voice confirms the speaker is of South African descent, highly educated, and speaks with a dialect typical of the city of Cape Town. That would match the biographical information we have on Johannes Broodryk in terms of his background. The other individual in the video is Elvis Zimmerman, currently employed at ComQuest in Baltimore, and a former employee at the NSA. Just a note, his position and vast knowledge of the inner workings of the government's sensitive networks at the highest levels presents a significant threat of its own, even if he hasn't been employed at the agency for a couple of years."

Mark shot a nervous glance at Woodward, who frowned at him. Although I'm not much on reading emotions, I sensed there had been a disagreement as to the importance of rescuing Elvis. Mark was a computer guy and he understood the importance and value of Elvis's knowledge and experience as only a tech head could.

Mark gulped some of his coffee and continued. "Those are the only two individuals in the video. The other interesting clue is a corner of a painting hanging on the right-hand wall. Although there is only one small part of the painting visible, a statistical analysis indicated there's an 89.6 percent chance that it's a replica of an oil painting by German artist, Hans Holbein."

"Hans Holbein?" I ran though the names of famous painters in my head but came up blank. "Never heard of him."

"Holbein, who lived from 1497 to 1543, titled the

painting *The Body of the Dead Christ in the Tomb*," Mark continued. "Here's what it looks like in its entirety."

Mark motioned to the guy at the laptop across from him and the painting appeared on the SMART board. Someone standing near the light flicked it off so we could have a clearer view.

I studied the painting. It depicted a side view of Jesus Christ clad in a loincloth, lying in what looked like an enclosed coffin. Wounds were evident on his hands and feet. His face and extremities showed early signs of discoloration and decay, but the rest of the body looked intact.

"Before the Resurrection," Slash murmured.

We all stared at it for another minute and then the light flicked back on.

"We will continue to collect data on the painting and the artist," Mark said. "We are also analyzing the remaining visual clues, the chair, ropes, the clothing of both men and every piece of data that becomes visible at one point or the other in the video."

I made a few notes and then looked up. "What about the audio? Did you use digital signal processing, adaptive filtering and discrete Fourier transforms to isolate and separate sounds?"

Mark looked surprised by my cyber forensics knowledge. "Ah, yes, we did. We're still gathering data, but we haven't found anything significant on that front yet. But I'm not sure further analysis will be necessary."

"Why not?"

"Because we think we already know where Broodryk is located."

"What?"

"Here." Slash pushed a piece of paper at me. "Broodryk took the video with his cell phone and a tripod. He left the GPS on. We've tracked his location."

My mouth fell open. "You've got to be kidding. Broodryk left the GPS on his cell on?"

"Apparently so. These coordinates put him squarely in Kenya."

THIRTEEN

MY MIND RACED, trying to determine the significance of the location. "Kenya? We have a lock on his location? That's way too easy."

Slash shrugged. I could see he wasn't convinced either, but Mark was running with it.

"That's not to say there isn't a problem with the coordinates. We entered them into our system. While the location is definitely in Kenya, a closer examination via Google Earth indicates there is no city, town, village or permanent structure within thirty miles. It's the middle of nowhere. However, we have a satellite passing over in exactly thirty-one minutes, so we intend to get a closer, real-time view of the area."

I considered the information. "Clearly, the video was either shot from a temporary location that was set up and taken down, or Broodryk spoofed the GPS system somehow. But why? What would be the purpose?"

The FBI cybercrimes agent who had briefed me after my first encounter with Broodryk spoke up. "It's got to be a clue if he didn't leave it on by accident. It seems unlikely someone of his ability would forget something like that."

I was in full agreement. "I don't buy that he left the GPS on by accident. It was for a reason. But why, I'm not sure yet."

I glanced down at my notes. "So, we've got forty-eight hours and a plethora of clues—an obscure German painting, a geographically desolate location in Africa, and four minutes and thirty-two seconds of a video conversation that might hold more information than is readily observable. That's a lot of ground to cover. He wants me to fail, yet I think he's genuinely excited by the prospect I might succeed."

Slash growled and I glanced sideways at him.

"Well, what do *you* suggest we do next, Ms. Carmichael?" Woodward asked. "Since no one knows him like you do."

I drew a line between several of the little boxes I had drawn on my paper. "First, I think the forensics team should continue to focus on the audio. Run the gamut of techniques, both forward and backward, and see if there are any abnormalities. Isolate any unusual sounds. Not sure if we'll find anything, but we have to check."

Several people scribbled notes as I continued. "Next, we need a closer look at those GPS coordinates. Get your best crypt heads on it. If the location ends up a dead end, we have to consider the possibility it's a code. Broodryk likely knows I have a background in cryptology, so we need to play that angle."

I rubbed my temples, wishing the tension away. "We also need a dedicated team of analysts on the painting. Where does the painting hang now? What is culturally or artistically significant about it? Who the hell is Hans Holbein?"

Woodward made notes of his own. "Okay, what else?"

"Well, we could use an update on Abri Pentz and his current whereabouts. What do we know about his relationship with Broodryk? Have they worked together before? How does Broodryk pay him? In bitcoins or some other currency? Can we follow the money trail? How long have they known each other?"

I thought of something else. "I also need to see everything you've got on Broodryk. What's his background, his likes and dislikes, his favorite food? No detail is unimportant."

I glanced down at my paper and saw I had circled the word *me* several times. I was the center of this entire operation in both terms of what Broodryk wanted and where the team looked for guidance. Leadership was not my forte, but I would step up for Elvis.

"Finally, I'm going to need a secure laptop, more paper, a place to spread out my notes and a quiet location to review the video again. I'd also like the assistance of a forensics expert as I'm not overly familiar with the software and have no time to bring myself up to speed."

Mark held up a hand. "I'll be your guy. I'll have my assistant get the rest of the team started on the other tasks you mentioned."

I nodded. "Thank you. Slash, I want your take on the satellite feed from those coordinates if possible."

"Done. I have some ideas of my own to pursue, as well."

"Excellent. I'm going to need all the help I can get. Also if anyone has a couple of ibuprofen, I'd appreciate it."

Woodward stood. "Okay, team, you heard the woman. Let's get to work."

Everyone filed out of the conference room except for Slash and Mark.

Mark walked over, handing me his laptop. "Take this. It's all set up, has a copy of the video and is wired for access to all the internal resources you will need. I'll get you some painkillers, grab another laptop for myself, and be back shortly."

"Thanks. Where can we work?"

Mark looked around. "I think we can work right here. There's lots of room and access to the SMART board, so we can have an oversized view of the video as needed. Does that work for you?"

"Okay. I just need it to be quiet."

"Shouldn't be a problem." He walked out of the room, leaving Slash and me alone.

Slash put his hands on my shoulders. "Are you okay, *cara*?"

"Not really, but I'm holding it together the best I can."

"You're magnificent." He kissed my cheek. "My girl." He murmured something else in Italian and then left the room.

I sat down at the conference table, pulling out the notes I'd compiled on Broodryk and his methods. I had to think like him, get in his head. In order to beat him, I had to *be* him if I wanted to understand and anticipate his actions.

What did he want?

To humiliate me—his ego is bruised, his operations disrupted. Payback is sweet.

To outwit me—to show he cannot be fooled twice.

To hurt me—I've hurt him badly both in terms of money and professional pride. He wants to hurt me back and make me look like a fool in front of my peers. I can't rule out physical harm, perhaps even torture and/or sexual assault, because he's a sociopath.

He won't be satisfied unless I play the game. If I refuse, he will kill Elvis and then kidnap and kill again.

Opening my eyes, I quickly jotted those ideas down and folded the paper in half so it stood to the side of my laptop. As repugnant as those motives were, they'd be good reminders for me.

Mark came back in the room, a laptop under one arm

and a cup of water in the other hand. He offered me the water and then deposited two pills in my palm.

"Ibuprofen."

"Thanks." As I washed them down with the water, he took the chair two spots down from me and set up. When he was ready, he looked over expectantly.

"What do you want to do first?"

"I want to listen to the audio. No visual, just audio."

"Got it."

He ran the video without picture and I listened to it three times in a row. I had Mark isolate sounds in certain spots and made notes. I was getting ready to listen a fourth time when Slash came in, carrying a steaming mug of coffee and what looked like a bagel.

"Did you discover anything from the satellite footage?" I asked hopefully.

"Unfortunately, no. There was no evidence that anyone had been there recently. No roads, no tire tracks, no crushed brush, no evidence of life whatsoever. It's bogus. He manipulated the GPS data."

I sighed, trying not to be too disappointed. I hadn't believed it could be that easy, but a part of me had hoped Broodryk would be arrogant enough to slip up.

"Okay, well, now we know what it's not. Doesn't mean we still can't guess what his true purpose was in giving it to us."

"*Si.* I have some ideas of my own. I have to go, but I'll be back." He set the coffee and bagel in front of me. "Eat. You need to keep up your energy, okay?"

As he set down the food, he noticed my notes about Broodryk's goals. He read them and then raised his gaze to meet mine. I could see by the hardness in his eyes he didn't like what I'd written, even though he might have agreed with it.

I didn't know what I could say to assuage his concern, so I picked up the coffee and took a sip. He fixed it just the way I liked it—weak with lots of milk and sugar. He knew me well.

"Thanks for the food."

"You're welcome. I'll be back soon."

After he left, Mark and I reviewed the tape about thirty times more. I compared the transcript to the audio. I made notes of inflections and pauses, considered patterns, rhythm, emphasis, word choice and intonation. Nothing stood out. After I had taken all the notes I could, we moved on.

Next I watched the video without the sound. Watching the video was significantly harder than listening to it, so I had to pause several times and take an emotional break. I wanted to watch it at least a dozen more times, but I decided to give myself a breather and come back later for a fresh look. I wanted to turn my attention to the GPS coordinates and what they might represent other than a geographical location.

Focusing on the numbers helped. They were simple, devoid of emotion and logical. Right up my alley.

Five hours passed. Mark bought us a couple of sandwiches and more coffee at the small café in the lobby of the building. I forced myself to eat some of it. Woodward stopped by to check on our progress, or lack thereof, a couple of times. On his last visit, he'd told me that we'd reconvene in the conference room in one hour to report on our findings.

At some point, Mark removed his tie. His blue dress shirt was now open at the throat, revealing a white undershirt. His hair was rumpled because he'd been running his fingers through it repeatedly, and his eyes looked bloodshot. I'd avoided the mirror the last time I'd been to the bathroom.

"Do you want to watch the video again?" he asked.

I'd spent the last two hours crunching the GPS numbers six ways to Sunday, but was having no success. Frustration bubbled in my throat. I wasn't able to look at the evidence dispassionately and it seemed to be adversely affecting my judgment and thought processes.

I sighed, pushing away the paper. I had filled several pages with equations and code. Nothing was working for me.

I took a big slug of water. "No, I don't want to watch it again, but I should. You come up with anything?"

"Not much. I've run a pretty exhaustive aural analysis of the background noises. I identified a sound compatible with a window air-conditioner, which likely means he was in a warm location when he shot the video. Seeing as how it's February, that does give us some geographical exclusion, unless he was keeping the room specifically cold on purpose. You know, for special computer equipment or to keep the prisoner cold for torture purposes or something." He must have seen something in my expression, because he backtracked, clearing his throat. "Uh, the torture thing is a stretch, of course. Sorry."

It wasn't a stretch and we both knew it. "Anything else?"

"There's the hum of a refrigerator—it's low-grade, given the grinds and groans—and a soft purr, likely from nearby electronic equipment, probably a computer. The place had electricity, which rules out the coordinates we got from Kenya unless he used a portable generator. Except, I can't isolate any noises a generator would make, so I think we stay with electricity. Maybe my team will have discovered something else I missed." He didn't look hopeful, which scared me.

I had zip. *Nada*. Hours were slipping by and I had absolutely freaking nothing to go on.

I glanced up at the clock on the wall. "We've got about fifty minutes until the team convenes. I'll take another look at the video."

"You want audio, too?"

The thought of hearing the whip strike Elvis's face again made my stomach turn. "No. Just visual."

"Got it."

He started the video and I stood up and turned off the light. This time I stood next to the screen, eyeball-to-eyeball with my nightmare.

For the previous viewings, I'd concentrated on everything in the room except Elvis. This time I prepared myself and focused exclusively on him.

My heart felt like it was being shredded to tiny pieces as the video played. I clenched my fists to keep steady and observant. He was injured, possibly badly. There was blood spatter on his T-shirt, but at least I didn't see any area that indicated saturation or a significant wound beneath his shirt. Of course, I couldn't rule out internal bleeding, but I didn't dare go down that road now.

I took a breath and kept watching. He'd been hit particularly hard on the left side of his face. There were smears of blood across his cheek, chin and neck, possibly the result of a broken or bloody nose. Bruises bloomed across his left cheek. His left eye was swollen shut.

Nonetheless, he sat defiant, calm and angry. He wasn't broken, he was angry. I could see it clearly in his one good eye and the set of the jaw I knew so well.

Not realizing I was doing it, I reached up to touch his face. That's when I saw it.

"Stop," I shouted.

FOURTEEN

MARK MUST HAVE been dozing, because he started so violently he nearly knocked the laptop off the table.

"What?" He hit the pause button. "What is it?"

"Here." I pointed to the screen. "Back it up a little."

Mark backed it up.

"A little more, then push Play."

Mark played the video and I stared at the space. "There. Did you see it?"

"See what?"

I pointed to a blank spot on the wall about two centimeters above Elvis's left shoulder. "Enlarge this space by two-hundred twenty-five percent. Back it up and play it again. Slow it down if possible."

Mark saw it at the same time I did. "A light. A barely perceptible flash of light. Damn, I didn't see it."

I tapped the screen. "I never noticed it before either. Keep playing and watch this spot exclusively.

He played it to the end and we counted twenty-nine flashes, with the last flash occurring seconds before Broodryk walked into the video.

"Start it over," I said excitedly. "He may have been doing it from the beginning, but I didn't catch it."

Sure enough, the pattern of lights started exactly eighteen seconds into the video.

We played it all the way through, taking notes to make sure we didn't miss anything, then I turned on the light switch, jumped into my chair and woke up my laptop.

"Now we're talking. Okay, Mark, give me those light sequences. Note the time in the video, whether they are long or short flashes, and the elapsed time between the flashes. You know the drill."

"Already ahead of you. Wow, this is good. We needed a break."

My fingers flew over the keyboard as he recited the data. My spirits soared. Numbers in, numbers out. Now I was in my element.

"What are you thinking?" Mark asked as he finished giving me the sequences. "Flashes of light conjure up images of World War II sailors flashing SOS messages. Do you think he's using Morse code?"

"That's where I'm going first. It's the most logical. I'm running the analysis right now. Give me a moment. I'm in the zone." My fingers ached from the typing.

After a few minutes, I sat back in my chair. My spirits, which moments before had been in the stratosphere, crashed and burned. "It's not Morse code."

Mark slumped. "Guess I shouldn't be surprised. It would have been too easy for a nutcase like him."

I swept my notes onto the floor in frustration. "Damn it. He's playing me. He knows I'm never going to find it in time. I thought we had it."

"Hey, don't beat yourself up. He probably altered or switched it up. He wants to keep you on your toes."

Pushing my hands through my hair, I kneaded my scalp. "I know. You're right. I'm sorry. I'm tired and scared, not to mention way too emotionally invested in this situation. I just thought I had it." I knelt to pick up the sheets of paper.

Mark joined me on the floor, helping me. "Look, I don't know if it will make you feel better, but if I were in your shoes, I'd be a complete basket case by now. I'm surprised you're still able to hold a coherent thought."

I sighed as he handed me some papers. "I'm a freaking mess."

"Well, you don't show it. Hang in there. We're going to figure it out and save your friend. We have to. At least we have something to work with now."

"I know. It's just everything takes time. It's the one thing we don't have in abundance. Come on, let's take another crack at it."

We sat back at our respective laptops and got to work. Mark was typing something while I sorted through the next best approach to tackling the coding sequence. I was leaning toward working up a Caesar Shift Cipher when Mark spoke.

"Did you know the world doesn't even use Morse code anymore? It was officially retired in 1999 when the Global Maritime Distress Safety System globally replaced it on a whim. I tried the GMDSS with what we've got, but nothing panned out either. I thought it was worth a shot."

"That was good thinking," I said and then froze. "Wait, that gave me an idea." I started typing.

Mark peered around his screen. "What idea?"

"Global. You said globally. That reminded me I used the global or international Morse code key, the ITU. But I forgot. There's another key. A historical key exclusive to America."

"Hey, now that you mention it, I think I actually knew that." He started typing, but I was way ahead of him. After a moment, I pushed back my chair.

"Holy crap. I think we've got it."

FIFTEEN

MARK LEAPED FROM his chair and stared at the screen over my shoulder, reading my translation.

"We've got what? A message? What does it say?" He read aloud from my screen. "'A man's faith might be ruined by looking at that picture.' Huh? What does that mean?"

I didn't have a chance to answer him because Dex Woodward stepped into the room followed by several more people.

All the same crowd from yesterday filed in except I saw a young woman who hadn't been in here before. She was probably in her early thirties with long chestnut hair pulled back in a bun and eyes so light brown they were almost gold. She carried a large file stuffed with papers and was dressed in a navy suit with a photo badge hanging around her neck. She gave me a small smile as she came in and sat next to Woodward.

I gathered up my notes and laptop and made room for the others. I didn't see Slash, and some guy took his seat next to me. After waiting a moment, Woodward made a motion and someone closed the door.

"Okay, we've all had several hours to attend to our respective tasks. Let's share what we know. First up, Steve Levy. He's Mark's second-in-command. What do you have on those GPS coordinates, Steve?"

Steve consulted his notes. "Well, we reviewed the GPS coordinates and the satellite images of the site. We considered that the subject might have had a portable residence of some kind. However, extensive review of the site indicated no evidence that a physical structure of any kind had been constructed and no sign that anyone had even been in the area recently.

"We then did a thorough background check on the location to see if it held any kind of historical, environmental or astrological significance. We came up empty. So we ran a transposition between latitude and longitude to see if we could come up with a meaningful location there, but it put us in the middle of the ocean.

"After that we tried applying a Vigenère Cipher, various steganography techniques and a monoalphabetic substitution to the numbers. Basically we've got nothing. I'm sorry. Could be he just spoofed the system and sent us on a goose chase."

I tried not to show my disappointment. They'd done everything I would have, so I couldn't fault their technique. Still, I didn't buy it. I couldn't explain why, but I knew Broodryk had a very deliberate reason for selecting those coordinates. I just couldn't prove it yet.

Woodward thanked Levy and then leaned back so I could better see the woman sitting beside him.

"Lexi, I'd like to introduce you to Grayson Reese. Ms. Reese is a CIA analyst. She's been tracking Johannes Broodryk for more than four years. She's just returned from out of town and has gathered all the intel we have on him. She's prepared to give us a quick background briefing now."

She tilted her head toward me, looking directly at me as she spoke. "Johannes Peter Broodryk was born on February 19, 1977 in Cape Town, South Africa. His father, Drake, was a computer engineer and designed software for one of the early microprocessors for the popular Anati

6600 computer at a company called Dynamica Tech located in Cape Town. His mother, Alina Pogova, was the daughter of Russian immigrants. She taught Russian literature at the University of Cape Town. Both of Broodryk's parents were killed in an automobile accident when Johannes was eleven. He lived with his single uncle, Boni Broodryk, a ship engineer, until he graduated. Johannes attended the University of Cape Town for four years and graduated with the equivalent of a BS in Computer Science with a specialty in network security and neural networks. His grades indicate he was a so-so student. Didn't show up for class much, but got the work done."

I made some notes on my paper. "Did he get a higher degree?"

"He started, but got kicked out. Got a taste for hacking. He stole about four hundred thousand dollars from a local bank and had blown through most of it by the time he was caught. He got three years in a minimum-security facility where he apparently honed his skills even further in the prison computer lab and got his hate on for authority in general."

I nodded and she continued without looking at her notes.

"Once out of prison, he went to live with a friend of a friend he'd met in prison. They needed a computer guy for their underground business and Broodryk fit the bill perfectly. Drugs, money laundering, forgery, extortion and robbery were just a start for him. His friend in prison, Gregor Muller, eventually got out and re-joined the operation. The two of them renamed their organization *Skelm*, which in Afrikaans slang can mean either troublemaker or a lover on the sly. Somewhere along the line Broodryk and Muller had an ugly falling out and the group split. Broodryk renamed his group the Veiled Knights and moved his operation to Johannesburg."

I interrupted. "The Veiled Knights—Broodryk's group—were the ones who masterminded the hit on the high school."

"Yes. Broodryk moved in a new direction and put the word out that the Veiled Knights are cyber mercenaries or hackers for hire. Cyber terrorism, fraud, documents, assassinations and drugs. You name it—he'll do it...for a price. He's amassed a fortune."

"What do we know about Broodryk's most recent whereabouts?"

"Intelligence indicates he prefers to operate out of Africa in general. Not only is it home, it's easier for him to move from country to country without detection. We do know that at one time or the other, he has had compounds in Johannesburg and Port Elizabeth, both of which are in South Africa. He also has been traced to the cities of Luanda in Angola, Niamey in Niger and Victoria in Seychelles. Most recently, we have determined he was operating out of Gabon during his attack on the high school in Washington, DC. The odds are extremely high he's still on the African continent. However, we are unable to isolate his specific location at this time."

I jotted some notes. "Does he have a family? Wife, children or a significant other?"

"None that we know of. We obtained his psychological reports from the prison, where he was required to undergo monthly examinations. The reports indicate he has a highly narcissistic personality with an overstated sense of self, a deep-seated need for admiration and a complete lack of empathy, among a range of other sociopathic tendencies. That kind of personality doesn't lend itself to long-lasting relationships, although we can't rule it out. We just don't know. However, despite his need for attention and admiration, the last photo we have of him is the one of him taken in prison." She nodded to a guy with a laptop and Broodryk's photo appeared on the smart board.

I shuddered. Broodryk's albinism—his white hair and pale skin—caused his face to blend into the stark white backdrop. His eyes freaked me out the most. They should have been a beautiful bluish white, but they were utterly devoid of emotion. Sociopath was an apt description for him.

"No one that we know of has seen him in person since this picture was taken." She cleared her throat gently. "No one except you. Can you advise us on his appearance?"

I set my pen down. "The fact that I saw him via a computer screen filters it some. But he looks very much the same. A little thinner in the cheeks and face—perhaps from age and maturity. But the eyes are identical. As of a few weeks ago, he hadn't changed the color or style of his hair. He still presented as albino."

She made a note of her own. "Okay, thanks. Doesn't mean he hasn't changed things up by now, but it's good to know."

Slash stepped into the room. Our eyes met and he gave me a small nod. Woodward acknowledged him and then motioned to a thin, red-headed guy who sat farther down the table.

The guy lifted a hand. "I'm Stuart Levy and I work with the NSA. My team was assigned the analysis of the painting in the video and the potential significance of it as part of a code. This is what we know so far from the video itself and the research we compiled in the short time we had."

He clicked on his laptop. The painting appeared on

the smart board. "We think this is the painting hanging on the wall. It's a replica, of course, and it's called *The Body of the Dead Christ in the Tomb*. German painter Hans Holbein is believed to have painted it in 1521. The painting is oil on wood and is 30.5 by 200 centimeters. It currently hangs in the Kunstmuseum in Basel, Switzerland. The painting depicts a life-size, biologically accurate rendering of Jesus Christ lying in his tomb. Art critics agree that Holbein, who reportedly unearthed a dead body to use as a model for the painting, wanted to show a realistic view of Jesus suffering the fate of an ordinary man. The decay and malformation of the body is consistent with what a body might look like after twenty-four to forty-eight hours in a warm environment. We ran several algorithms on the digital files of the painting to see if we could detect any abnormal or unusual use of color, paint, techniques or significant objects. We came up empty-handed. Scholarly research on the painting is limited mostly to an examination of Holbein's art techniques—none of which appear to be out of the ordinary—and his influence on modern literature."

I looked up from taking notes. "He had an influence on modern literature?"

He nodded. "Specifically Russian author Fyodor Dostoyevsky. Dostoyevsky refers to the painting in his novel *The Idiot*. He apparently viewed the painting in person in 1867. He spent so long staring at it that his wife feared it would induce an epileptic incident. The painting made such an impression on him that he later incorporated a viewing of it among his characters in the novel."

"Wait." My thoughts whirled. I held up a hand so no one else would talk while I tried to sort out the significance. "Broodryk's mother was Russian and taught Russian Literature at the university. 'A man's faith might be ruined by looking at that picture.'"

Levy frowned, puzzled. "Excuse me?"

I grabbed my laptop, typed in the phrase and then grinned in excitement. "That's it. Dostoyevsky wrote this exact phrase on page four, paragraph nine of his novel *The Idiot*. It happens when two characters are looking at the painting The Body of the Dead Christ by Hans Holbein. One character asks the other if he believes in God. The first character, apparently horrified by the painting, cries out that a man's faith might be ruined looking at that picture."

I glanced up and realized everyone in the room, except for Mark and Slash, was looking at me as if I'd completely lost my mind.

"What the hell does any of that mean?" Woodward asked.

"It means she found the first clue," Slash said.

SIXTEEN

EVERYONE STARTED TALKING at once. Woodward had to get everyone quiet so I could bring them up to speed on the flashes of light Mark and I had discovered on the video and how we'd translated it.

"So, the bottom line is that Broodryk sent me a message in the form of a Dostoyevsky quote," I finished. "What it means, I don't know yet."

"Dostoyevsky's book *The Idiot*?" Woodward asked. "Do you think the title of the book is significant? Like he's referring to us as idiots or something?"

I shifted impatiently. "Sure, he's poking at us, but I don't think that's what's paramount here. He now references Dostoyevsky twice, which means he's making it clear that whatever we need to do has to involve him somehow."

"I'm not following you," Woodward said. "Dostoyevsky is a dead Russian novelist. How does this factor in to our situation?"

Mark suddenly pumped his fist in the air. "Got something. I just ran the transcript of the video against a cross-reference of Dostoyevsky quotes and came up with another match. Broodryk said, 'I've plenty of time... my time is entirely my own.' Dostoyevsky wrote that as well—word for word. And it also came from *The Idiot*."

My mind raced as I organized the information, trying to sort through the significance. "That's three times he cites Dostoyevsky—twice from the same novel. Three times is the charm. Now I have to put it all together. What's he trying to tell me? I'm still missing a piece of the puzzle. It's got to be those GPS coordinates. They weren't a spoof or misdirection—they mean something."

Slash pushed off the wall. "You're right. They do mean something."

"And you know this how?" Woodward asked.

"I know because while Broodryk may be a psychopath, he's isn't stupid. Those coordinates were chosen specifically for a reason. He didn't just forget his GPS was on when he took the video. He knew that'd be the first thing we checked. Once we viewed the satellite images and ruled out the location, it was game on. I figured Levy's team would take the required path, examining and ruling out the obvious codes and ciphers. Tedious, but necessary work. I knew Broodryk would know that, too, so I decided not to waste time there."

"So, what did you do?" I asked.

"I tried something completely different. I started by converting the coordinates to binary language. I tried "Wow. That was smart thinking, Slash."

"Not smart enough if it didn't work. So, I thought for a while longer and had another idea."

I held my breath. Slash was good, very good, so I knew whatever he said would be vital.

He looked at me. "This time, I put myself in Broodryk's shoes. He wants you to play his game. He has to engage you, draw you in, so what does he need in order to do that?"

I considered. "Communicate. He's got to figure a way to communicate with me. It has to be a back and forth exchange, so he can make certain I'm involved personally and issue appropriate taunts in order to feel superior to me."

"Exactly. Now what's the easiest way for a man like him to do that?"

"A phone number?" Woodward offered. "The GPS numbers could be configured into a phone number. It's too long for a US number, but maybe a variation of an international one? Maybe he wants to talk on the phone."

Mark started typing, but Slash held up a hand, stopping him. "Don't bother. That's not it."

I suddenly knew where Slash was going with this. I almost jumped out of my chair and planted a big one right on his mouth.

"Holy cow." My eyes widened. "It's deceptively simple. I should have thought of it sooner."

"Holy cow, what?" Woodward frowned. "Can someone please clue me in?"

I kept my eyes on Slash. "It's an IP address, right?"

Slash smiled. "Exactly. I had to go to a seven-digit latitude and longitude string and convert east/west into numbers, but that was the easy part. Once I had the formula it was only a matter of time before I came up with the answer."

"Oh my God. You're a freaking genius. What did you find?"

"I came up with several possibilities, depending on which way I crunched the numbers. But hearing what you and Mark have found, I think we can narrow it to one optimum choice."

Hope soared through me. "What is it?"

Slash put his hands on the table. "A private chat room set up to discuss the literary works of Fyodor Dostoyevsky."

SEVENTEEN

ONCE AGAIN EVERYONE started talking. Woodward had to thump the table to get people quieted down.

Slash walked behind my chair. "First order of business is finding out who owns the address. It's private, but it's likely legit. I had time only for a quick overview, but it looks like the chat room was established about four years ago and has about one hundred and twenty members who visit on and off to discuss their views on the works of Dostoyevsky. My best guess is that Broodryk intends to simply to co-opt the chat room and use it as a place to talk. If I were him, that's what I would do. I don't think we'll get anywhere with discovering the source of the IP address, but we'll have to investigate it anyway."

I glanced up at the clock. "How much time do we have left?"

Woodward scrawled something on his notepad. "Four damn hours. Not much time."

"It's enough." I sat back in my chair. "He knows we'll be tracing him with everything we've got. No doubt he'll take every precaution."

"No doubt," Slash agreed. "If he chats, it will be short and sweet. He already knows what he wants to say... Where he wants things to go."

Grayson Reese's eyes widened. "How can we find him in a public chat room? How will you track him?"

"Very carefully," I answered. "We'll put the best we've got on him. He'll throw every trick in the book at us, but we'll be ready and tracing him in multiple ways. It's a crap shoot, but hopefully we'll get lucky."

Mark stood up. "I've already got my team on the IP address, tracking it down, finding out what we can about it in the most discreet way possible."

Slash nodded. "Good. We'll need to convene a separate tech meeting to discuss our strategy for the chat. First order of business is to get her approved to join the chat room, as it's both moderated and private. Get a couple of spots for us, too."

"I'm on it," Mark said.

I blew out a breath. "I need to think through what I should say to keep him chatting. Every second will count." I turned to Grayson. "You've compiled the most information on him and have been studying him for more than four years. You probably have the best handle on his mental state, his likes and dislikes, and what pushes his buttons. I need you to brief me in detail and sit next to me during the chat in case I need advice."

"Of course."

"So, when do we conduct this chat?" Woodward asked. "How will we know when or if he'll appear?"

I rubbed the back of my neck. "I guarantee he's already there—in and out—checking for me, which will be a good place for the tech team to start. They'll begin tracing those people who have been active for the past few days. We'll go in when we're ready, but at least an hour before the cut-off time. For an initial post, I'll provide a clear identifier so he'll know it's me. If he responds, then we're off."

"And from this chat, we should be able to isolate his location?"

I lifted my shoulders. "I don't know. Maybe. It depends

on what he does and what precautions he has in place. There are no guarantees. But what choice do we have?"

Woodward looked around the table at the somber faces. "Apparently none. Okay, let's do it."

WHILE THE TEAM PREPARED, Grayson Reese gave me more details on Broodryk. I liked the analytical bent of her mind. Two hours and four cups of coffee later, I felt like I knew Broodryk better than I ever wanted. All the information was useful, but I had a stomachache and a serious case of the jitters.

Minutes were ticking past. How could I be certain whether the Dostoyevsky chat room was Broodryk's true plan, whether he would even show, or if he'd just kill Elvis to spite me?

Broodryk would never make it easy.

I stood and started walking around the room, trying to burn off some of the nervous energy. Grayson watched me thoughtfully.

"It sucks to be you right now." She took a sip of her coffee. "On the other hand, it's a stroke of good luck for us that Broodryk has this crazy obsession with you. It's the most activity at one time we've ever seen out of him. You've helped generate more material on him in a few weeks than we've been able to accumulate for the past four years. You really pissed him off."

"Hooray for me. How is it that you got stuck following his every move?"

"Wrong place and the wrong time, I guess. His file got dumped on my desk. Who knew he'd turn out to be such a major threat to the world?"

"It's funny how things like that work."

"Well, it turned out I was a good choice. No husband,

kids or social life to speak of, so I have the time to devote to tracking his every move."

"That's a break for me. I'm glad you're on our side."

She smiled. "Look, Lexi, I know you're worried, but we're going to catch him. Eventually. Everyone said Osama bin Laden would be impossible to find and we nailed him. If we really want him—and we do—we'll get him. Broodryk is now the number-one priority of the American government, not to mention most of our allies. His days are numbered."

I put my hands on the back of one of the chairs. "The real question is time. Will we be able to find him in time to save Elvis?"

I knew her answer when she wouldn't meet my gaze. "That's what I thought. But I'm not giving up."

"You shouldn't. I'm going to do everything I can to help you. Trust me, weirder things have happened."

I nodded. "Let's just hope this is one of them."

"ARE WE READY?" I asked, my stomach clenching.

The room was packed. We'd moved to a bigger conference room to accommodate more people and equipment. Someone had decided it was necessary to film the proceedings. There were cameras pointed at me from all four corners of the room. Slash sat to my left and Grayson to my right. Woodward paced behind me and acted like the conductor of the operation.

I wanted to throw up, but I swallowed hard and kept my game face on. In minutes I would know whether I'd properly unraveled the clues or if Elvis would die because I'd screwed up.

I felt a trickle of sweat bead on my temple. All these people and the pressure were making me physically ill. Slash reached under the table and patted my thigh.

"You've got this, *cara*," he murmured.

I pressed my lips together and poised my fingers over the keyboard. "Am I good to go?"

Mark checked something on his screen and flashed me a thumbs-up. "You're ready, Lexi. I count four active accounts in the room right now. We've already started a trace on all of them. Good luck. Team, stand by."

It was as if the entire room held its collective breath as I started typing. No pressure there...

I popped into the chat room using my personal account and typed.

Hello. I'm new here. I'm a big fan of Dostoyevsky, especially his novel The Idiot. Anyone else like this book?

I waited and watched the blinking cursor.

Grayson leaned over and asked, "What's your call name again?"

"The Idiot," I replied. "Nothing like a little overkill, just in case."

"Good plan."

It took exactly three minutes and four seconds to elicit a reply.

Hey! Nice to have you here. I enjoyed The Idiot, too. I felt like this was Dostoyevsky's best work in terms of depicting actual Russian life rather than just providing an aloof intellectual commentary disguised as a literary novel.

"I'm on it," Mark said. "Appears to be the registered moderator. Running the trace now. Looks straight and clean so far. Narrowing it to New England. To Rhode Island. To a residence in the city of Cranston. No evidence of evasion or unusual protection."

Slash shook his head. "It's not him."

"Put someone in Rhode Island on stand-by anyway," Woodward ordered.

Mark nodded. "Check."

"Okay, I'm responding," I said, and started typing.

I agree. My favorite part is when Myshkin tells Rogozhin that a man's faith could be ruined by looking at Hans Holbein's painting of the Body of the Dead Christ in the Tomb.

"Come on, come on," I murmured. "I'm here."

Wow. That's kind of an odd part of the novel to be your favorite. What prompted you to pick that?

"It's the same guy responding," I reported. "Are there still three other people in the room?"

Mark typed some commands. "Yes. But they are different than those who were logged in just minutes ago. We are running traces on all of them. The most recent activity in the room, other than the chat you are having right now, was eleven minutes ago. It surprises me that it's a pretty active group for such an archaic topic."

"Go figure," I muttered. "Okay. I'm responding."

I guess it's because I struggle with the concept of faith myself. Is God real? Can we better ourselves through his teachings? Is death the end for us or is there life beyond our existence as we know it?

Slash glanced sideways at me, his fingers pausing over the keyboard. I shrugged, then focused my screen as the moderator typed something else.

Ah, now I see your reasoning. There are some critics who say that Prince Myshkin is a Christlike figure and represents all that which is pure and noble in the human spirit. But Rogozhin is struggling with his faith, too.

Mark straightened in his chair. "Hello. We've got a sudden influx of chatters. Sixteen so far."

My heart started pounding. "It's Broodryk. He's flooding the room on purpose."

"Stay calm," Slash warned. "Pick them off, one by one. He's got to choose at least one identity to chat with her."

"He'll mix it up," Mark said, his voice containing a trace of panic. "He'll hop from one to the next. God, he's added more. We're up to thirty-four chatters now."

"Steady," Slash said. "Take them in order. We're still in control."

Well, hello, new member. It took you long enough. I didn't think you'd show, but I'm impressed you did. Well done.

"It's Broodryk," I said, the calmness of my voice contrasting the way my hands trembled. "We have contact."

Woodward peered over my shoulder. "Someone find me that son of a bitch."

I inhaled a steadying breath and typed my response.

I'm usually late to parties, if I come at all.

Grayson nodded approvingly. "Good. Casual, a bit uncaring. Challenge his superiority, his manhood. Don't let him know how scared you are. You must be a worthy opponent."

Broodryk's response was immediate.

You passed the first test. Congratulations. Your friend is glad you came, too. He can't wait to see you. Neither can I for that matter. Ready for a rocking good time? A threesome perhaps?

Slash stiffened beside me.

"Ignore the sexual overtones and go straight to the heart of the matter," Grayson advised. "He's trying to intimidate you. Ask about Elvis."

I pushed aside my revulsion and typed.

How's Elvis?

There was a pause, then a message popped up.

Hey, are you guys talking about Dostoyevsky or setting up a date? Take it offline if you are getting hot and heavy.

"It's the moderator. He's pissed. How are we doing on the trace?" I asked.

"Broodryk has help," Slash said, his fingers flying across the keyboard. "No way he's doing this himself. Too many moving pieces. But that's good news. Could be whoever is helping him isn't as well protected. We're tracing both him and his accomplice or accomplices. But he's throwing up a lot of smoke screens."

"He is switching identities," Mark said. "He's all over the place."

A message popped up.

Elvis is fine and ready to dance in his blue suede shoes. Waiting to see if you will come through for him or let him expire in a most unfortunate way.

Grayson heard the catch in my breath. "Keep him talking. Remain aloof. Cool."

I'm not much for games. What do you want, Broodryk?

I already knew the answer, but I watched the letters appear on my screen anyway.

You, of course.

"Keep him going," Slash said. "He's exhausting his time. We're closing in."

"Tell him you want to make sure Elvis is still alive before you'll play his game," Grayson advised.

I'm not playing your game until I know Elvis is okay. Prove it to me.

I lifted my fingers from the keyboard. Sweat trickled down my temples. Words popped up on the screen.

Okay that's it. I'm terminating you guys. This is getting too creepy.

"It's the moderator." My voice shook. "He's throwing us out."

"Damn," Mark said. "We're making progress here."

"Can't you stop him?" Woodward asked. "Someone stop that moderator."

"Wait, Broodryk uploaded a file," I said, staring at the screen. Grayson leaned in to look, practically lying on me.

Come to these coordinates. You have four days and not a minute more to obtain the next clue. Ask for the elder, as he has it. However, he requires the current location of the Kwabano in exchange for his cooperation. I suggest you bring that information with you. You may bring whomever else you want with you, as long as it includes Hands. Pentz wants to play, too. You must come in person, Lexi Carmichael. If you send someone else, it's game end. I will know. Your next clue is there. Here is proof of condition. See you soon.

I tried to type something, but nothing happened. "I've been blocked. Damn."

"Broodryk's gone, too," Mark reported. "Vanished."

"Did we get him?" Woodward asked. "Someone explain to me what the hell is happening."

Mark rubbed his forehead. "We didn't get him exactly, but we've got a boatload of data to examine. He's in there somewhere."

"I didn't get to see what he left." Panic made my voice shrill. "What proof did he leave? Where are the coordinates? Did anyone get it?"

Slash put a hand on my arm. "It's okay, *cara.* I'm still in the chat room. We're good. I've got it."

"Oh, jeez. Thank goodness. What is it? What did he leave?"

Slash turned his laptop towards me. He opened a file and a picture of Elvis appeared. He was bruised and gagged, but clearly alive. A newspaper in a foreign language, Arabic perhaps, had been propped on his lap. Slash enlarged the photo and I saw it had today's date on it. On the bottom of the photo were a set of coordinates, clearly marked as longitude and latitude.

"Where is it?" I asked. "Did you have time to plug it in? Where does he want me to go?"

Slash ran his fingers through his hair. "The Central African Republic."

EIGHTEEN

"WHAT?" WOODWARD EXCLAIMED. "What the hell? That guy is completely certifiable."

My heart was pounding. I needed to calm down or I'd pass out.

Grayson frowned. "Forget Africa for a moment. What did he mean about Hands? Is that a person? Why did he reference Abri Pentz?"

Slash pushed back from the table, stood up. "We don't know. We'll have to analyze that, too. But first, we need to strike while the iron is hot. We're moving this operation to the NSA, where we can plug all the data into the big-boy equipment."

"I'll obtain current satellite imaging of the new coordinates," another man offered.

"Wait. Who's the Kwabano?" I asked.

Grayson answered. "It's a violent extremist group that operates in the Central African Republic. It has a history of raiding villages and kidnapping children as young as ten in order to force them into slavery."

My stomach turned over. "Do we know the Kwabano's location?"

Woodward put a hand on the back of my chair. "We will."

"Okay, team. I'll report back as soon as I know something." Mark closed up his laptop and stood.

Everyone started packing up equipment.

I closed my laptop and rose. "I'm coming with you to the NSA, Slash."

Woodward put a hand on my shoulder. "No. I need you here. The bigwigs are waiting for a report and I don't know what the hell to tell them."

"There are a dozen other people in the room right now who have a better idea. Have *them* tell you what's going on."

Woodward lowered his voice. "You want to keep government resources invested in rescuing Elvis Zimmerman? Then I suggest you sit here and tell me what is going on."

It pissed me off, his not-so-subtle suggestion of what would happen to Elvis if I didn't cooperate. I exchanged a glance with Slash and he nodded slightly.

I frowned, but sat back down. "Fine."

Everyone filed out except for Woodward and Grayson Reese. I brought them up to speed on the tech side of what had happened, although it was a sheer waste of time. Neither of them were tech heads, so any discussion of techniques, style or smoke screens wasn't helpful. I tried not to be impatient, but time was ticking. I felt trapped babysitting Woodward, instead of working on what I knew best.

I stopped myself from incessantly tapping my pen and tried to look interested in what they were saying.

"I'm puzzled by why he's chosen the Central African Republic," Grayson said, flipping through some papers in her file. "As far as I can tell, he's never had a residence there. He's definitely funneled money through the banks and had occasional dealings on a low level with a few local warlords, but honestly it doesn't fit his *modus operandi*."

"Isn't it clear why he wants her to go there?" Woodward said, picking up his coffee mug and taking a drink of what had to be stone-cold coffee. "Death, kidnapping, rape, torture—or all of the above."

"He doesn't want me dead," I said absently. "Not yet, anyway."

"You don't know that for sure," Woodward said.

"I do. He could have had Pentz shoot me at any given time. But that would have taken the fun out of it. The entire shoot-out was calculated. He shot at me in front of my parents and boyfriend to let me know that no one I love is safe."

"Agreed," said Grayson. "That was pretty dramatic. He'd love that."

I shrugged. "Only Broodryk didn't do his homework very well. He didn't know anything about Slash. *Couldn't* find anything, I'll bet. Probably figured he was just a tech head. He had no idea Slash would fire back. Surprised the heck out of Pentz for sure."

"Yes," Grayson agreed. "But it didn't stop the plan."

"No. Broodryk wanted a big show and instructed Pentz to leave the thumb drive, so that's what he did. It wasn't pretty, though, and that probably pissed both of them off. Now Pentz probably feels like I'm unfinished business as well, which is why he wants in on the so-called fun."

Grayson frowned. "So, who is this Hands that Broodryk referenced? He said he doesn't care who comes with you as long as you include Hands."

I lifted my hands. "I have no clue."

"I know who he's referring to."

We looked up and saw a lean middle-aged man dressed in a military uniform in the doorway. His wiry black hair had silver streaks and his jacket had an impressive load of medals.

Woodward rose. "Jack. Glad you could make it."

"Wouldn't have missed it." Jack stepped forward and shook hands with Woodward. "I was next door when word came down that you might need my assistance."

"Yes, indeed. This is Lexi Carmichael, the target of the operation, and Grayson Reese, an analyst and political profiler at the CIA. Ladies, meet Naval Rear Admiral Jack Spearman. I assume you've been read in, Jack?"

"Very briefly. Interesting turn of events."

"To say the least."

Grayson and I shook his hand. I wondered why word had come down that we needed the Navy's help, but it looked like I was about to find out.

"Sit down," Woodward urged. "We were just talking about someone named Hands."

"So I heard."

We all sat back down and I leaned forward. "So, do you know who this Hands is?"

"I do. He's one of my men."

"Your men?"

"The Navy SEALs."

I blinked. "Hands is a Navy SEAL?"

"Not just any Navy SEAL. Hands—which obviously isn't his real name—is one of the Navy's best snipers."

NINETEEN

"A SNIPER?" I repeated in surprise.

Jack nodded. "Yes. He's one of the best shots in the world."

I took a moment to try and wrap my mind around it. "Whoa. I don't get it. Why would Broodryk mention a Navy SEAL sniper?"

Jack set his elbows on the table. "My guess is that this is not about Broodryk. It's about Abri Pentz."

"Wait. This Hands guy knows Pentz?"

"He does. They have a long-standing feud going back when they were just starting out in their respective military careers. Hands was with us, and Pentz with the British. They competed against one another in numerous international and military sniper competitions as they completed their training. More often than not, it came down to them as the final two. Later, they kept track of each other's tallies in terms of confirmed kills in overseas missions."

"What's with this obsession over kill tallies?" It seemed totally repugnant, but war and conflict were repugnant to me, so what did I really know?

"It's not an obsession. It's all about accuracy for snipers. Anyway, Hands is the better sniper. He's always been one step ahead of Pentz. Don't get me wrong, Pentz is damn good, but he was a bit quick on the trigger. He lacked emotional control, which became evident when he eventually snapped. After his dishonorable discharge, he went rogue and became a gun for hire. He's been working for Broodryk for some time. Apparently he hasn't lost his hate for Hands."

I rubbed my temples. "Apparently I'm really tired, because I'm having trouble seeing how that fits with the big picture here."

"Give me fifteen minutes to chat with Jack," Woodward said, waving his hand at Grayson and me. "You ladies take a bathroom break and grab a sandwich downstairs at the café. Then I'll give you the big picture, okay?"

"How about me going to the NSA to work on the tech side instead?" I asked.

"We've got plenty of experts over there for now. Stay with me, okay? I need you here."

I sighed and glanced at Grayson, who shrugged.

"I could use some fuel," she said. "And another cup of coffee. Come on, I'll treat you."

I didn't feel like eating or drinking more coffee, but Woodward and Spearman had disappeared, so I followed her down to the café. We bought a couple of turkey sandwiches and chips. Grayson got more coffee while I opted for bottled water and more ibuprofen. We ate in silence and I chewed without tasting anything. I was seriously dragging, my brain nearing shutdown from sheer exhaustion and emotional distress. The short nap induced by a tranquilizer seemed years ago. The only thing that kept me going was that—as far as I knew—Elvis was still alive and had been spared for the time being. Still, I wasn't sure how much longer I could keep working without face planting on the table.

When Grayson and I returned to the conference room about fifteen minutes later, a few guys I hadn't seen before had joined Woodward and Jack. They sat behind laptops typing and didn't say a word to us as we sat down. I looked questioningly at Woodward, but he insisted everyone else take a chair and then he closed the door himself.

"We're going to go ahead and get started," he said.

"Get started with what?" I asked.

"We're going to talk action plans. We've analyzed the coordinates in the Central African Republic, the satellite feed of the location, the data from the chat room, and we've uncovered some additional interesting information."

"That was fast. Shouldn't we wait for Slash and the others?"

"They've been delayed, so we're going to press forward."

I wasn't sure what would have caused Slash and the others to be delayed for such an important briefing, but I didn't have a chance to ask because Woodward was already talking.

"We've analyzed the target location," he said, motioning to one of the guys with the laptop. A map popped up on the SMART board and then zeroed in on the coordinates.

"According to the National Geospatial-Intelligence Agency, the coordinates are squarely in a rural, unnamed grazing village about thirty-five kilometers from the town of Boda. The village appears to have no more than a hundred or so full-time inhabitants, most of whom herd goats and sheep and live in shacks. Unfortunately the village recently fell victim to the Kwabano, a group of armed militants who kidnapped more than two-dozen of their children—many as young as ten years old. As a result, the villagers have been arming themselves for a fight to get the children back. It's not a good place to be right now."

I pushed aside the remains of my sandwich. "Broodryk said the elder will cooperate if we provide the information on the whereabouts of the Kwabano. That's why they want the information. They are trying to rescue their children."

"Yes. But it doesn't make the situation any less dangerous. There is no love for Americans in that part of the world."

"Broodryk said to find the elder. I assume that would be a village elder, right?"

"I think that's a safe assumption."

Grayson made a noise of disapproval. "I don't want to be the one to draw attention to the oversized elephant in the room, but I don't like where this is headed. I think it's obvious to everyone that Broodryk is trying to draw us into a trap where he'll employ Abri Pentz to pick everyone off one by one or sell us out to whichever armed group is willing to pay a fee. That is, if whoever is supposed to talk to the so-called elder to get the clue even survives the initial journey past unfamiliar terrain patrolled by extremely hostile and heavily armed extremists and gangs. Doesn't anyone else think this is completely insane?"

"I'm going to give it you straight." Woodward ignored Grayson and focused in on me. His eyes gleamed. "We *must* get Broodryk. His little game with you is generating the best leads we've ever had in regards to his possible location, methods and style. Network specialists are pouring over every byte, adjusting and anticipating what he's going to put in Pruxrat. But it's not going to be enough. We must stop him before he releases that virus."

I narrowed my eyes. "Fine. Just so we're clear, my priority is getting Elvis back alive."

"And we can help you do it. I assure you, without us, you don't have a chance."

I studied him for a moment. "You kept Slash out of this on purpose."

"Yes. He's not going to agree to let you go. Or he'll want to be a part of this. You understand why we cannot permit that."

"Because you're willing to sacrifice both me and Elvis if it comes down to a choice between extracting us or taking Broodryk down."

"Yes."

"Slash is not going to like this."

"No, he will not. Which is why he's not here right now. We needed a chance to put everything on the table for you, unclouded by his frustration and certain hostility."

Once Slash figured out what Woodward had done, hostile would be an understatement. But I was here and Woodward had something to offer that might save Elvis, so I'd listen.

"Fine. What's your plan?"

TWENTY

I LISTENED TO Woodward outline his strategy. Although in the very early stages, it had a straightforward, but breathtakingly dangerous approach. Dangerous because it involved me traveling to the Central African Republic and participating in a military operation that had less than a twenty percent chance of success.

Now I totally understood why Woodward had kept Slash out of the conversation. Despite our progress with engaging Broodryk, I don't think it ever crossed Slash's mind that I'd be asked to go abroad and be physically involved in an operation to secure Elvis's release. I had no military training whatsoever, but here I was considering my role in an armed operation.

Grayson asked a lot of probing questions, which I appreciated. But in the end, nothing remained certain except that, if I did nothing, Elvis would die.

I desperately needed a few hours of sleep so I could make a thoughtful decision. But where? I couldn't go home to my parents and face their interrogation about what was going on. I couldn't face Slash while I was still contemplating Woodward's secret plan. He'd talk me out of it before I had time to think through all of my options clearly and without bias.

Grayson must have sensed my indecision.

"You can come home with me for a few hours. I live close by and I've got a perfectly comfortable couch, if you need to crash."

It was my best option at the moment and I was too tired to try to figure out anything else. "Thanks, Grayson, that would be great."

"Call me Gray," she said.

"Sure, okay."

A security detail of two FBI agents was assigned to us and they followed us to her condo.

"We've got four hours before we have to report back," Gray said when we got inside. "Will that be enough?"

"We don't have a choice."

Her condo was small—one bedroom with a decent-sized kitchen and living room. The couch looked comfortable. She gave me a towel, a spare toothbrush and an oversized T-shirt to sleep in.

I stood in front of a bookshelf stuffed with books and mementos from overseas. "You like to travel."

"Yes. I don't get to do as much of it as I'd like given my current employer."

I picked up a framed photograph. "Your family?"

"My folks and two younger brothers. I'm not married. Hell, I haven't had a date for two years. My job doesn't lend itself to that kind of level of commitment, or *any* level of commitment, really. I work crazy hours and can't talk about what I do. You probably know the drill."

"I guess."

"So, what's with you and that Slash guy? He's your boyfriend, right?"

"Yes."

"He's pretty smart, not to mention hot."

"Yeah, he's good like that."

"He's going to be royally pissed at Woodward."

"Yes, he will."

She hesitated, looking at me. She probably wanted to

ask me a lot more questions, but we were both desperate for sleep.

"Well, let me know if you need anything else, Lexi."

"I will. Thanks."

Before I went to sleep, I plugged in my cell. I had several texts and phone calls—a couple from my parents, but most of them were from Slash.

Where are you, cara? What did Woodward say to you?

I wanted more than anything to lean into his strength, but I had to think things through on my own. These decisions were mine to make. If things went wrong and people died—myself included—he couldn't blame himself. I wouldn't put the responsibility of those decisions on him. I cared too much about him to do that.

I texted him back.

I'm fine and safe. I need a few hours of sleep. Woodward proposed a plan in your absence. We're meeting back at the conference room in four hours. See you then.

I re-read it before I sent. It seemed sterile. I sucked at texting, but I pressed Send anyway.

Then, since I was on a roll, I sent my mom a text saying I was okay and would call her and Dad soon. Sighing, I turned off my phone and stretched out on the couch.

I don't remember falling asleep or dreaming, but in what seemed like an impossibly short time, Gray tapped me awake.

"Hey, Lexi. Time to get up. We've got about an hour until our meeting."

I struggled to sit up and pushed the hair out of my face. "Really? It's been four hours already?"

"Yep. You want some coffee?"

She had already started brewing it. The aroma wafted through the room.

"Sure." My stomach growled and I realized I was hungry, too. I rubbed my eyes until she came into clearer focus. She moved around the kitchen dressed in a white T-shirt and soft shorts. Her dark hair was mussed and she looked really young without make-up and the suit.

I stretched my arms above my head. "Can I hop in the shower?"

"Sure, go ahead. I'm good to go for the day."

I showered and got dressed in the same jeans, T-shirt and sweater I'd had on earlier. Gray slipped into a new suit—this time a black pinstripe with a red blouse. She did her make-up, swept her hair into a bun at the back of her neck, and hung the security badge around her neck. She looked calm, rested and professional. I looked like a kid who had just rolled out of bed.

She pulled down two travel mugs from a cabinet and I filled both with coffee.

"Breakfast of champions." She tossed me a banana and I caught it against my stomach.

"Thanks."

We picked up our security detail in the lobby of the condo and they drove us back to the CIA satellite office.

Dex Woodward met me in the lobby and drew me aside. "Can I speak with you privately, please?"

I looked over at Gray. She shrugged and got on the elevator with the rest of the security detail.

I turned my attention back to Woodward. "What's up?"

"Have you thought about our conversation?"

"Sure, I've thought about it, but I haven't made a decision. I'm not going to do it without talking to Slash first."

"I'm afraid he's in an operational blackout at the moment. Just on the Central African Republic mission. I'm sorry, but we thought it best."

I looked at him incredulous. "Are you freaking serious? You can't keep him shut out of half the operation. He's vital to the mission."

Woodward frowned. "Yes, but we need him focused on Pruxrat, not you."

I clenched my jaw and counted to one hundred by sixes and then did it again backward. It was either that or smack some sense into Woodward.

"Look, Woodward, they are utterly intertwined." I didn't verbalize the implied 'you freaking idiot' at the end of that sentence even though I should have. "Let me give you a word of advice. You can't shut Slash out even if you wanted to. You have no idea what he can do. If he wants in, he's in. You try and go around him and you'll be sorry. What will you do if he quits?"

Woodward paled. "We thought he'd unduly influence you."

"Slash doesn't make my decisions for me, but I value his insight and support. Bring him back in."

"He'll want to go on the operation. We can't allow him to do so."

"Fine, but shutting him out is the wrong way to approach this. You can't do this without him and I *won't* do it without his help. Slash and I are a team. Let's be clear about that, okay?"

"Well, you need to be clear then, too. Slash stays stateside. That's the bottom line. We won't let him accompany you if you decide to go."

"Understood. But now he's going to be royally pissed. It was a stupid strategic mistake. Bring him back now. I need him."

He hesitated. "I have to get approval from the top."

"Seeing as how my cooperation depends on it, I have every confidence you'll succeed in getting it."

TWENTY-ONE

SLASH PACED IN the confines of the small space adjoining the conference room. "You can't be seriously considering this."

"I have to evaluate every option."

"It's not an option. It's suicide."

I twirled my finger around my ponytail. Anxiety was causing my stomach to twist painfully. Because of Woodward's stupid decision, we'd wasted another hour of precious time catching Slash up. Slash got angrier with every word Woodward spoke. By the time Woodward finished, Slash was barely containing his fury. I'd asked to speak with him alone, so Woodward had led us to a small room.

Slash's jaw was clenched so tightly, I worried it might crack.

I didn't want to do it, but there was no sense in wasting more time. My throat seized up so badly, I had to choke out the words.

"I'm going to go, Slash."

He recoiled. "What?"

"I'm going to go. I've analyzed it six ways to Sunday and while it's risky, it's our best chance of saving him."

His expression indicated a mixture of ferocity and disbelief. "That's Woodward talking. It is *not* our best chance of saving him. You can still save him right here from the safety of Washington. There are a number of vital functions you can do from here."

"Such as?"

"Such as engaging Broodryk remotely. We have ways to make him believe you are where he wants you to be without you having to be physically present. You know that."

"Yes, I know that. But Broodryk would know it, too. He's a true wizard, not a kid or a novice. He wants me to engage personally, and he'll plan for that contingency."

"He won't find out. I'll construct an impenetrable cover."

I lifted my hands. "I can't tell you how desperately I want to believe that. But Broodryk will expect that. He'll be looking hard, probing for deception. You're good, Slash, maybe the best in the world, and I'd help you. But we don't have the time to create the kind of cover we'd need to stop someone like Broodryk. Besides, you have to focus on Pruxrat. You can't split your time and be everything to everyone at once."

"I'd figure it out."

"I believe you would try. I sincerely do. But if Broodryk finds a weakness in that cover, he'd kill Elvis on the spot. I can't risk it. There would be no second chances or do-overs. Broodryk hasn't gone to all this trouble so I can engage him remotely. My attempts to deceive him in that way would enrage him. I promise you, he'll have ways to ensure and verify my physical presence. Elvis's death would be worse than I could possibly imagine if I don't show up in Africa."

"You can't possibly go. You can't forfeit your life like this. If you go, that's what you'll be doing."

"It's not like I'm going into this alone. They're going to have the Navy SEALs accompany me."

"It won't be enough. It's still suicide. You won't come back. None of you will. That's Broodryk's end game. Listen carefully to me, *cara*. You're so upset, you're thinking with your emotions instead of your intellect."

So was he, but I didn't want to argue that with him, too.

"You're right, Slash. Emotions are factoring strongly in my decision. I know it's not like me, but I'm well aware there are serious risks. Woodward's an idiot, but he's got a plan."

"He's manipulating you. He doesn't give a damn about you."

"I know he's using me. He's doing his job. But he's correct that it's the best chance we have of finding Broodryk *and* saving Elvis. We *have* to play Broodryk's game."

"Then play it from here. I can multi-task. I swear."

I reached out, touched his cheek. "No, you can't. You're already exhausted, and you need to focus on Pruxrat. It's vital. Please. You do your part and I'll do mine to save Elvis."

His jaw hardened beneath my fingertips. "I didn't want to say this to you, *cara*, but it's time to put the truth on the table. Elvis is already as good as dead. No matter what he says, Broodryk is never going to let him go."

I stepped back, dropping my hand. The bluntness of his words hurt even though I knew he said them out of concern for me.

"I know, Slash. I've always known. But it doesn't mean we can't do everything in our power to save him." My voice shook. "I'm not giving up."

"I'm not giving up either, but I'd rather risk Broodryk exploiting my cover for you while you're here safely within arm's reach and not in Africa."

"I agree that would be safer for me, but it puts not only Elvis at risk, but billions of other people who might suffer as a result of Pruxrat."

"I've got Pruxrat covered."

"Not if you've got me and my impenetrable cover to worry about. Think rationally. We've got to come at Broodryk from both sides. I have to go."

He leaned forward, bracing his hands against the table. "Have you thought what Elvis would want? He wouldn't be on board with this plan either. You heard him. He told you not to come. He suffered that beating to tell you that himself. Don't make his suffering meaningless."

The anguish in his eyes cut at me, but I held my ground. "Playing the guilt card on me won't work. I heard what Elvis said. But this isn't just about you and me and Elvis anymore. It's bigger than that. This is our best chance to stop Broodryk for good, not just put a bandage on the problem. We both know he won't stop unless we get him. We've never been this close to him before and we may never get the opportunity again. We can't waste this opportunity."

"Please, *cara*, let the SEALs do their job in Africa. Stay here and work with me."

I pressed my hand to my forehead. Pain throbbed behind my eyes. "I wish I could, I really do. I understand the dangers, Slash, but I have to make the decision I think is right in the long run. I'm going to stop Broodryk... or die trying."

He swore, throwing up his hands. "*Mio dio!* Listen to me. You *will* die. Don't fool yourself into thinking you'll be safe because of a few men with specialized training. No one can keep you safe. Not even me. Not if you go there. I can't be there with you."

I blinked back the tears. "I know. You're too valuable. I'm expendable and so is Elvis. But we'll risk it if it means we can get Broodryk."

He grabbed my arm. "You're not expendable to me. Don't ever say that." His voice was rough with emotion. "Never."

"Please, Slash, I can't do this without you."

He slammed a forearm against the wall in frustration. "No. I won't be a willing party to your death."

"Then help keep me alive."

"You can't ask me to do this…help plan your suicide."

I swiped at the wetness on my eyelashes. "If it were me tied to that chair, you'd come."

"*Si*, I would. Because I could. I'm fully trained for this kind of operation. You're not. You have no idea of the things that could happen…*will* happen. This is war. It's brutal, vicious and ugly. Even if you survived, things like this change you. Permanently. I know, trust me. I'm speaking from experience."

I looked at him steadily. "You think I'm naive, but I understand what you're saying. I really do. Consider this, though. If I don't go, if I let Elvis die, then what? Who will Broodryk come after next? You? My parents? Basia? You want me to live with that? Because I've thought of that and I couldn't do it. If I lost Elvis and then you, *that* would change me permanently. We're both smart enough to know Broodryk can keep his promises to hurt my friends and family. It will *never* end until he sends someone to shoot me who won't miss. By that time, I'd probably welcome it."

He closed his eyes and said nothing.

"Slash, please. Have faith in me. I can do this. I *will* do this."

His fists clenched at his side. "Then you do it alone. I won't help you throw your life away. I can't."

I couldn't breathe. I couldn't move. My world shattered into tiny pieces.

I swallowed the lump in my throat. "I…understand."

But I didn't really. I hadn't created this set of lousy choices, but still I had to choose. I needed him to support me, even though I was risking my life. I wasn't on top of this relationship stuff yet, but he'd promised we were a team and I wasn't alone. Now…now he was leaving me.

He turned away, as if he could no longer look at me.

I choked out the words. "I have to do this. I'm sorry."

"So am I."

Without another word, he strode past me and slammed the door.

TWENTY-TWO

I WAS BARELY able to function, but since the decision to proceed with the operation had been made, it was now a matter of logistics. I'd been told to get my affairs in order, so I filled out a bunch of paperwork and had a strained telephone conversation with Finn. Two CIA agents had visited him earlier in the day and told him I'd been co-opted in a matter of national security. I could tell he wanted to ask me a lot of questions, but he knew better. I couldn't tell him anything except I would take the time off as vacation, and I fully intended to return to my job if he'd still have me. He'd sounded worried, but told me to take all the time I needed and my job would definitely be waiting.

Finally, I made a long overdue phone call to Basia and updated her as much as I could about Xavier and Elvis. I must have sounded pretty awful, because she stopped me mid-sentence.

"Lexi, are you okay?"

"Yes, I'm fine." My voice wavered and I fought back the emotion. "No, Basia, I'm not fine. I'm a mess. I'm beyond worried about Elvis, and Slash and I had an awful fight. It wasn't about leaving the toilet seat up either. He's totally not talking to me. In fact, he might never speak to me again."

"Oh, honey. I'm so sorry. Emotions are running high right now. He'll come around."

"I don't know that he will. He's really angry."

"He's running scared. We all are. We're coping the best we can in our own ways. Do you want me to talk to him?"

"No. It won't help. There's nothing you can do."

"Are you sure?"

"Yes." I was pretty darn sure that even Basia couldn't persuade Slash to feel okay about what I had to do.

"There has to be some way I can help."

"Well, there might be something. Do you have any idea how to contact Xavier's parents? I've never heard either Elvis or Xavier talk about them. Someone needs to tell them what's happened."

"Um… I don't know. Xavier never mentioned them."

"It's okay. I'll figure it out."

"Look, if you need to go to their house, Xavier told me they have a spare key in the backyard in the third stacked brick by the back steps. It's not a real brick, but a fake one. It will only open the side door. Hold on a sec and let me check the notepad on my phone. Ah, here it is. The alarm code for the house is #314159."

I smiled. "Pi."

"Huh?"

"Never mind. Thanks, Basia. I'll let you know what I discover."

"Hang in there. Love you. I really do."

This might be the last time I ever spoke to her. "Basia? I…want to tell you something. The first day we met and you walked into our dorm room dressed in pink and pulling monogrammed luggage, I thought we'd hate each other. But you turned out to be my first real friend. I'm not sure I can adequately explain how important your friendship has been to me."

"Oh, sweetie. I know and I feel the same way."

I clicked the off button and then stared at the phone for

a long moment. Putting it aside, I opened my laptop and did a quick search online for the Zimmermans' parents. I came up completely empty-handed. Guess it would require a visit to their house after all.

I found my security detail—two FBI agents—and told them where I needed to go. They were nice, but I was beginning to have a firsthand understanding of what it felt to be Slash. Being shadowed every moment of every day was beginning to feel seriously creepy.

The guys drove me to the twins' house and were happy enough to wait in the car after I'd retrieved the key, turned off the alarm and they'd cleared both the perimeter and the house. When they were done and had gone outside, I headed for Computer Central, aka the living room, which they had converted into a huge workstation.

The room remained freezing cold, even in their absence, in an effort to protect their equipment. I grabbed the blue blanket they kept for me and wrapped it around my shoulders.

I stood in the middle of the room looking between Xavier's and Elvis's desks. Xavier's desk was messy with papers, note pads, cables and thumb drives scattered around. Elvis's was like mine—everything in its place, perfectly organized with a maximum degree of functionality.

Sighing, I sat down in Elvis's chair and put my hands on his desktop, imagining him sitting here. It was such a familiar memory that I almost expected him to walk into the room and smile at me like he always did.

Reminding myself I'd come here for a purpose, I overcame my reluctance to go through Elvis's private things and got to work. I didn't fool myself into thinking I could penetrate their electronic network, so I'd have to do this the old-fashioned way. I pulled open the first drawer and started going through it.

It held mostly pens, pencils, mechanical drawing items and flash drives. On the right side of the drawer was a photograph. I picked it up. It was a picture taken of Elvis and me in Ocean City, Maryland, the place I had first met the twins. Basia or Xavier must have taken the photo, which I'd never seen before. Elvis and I stood on the Boardwalk with our backs to the sea. We were smiling and Elvis had his arm slung around me. Even though the photo wasn't quite a year old, we seemed so young and happy. I touched his cheek with my fingertip and then put the photo back where I'd found it. The second drawer held paper and a few small notepads. The third drawer was filled with files. I thumbed through them, feeling uncomfortable looking through his personal documents, but reminding myself it was necessary.

I figured he kept all his addresses electronically, but I hoped to find, at the very least, a mention of one of his parent's name on a document that could get me started in a more efficient online search. I opened a file labeled Garden Springs Resort and pulled out a colorful brochure with a colonial building and lots of pretty landscaping.

I scanned the brochure and realized it was an assisted living facility. I set the brochure aside and picked up the next document—a signed application for an Ottilie Zimmerman to be admitted to the facility. It was dated five years prior. My calculations put her at sixty-nine years old, and we shared the same birthday. I read the rest of the contract, but no medical information was provided. There was also no mention of a husband, and further investigation into the file didn't produce any more leads or information on him.

I put the file back and sat back in the chair. After a

moment, I got my cell out and dialed the number from the brochure.

"Hello. Garden Springs Resort. We offer the best in assisted living. May I help you?"

I cleared my throat. "Ah, yes. I'm calling about Ottilie Zimmerman. I'm a friend of her two sons, Elvis and Xavier."

"Oh, how nice. They are the two sweetest, most polite boys you'll ever meet. Their momma sure raised them right. Did you call to check up on her for them?"

"Ah...yes. How is she?"

"She's doing just fine."

I wanted to ask about her medical condition but knew the staff wouldn't be permitted to talk about it. "They're abroad right now."

"Yes, in Greece, I hear. Lucky ducks. I bet they're having the time of their lives. It's nice of you to check up on her for them."

"Ah, no problem. Say, do you think she'd be up for a visitor?"

"Why, she'd be delighted. She doesn't get many visitors. It would have to be supervised, of course, since only the boys are on the approved visitor list, but I think we can arrange something. And you are...?"

"Lexi Carmichael."

"I'm Marilyn Para, the Day Administrator at Garden Springs. When would you like to come?"

"Would now be okay?"

"Sure. How long will it take you to get here?"

"Fifteen minutes."

"Great. I'll be waiting."

TWENTY-THREE

GARDEN SPRINGS RESORT was situated in a beautiful and exclusive location, surrounded by trees, impeccable landscaping and several elaborate fountains. There was one large building and several smaller buildings surrounding it. The FBI guys drove me and, after some heated discussion, agreed to wait in the car while I went in by myself.

Marilyn Para was in her office when I arrived. She was a middle-aged woman with a short gray bob, red cheeks and a friendly smile. I introduced myself and she shook my hand enthusiastically. She led me down a hallway and we turned left onto a covered walkway to an adjoining building.

"So, Mrs. Zimmerman's husband doesn't live here with her?" I asked.

"I've never heard of a husband," Marilyn answered. "You'd have to ask her or the boys about that."

"Okay, thanks."

When we got to the entrance of the building, she waved a badge in front of an access panel and the door opened. Different smells assaulted my nose. A sweet sickly smell of scented candles mixed with the antiseptic smell of medicine and heavy-duty cleaners. Marilyn kept up a steady stream of chatter as we walked down a hallway, but I could hardly bring myself to respond. My mind was racing ahead to meeting Elvis's mom and what I would say to her about her sons.

"Here we are," Marilyn said, stopping in front of room

twenty-six. Before I could prepare myself, she knocked twice on the door. It opened, and a female version of the twins stood looking at me.

Ottilie Zimmerman didn't look sixty-nine. Her long brown hair had almost no gray, and there were only a few small lines around her eyes. She was dressed in a white nightgown and when she saw us, her fingers reached up to twirl the corner of a white gauzy scarf around her pinky finger.

"Hello?" she said softly. "Who are you people?"

Marilyn smiled. "Why, Ottilie, you know who I am. You just had lunch with me today. Remember? We ate the Mexican casserole. This is Lexi Carmichael. She's friends with the boys."

I held out my hand, but she didn't take it. She studied me for a long moment and then her face broke out into a smile. "Yes. I've seen you before. Elvis. Yes, Elvis showed me a photograph of you."

I blinked. "He did?"

"Can we come in, Ottilie?" Marilyn asked. "It would be much more comfortable talking inside than standing in the hall."

"Of course."

She stepped aside and we entered the room. It was the size of a small studio apartment minus the kitchen. She had a small couch facing a television and an adjoining room that likely led to a bedroom and bathroom. A small table and four chairs sat in one corner. It looked clean and comfortable. Marilyn headed straight for the table and sat down. I followed and took the chair next to her, but Ottilie remained on her feet.

"Where are my boys?" she asked, frowning.

Before I could answer, Marilyn spoke up. "The boys

are in Greece, remember? That's why Lexi's here. She's checking up on you for them."

She turned those Zimmerman-blue eyes on me and her expression crumbled. "They always bring me flowers and a book."

I lifted my empty hands. "I'm sorry I forgot. I'll bring them next time."

"Well, of course you will. Would you like some gelatin? I have lime. It's my favorite."

"No, thank you, but it's kind of you to offer."

She smiled. "Did you know Elvis and Xavier like to read to me when they visit? I sit on the couch and they sit there, too, and read to me in their beautiful voices. All kinds of different novels and poetry. They read until they're hoarse. They are my angels, you know."

A lump formed in my throat. I couldn't speak.

She walked across the room and took my hand. Her hand was cool. "You wish to tell me something, don't you, my dear?"

I found my voice. "Why do you say that?"

"I could always tell when my boys were hiding something from me. They had this look in their eyes. Just like you do now. So, tell me. It's okay."

I wasn't able to say it. The truth was locked inside me.

She sighed, releasing my hand. "Did they fall down again? They are always skinning their knees. They don't seem to have much in the way of balance, I'm afraid. They get that from me."

"Mrs. Zimmerman, where's your husband?" I blurted out.

She looked at me blankly. "My husband? I have a husband? Oh, dear, I think I forgot. My memory isn't what it used to be. Would you like some gelatin? I have lime. It's my favorite."

I stood, my heart breaking. "No, thank you. I'm sorry. I can't stay. I just wanted you to know your boys are thinking of you. I appreciate you permitting me to visit."

"Oh, dear. Oh, dear. We didn't have time to read. It's late I suppose." She began twirling the gauzy scarf around her finger again. "When are the boys coming? Sometimes I don't even remember that I have two boys. Where are they? Why didn't they come with you?" Her voice rose in agitation.

Marilyn stood and patted Ottilie's hand. "They'll come see you when they come back from Greece. Don't worry about it."

She nodded. "Yes, of course. They will bring me flowers and a book."

Marilyn opened the door but before we stepped out in the hall, Ottilie called out to me. "You'll bring me my Elvis the next time, won't you?"

I turned around as her eyes—Elvis's eyes—pleaded with me.

I swallowed hard. "I'm sure going to try."

TWENTY-FOUR

NEXT STOP WAS my parents' house. I called first to make sure they would be home and then I had my security detail take me. A police officer sat out front in my dad's rocker. My mom hugged me when she saw me. My dad looked older and scared. I gave him a hug, too, and we headed into the kitchen where my mom got busy fixing us hot chocolate.

"Where's Sasha?" I asked.

"It's his night off," Mom said. "You look tired. Are you okay?"

I felt anything except okay, but I didn't see the point in worrying her. "I'm good. Did Beau and Rock leave?"

"Hours ago," my dad said. "They went to work."

I swallowed my disappointment. I'd hoped to see my brothers one more time, but it wasn't to be. I couldn't tell them where I was going or what I was going to do anyway. It's just, I hadn't really had a chance to say goodbye.

Now it was just my parents and me. It might be the last time I saw them. What did you say in situations like this?

My heart squeezed in my chest. I couldn't fathom how military families did this all the time. How did they survive the stress?

I closed my eyes, took a deep breath. I wouldn't worry them. I would just be as truthful as possible.

"Mom, Dad… I want to thank you for everything you've done for me. I guess I'm not very good at saying or showing that. In fact, other than in a few notes when I was little, I'm not sure I've ever said it quite so frankly. I just want you to know how much I love you. I know it hasn't been easy with someone like me."

"Someone like you? Lexi, why are you saying this?" My dad looked suspicious. "What's going on?"

"Nothing. I'm just… I just wanted to say it. Lately it seems like my life is perpetually in danger. So, it just seemed the right time to let you know you've been great parents."

"Can't you just stay here with us?" my mom asked.

At that moment, I wanted nothing more. Life really did come full circle.

I patted her hand and felt a swell of love. "Thanks, Mom, but I have to go to work. I can stay the night and I definitely have time for a cup of hot chocolate if you'd get the kettle. It's whistling, by the way."

She glanced over in surprise at the stove and then kissed the top of my head. "Great, sweetheart. We'd love to have you, even if it's only for the night."

I WAS SCHEDULED to report to Andrews Air Force Base in Maryland at 0600, so my security detail drove me there. I hadn't been able to sleep. Instead, for the past several hours, I'd checked my phone constantly for a message from Slash.

Nothing.

So I focused on the mission instead, asking Woodward what I was supposed to bring. He told me everything except underclothes would be issued to me. I was to leave my identification, cell phone and everything else at home.

Therefore, I reported for duty with nothing more than the clothes on my back and a small backpack containing some extra underwear and a couple of bras. I was taken to a building for what they referred to as "in-processing" and ushered to a waiting area. I was surprised to see Gray there, sitting on a bench, dressed in her usual three-piece suit with her hair pulled back into a bun and looking as professional and impeccable as ever.

"Hey, Gray. Come to say goodbye?"

"I wish. I'm here for in processing, too. I'm going on the mission with you."

"What? You are?"

She squeezed her hands together in her lap. "Well, it makes sense, I guess. I've lived and breathed Johannes Broodryk for four years. I've gathered the most collective information about him, most of which is burned into my brain. I've been told I need to be on hand in case Broodryk's choices or movements require an immediate and intuitive prediction based on my insightful knowledge of him."

"Wow. You can't do that remotely?"

"Apparently not as effectively."

"Oh." I stared at her. I didn't want to say I was glad she was coming. I wasn't. The odds were, neither she nor I would come home alive, so how could I be glad about that? We'd both been sucked into Johannes Broodryk's sick world and there wasn't a lot we could do about it.

I sat down next to her and said nothing. That probably wasn't socially acceptable, but we are who we are.

While we were sitting there in silence, a guy dressed in camouflage and boots with a backpack slung over one shoulder approached. He was tall, at least six feet three, with light brown hair cut so close, his scalp was visible. He dropped his backpack at our feet, put one booted foot on the bench and studied us.

"Well, hello, ladies," he said in a southern drawl. "Reporting for duty?"

I nodded. "We sure are. Are you one of the Navy SEALs?"

"Yes, ma'am, I am."

We looked over as a guy in a blue uniform stepped out of the office. He glanced at a clipboard. "Lexi Carmichael?"

I stood. "Right here."

"Come with me, please."

With a last look over my shoulder at Gray and the soldier, I followed him into a room. Once in, I was introduced to a female soldier, also in a blue uniform, who took me aside and gave me camouflage to wear, a couple of olive-colored T-shirts, boots, a jacket, wool socks, gloves, a toilet kit and a bunch of other items.

She started stuffing everything into a backpack similar to the one the soldier had been carrying. "We were provided with your measurements and weight, so you should be good to go. You don't have to change for the flight, unless you want to. I'd just ask that you try the boots on to make sure they're a good fit."

"Okay. Sure."

I tried the boots and found them surprisingly comfortable. I walked around a bit. "They're good."

"Excellent." She patted my shoulder. "You'll be provided a brief on all of your equipment during the flight. Good luck. We're all pulling for you."

"Appreciate it."

I picked up my backpack and she led me to a room behind the office where Woodward, Spearman, Mark and a couple of other men dressed in uniform were waiting.

Mark approached, then handed me a laptop bag. "You'll have everything you need here. It's secure."

He handed me a business card. On the back were a series of numbers and symbols.

"Passwords," he explained. "Carry them separately from the laptop, but it's better if you memorize."

"Already did." I tapped my temple. "Photographic memory."

"Excellent. You know we've got your back, right? I'm on this 24/7 until you come home."

"Thanks, Mark. That makes me feel better."

He gave me an awkward hug—which was strangely comforting—then whispered in my ear, "Follow me."

He pulled away and left the room.

I glanced over at Woodward. "I'll be right back. Bathroom."

Woodward nodded and I exited the room. Mark was waiting in the hallway looking really nervous.

"What's this all about?" I asked.

He led me down the hallway to a room about three doors down.

"Go in." He motioned toward the handle and then disappeared down the hall.

I opened the door.

A man stood by the window, dressed in a black leather jacket and jeans. He turned when he saw me.

My heart skipped a beat. "Slash."

I started to go to him and then stopped, unsure if things had changed after our big fight.

I shouldn't have worried. In three steps he'd closed the ground between us and wrapped me in a hug so tight I could hardly breathe. I wound my arms around his waist and held on, pressing my face against his chest.

"You came," I mumbled, holding him tighter. "I didn't think you would."

"How could I stay away? I don't like what's happening, but I'm with you. I'm always with you, *cara*."

He pulled back and studied my face, tucking a strand of hair behind my ear and touching one of the diamond stud earrings he'd given me for Christmas. "I understand why you have to do this, even if I don't agree with it."

I looked at him. He hadn't shaved and looked like he'd spent the last several hours like I had, wide awake and troubled.

I touched his stubbly cheeks with my fingertips. "I can't tell you how much it means to me that you came. I thought you were never going to speak to me again."

"You've made your stand, so I'm making mine next to you. Do what you need to do to get Broodryk and I'll work my end. We'll meet in the middle, okay?"

I knew how much it cost him to say that. "I'm sorry, Slash. I never wanted to force you into this position."

"You didn't force me. I'm here of my own volition."

"Are you sure?"

He caressed my check. "Never surer of anything in my life."

"I'm glad. I'm really scared. It helps immeasurably to know you're still in this with me and you understand. Everyone else is depending on me."

"You were right." He rested his chin on the top of my head. "You can do this, and so can I."

I managed a small smile. "That's the spirit."

He pressed his lips to my hair. "Do you want to know what I really want? I want to stop time and keep you safe in my arms. Freeze time right at this moment. I never want to lose you. But you were right. This *is* bigger than us. I didn't want to acknowledge it because of the risk to you, but Broodryk won't ever stop. I might be able to protect you for a while, but I couldn't be everywhere all the time. I don't like any part of this, but I understand why you made the call you did."

My throat tightened. I had to go soon or I might change my mind after all, something I knew I'd regret for the rest of my life.

"Thank you for coming," I whispered. "Thank you for staying with me."

"For as long as you want me."

We stood for another minute in silence. "I have to go. They're waiting for me."

"I know." His arms tightened around me. "Go bring Elvis home. Be smart, be careful, but more than anything, don't let anyone manipulate you. You may have to play the game, but you don't have to let Broodryk or anyone else push you around. You're smarter and a lot more in charge of this operation than you know. Follow your head and your heart. They are your greatest strengths. Broodryk won't stand a chance against that combination. More importantly, remember I love you. No matter what happens."

He kissed me with both tenderness and fire and then let his lips linger a moment more. Without another word, he released me and strode out of the room.

As the door clicked behind him, my heart hurt so much I staggered sideways and braced a hand against the wall.

"I love you, too," I whispered.

TWENTY-FIVE

I RETURNED TO the briefing room. Gray and the SEAL we'd been talking with were now there, along with two new guys dressed in camouflage. One of the men was about six feet tall with shaggy blond hair, a surprise because I thought all military guys had to have short haircuts. The other man was extremely large and muscular with bulging biceps. His teeth flashed white against his dark skin as he gave me the most charming smile I'd ever seen. I couldn't help but smile back. He was the first to approach me.

"Hey there, I'm Hulk," he said, holding out a hand. His palm was two sizes bigger than my entire hand, but his handshake didn't crush me.

"Nice to meet you, Hulk. I don't even have to ask why they call you that."

He grinned. "I like a woman with smarts."

Wow. His smile was really infectious. "I'm Lexi Carmichael."

"Hello, Lexi Carmichael. The pleasure is mine."

The blond guy joined us. "Hello, ma'am. I'm Wills. Nice to meet you."

"Hi, Wills." I shook his hand, too. "Glad to meet you, as well."

I glanced over at the first SEAL Gray and I had met in the waiting room. He was chatting with Gray, who'd changed out of her suit and had dressed in camouflage pants and a T-shirt.

"I bet that's Hands." I tipped my head toward the guy.

Wills nodded. "The one and only. So, you're the asset."

"What do you mean, asset?"

"Our pot of gold." Wills tapped my shoulder. "It's our job to protect you. We've only gotten a quick briefing so far."

"Oh. Right. I guess that's how it will work."

"Who's the woman talking to Hands?" Wills asked.

"Grayson Reese. She's coming with us. She's an analyst with the CIA."

"Ah, a spook."

Wills leaned over to me and lowered his voice. "Just a heads-up, Hands isn't much for babysitting, which is how he sees this mission. He doesn't have much of a bedside manner either, if you get my drift. But he's a damn good SEAL and an even better leader."

I stiffened. "He doesn't have to babysit me. I can take care of myself."

Will grinned. "Well, at least you've got spirit. Guess we'll see what you're made of soon enough."

Woodward made a farewell speech and gave us some final instructions before we were loaded onto the plane. I looked out the plane window as Andrews Air Force Base disappeared below me and thought of my parents, brothers and Slash.

Once we'd taken off, Wills gave Gray and me a briefing on our equipment and some basic survival tactics. It was hardly exhaustive, but he gave us some good pointers. I discovered that Wills was a medic and a communications specialist. It seemed an odd combination, but Wills told us the SEALs were trained in numerous areas. Hulk was a killing machine—an expert in martial arts and jujitsu. I decided I never wanted to get on his bad side. He was so large he wouldn't have even had to use any of his moves on me. He'd just sit on me and I'd be squashed. Hands was the team leader and sniper, although according to Wills, he'd officially hung up his sniper role when he was promoted to team leader.

After that I sat in an uncomfortable jump seat with the laptop balanced on my knees, getting familiar with Broodryk's techniques and reading all I could about his life and methods.

"How is it going, Keys?"

I looked up from the laptop and saw Hands looking at me. "What did you say?"

"I asked how it was going."

"No, I mean what did you call me?"

"Keys. That's what you've been doing for the past hour. Banging on those keys."

I looked down at the keyboard. "Oh, right."

"I didn't officially introduce myself. I'm Hands."

"Hi, Hands. Nice to meet you. I'm Lexi."

"I know. You're the asset."

"So I understand."

"You ever been to Africa?"

"No."

"You know how to shoot?"

"I've had a couple of lessons."

"You any good at following orders?"

I thought about my fight with Slash and how by just being here, I was going against Elvis's wishes, too. "Probably not."

"You better get used to it."

I sighed. "Don't worry. I know what I have to do on this mission. You don't need to hold my hand."

"I'm counting on that."

It wasn't the start I'd hoped to have with the team

leader, but he leaned back in his seat and closed his eyes, so I resumed my work on the keyboard.

The entire flight lasted seventeen hours, including a refueling stop at Ramstein Air Force Base in Frankfurt, Germany. By the time we arrived in Djibouti at Camp Lemonnier I was exhausted. We landed at eleven o'clock in the morning local time. I had dozed on and off for a good chunk of the flight, but never quite reached REM. Altitude, stress and emotional exhaustion all worked against me.

After grabbing our gear, we filed off the plane and were greeted by a sailor who stood stiffly next to an un-marked white van. Oppressive heat enveloped me, and the landscape shimmered so brightly it hurt my eyes. We climbed into the van and headed out.

Gray looked out the window as we drove. "This is a pretty impressive base. Paved roads and real buildings. What's that over there?" She pointed to a huge, white, domed structure.

"It's the Thunder Dome," Wills answered. "A huge meeting place, but also a basketball court. They've re-ally built this place up the past several years."

"Have you guys been here before?" I asked.

"More times than I can count," Hands replied. "It's even got a swimming pool."

"Cool." Gray squinted as she looked out the window. "Is this an Army base?"

"Navy," Hands replied. "The best of the best. Actu-ally, it's the only US military base in Africa."

The guy driving us stopped in front of a two-story white building with air conditioning units in every win-dow. I sincerely hoped they worked. Even with the air con-ditioning going full blast in the van, I was sweating like a pig and had concerns about my computer equipment.

We exited the van and entered the building, where the air was definitely cooler, but not by much. A red-haired man in camouflage stepped out of an office and the SEALs snapped to attention.

"At ease." They relaxed slightly as he moved to greet Gray and me first.

"Welcome to Djibouti and Camp Lemonnier. I'm Captain Nathan Bischoff. Be advised that your mission here takes top priority."

"Thank you, Captain," I said.

A weird hissing came from somewhere behind Hulk. We all turned around in surprise as a furry, white animal leaped out of nowhere and landed near his feet. Hulk made a startled noise, whipped out his gun and pointed it at the creature.

"Stand down, sailor," the captain barked. "He's not dangerous."

Hulk lowered his gun and we all took a closer look at the animal.

"Is that a fox?" I asked.

The commander reached down and picked it up. "Yes. It's a species native to Africa and can be somewhat domesticated. Don't worry, he's had all his shots. I call him Fennie. You can pet him if you want."

Hulk eyed it with mistrust and none of us offered to pet it. For some reason, the fox stared balefully at me from the captain's arms, as if daring me to try. I didn't. Pets and I didn't have a good history. Somehow they seemed to sense my indecision regarding animals and took it as a signal to try and dominate me.

The captain cleared his throat. "Well, anyway, I've had quarters arranged for you. You'll want to rest a bit and eat. I have scheduled a meeting here in two hours with all the necessary players. I'll see you then. Dismissed."

Gray and I exited first, followed by the SEALs. The same sailor who'd driven us from the plane stood outside waiting for us. "Gather your gear and follow me, please. I'll walk you to the barracks. They aren't far."

We retrieved our stuff from the van and filed in behind him. My eyes hurt from the brightness and I wished I'd thought to get my military-issued sunglasses out. But because I hadn't, I squinted down at my feet.

That's when I saw it.

TWENTY-SIX

I LET OUT a strangled scream and bumped into Hands.

Guns were drawn and the men formed a protective circle around Gray and me.

"What is it?" Wills barked over his shoulder. "What's going on?"

I pointed to the ground. "There. What's that?"

They turned around slowly and looked where I was pointing. Hands pushed his boot against it. "It's a damn desert spider, Keys."

I scooted as far away from it as I could get. "Scientifically speaking, that's not a spider. It's the size of a small dog. Shoot it."

Hands picked it up with the butt of his rifle, carrying it away from us. He set it down a good ten feet away and then came back.

He lowered his sunglasses and gave me a long stare. "Let me give you a word of advice. Stop being so jumpy around a bunch of guys with guns. Come on."

Gritting my teeth, I followed him.

The sailor escorting us stopped in front of a building and opened the door, motioning us inside. These barracks had a sparse living area in the center of the structure with two couches facing each other and a coffee table in the middle. An end table on either side of the couches held a lamp and there was a small television. Separate sleeping quarters were visible through open doors on either side of the living space.

Hands looked around, whistling. "Well, look at that. We got the VIP suite."

It hardly looked impressive, but what did I know?

The sailor cleared his throat. "The mess hall is to your right and the latrine to your left. The ladies' latrine is a bit farther down than the men's." He pointed to a door to his right. "Seeing how this is the VIP suite, there's a half bath here if you need it. No tub or shower, but it saves you from having to trek down to the latrine in the middle of the night."

We dumped our gear, cleaned up and then headed to mess hall together without saying much. After eating we returned to headquarters, where we were ushered into a crowded conference room. Someone had a laptop set up to display a map of Africa on a large screen. As soon as Gray and I took our seats, the captain got started.

"Operation Nightcrawler is a go. The teams will leave tonight at 2400 local time, putting us at the hot zone about 0230."

"Tonight?" I interrupted. "Isn't an operation like this more dangerous to conduct at night?"

Captain Bischoff looked like he wasn't used to being questioned, but he answered anyway. "Yes and no. Darkness will offer our insertion team some additional cover, but Broodryk and Pentz will likely expect us to come at night, so they'll be ready. We're going tonight because we have to assume they are tracking your movements. It's likely they'd expect us to give you a full day and night to rest and recover from the journey. So we won't. Are you up for that?"

"Yes."

"Good. We can expect they'll be waiting but may not be on full alert, which gives us a slight edge. We'll take it. We're going in small because the location and transportation limit our scope. We'll have seven plus the asset for the insertion team. Six more for recovery. The rest of us sit tight and watch from here."

Being constantly referred to as an asset felt weird, but I tried to go with it. I wasn't crazy about the thought of running around in hostile territory in the middle of Africa in pitch black darkness either, but I wasn't seeing any other options.

"We'll split into two three-man teams on the ground, Alpha and Bravo," Bischoff continued. "The asset is assigned to Alpha Team. Both teams will drop via a V-22 Osprey aircraft approximately two kilometers from the hotspot.

I held up my hand. "Whoa. Exactly what do you mean by *drop*?"

I glanced sideways at Hulk, who was shaking his head as if I were doing something wrong. It occurred to me that perhaps I was interrupting the flow by asking too many questions. However, seeing how it was my first military briefing, I had no idea if there was a special protocol that detailed who could and could not ask questions. We didn't have time for that now. These were important details that could mean life and death. My life. My death. As the asset I not only needed to *know* what was going on, but *understand* it. Questions and the subsequent answers were vital. Protocol would just have to take a back seat.

"Ms. Carmichael, you're going to do a tandem jump with one of the SEALs," the captain explained.

"Wait. You mean jump, as in jump from a plane?"

"Don't worry. These guys are pros."

I swallowed hard. "Can't we get dropped off by a helicopter or something that actually lands on the ground?"

The captain shook his head. "We need to go in silent.

A helicopter is too loud, especially in the desert, and so is a convoy. They'd hear us coming for miles. It will be safer to make a high altitude drop from about ten to twelve thousand feet."

Twelve thousand feet?

Panic gripped my throat. Now probably wasn't the time to mention I was prone to carsickness, seasickness, and harbored a deathly fear of heights.

Hands must have noticed my concern, because he turned his laser green stare on me. "Don't tell me you're scared of heights."

I shrugged. "Of course not."

It wasn't a lie. Technically I was only afraid of standing on anything higher than a dining room chair.

Hands's eyes narrowed and I could tell he wasn't buying any of it.

The captain tapped on the map with a pointer. "Anyway, we will have Team Charlie as the reserve and recovery force located on a second V-22 Osprey aircraft, which will follow and circle while waiting for mission completion."

"Speaking of mission completion—if we parachute in, how do we get out?" I asked.

I caught a movement near the door, which was slightly ajar. Fennie the fox slunk into the room. The captain picked him up and began stroking him while talking.

"The Osprey has a short vertical takeoff and landing capability. Team Charlie will drop off and provide cover fire as necessary for you to re-board. But once Team Charlie lands, everyone will know we're there."

I felt ill as he described the set up. I couldn't even begin to statistically calculate how my ineptness might affect the mission. Hands was right to be concerned about me.

"What do we know about the village?" Wills asked.

The captain clicked a remote and the map changed to a satellite photo of the village.

"Satellite images indicate about fifty structures. One structure is set apart from the main residential area and has what looks like a place for a bonfire in the center. It's a courtyard where they may hold festivals, gatherings and perhaps a market. Our best guess is that the big building serves as a community center, a meeting place or the town center. There are two fairly large structures on either side of the building. To the right is a barn and animal corral of some kind. To the left and across the courtyard is a garage. There are a few cars, parts and loose tires visible. Stretching between the garage and the meeting building is a wall that looks like it might be made of cinder blocks. It's too hard to judge the height of the wall at this point."

He tapped at on a small white building attached to the far left corner of the meeting building. This is our target. We think the village elder is most likely going to be here."

"How do we get in?" Hands asked.

"Right now there appears to be only one door to the structure. It's on the backside of the meeting house here. It directly faces the residential area where the largest cluster of homes are located. There should be an interior door that connects to the meeting house, which you can use for egress."

He trailed the pointer to a tall structure behind the houses. "Here's where the water tower is located. Conveniently situated directly across from the door. I figure it's about four hundred yards."

"Damn," Hands swore.

I didn't understand. "What? Why is the location of the water tower a problem?"

Hands shifted in his seat, a look of annoyance on his face. It seemed pretty clear that, given all my novice questions, he considered me a liability rather than an asset.

"Because that's the highest vantage point in the village and makes it the premium spot for Pentz to shoot from," Hands said as patiently as he could manage.

I still wanted to be clear. "But that's a good thing, right? We'll know where he is. We can just shoot him ourselves."

"It's not so easy, Keys. He could be anywhere on that tower. We can't go in with blazing guns and massive explosions. Plus we can't blow up the only water tower this village has. Add to that, we don't know how many hostiles are in the village or how well they're armed. We have to get you in quietly so you can get the information. Getting out is another story. But Pentz, too, has to be careful not to start blasting. It would be game-over too quickly for him, too, and you wouldn't be able to extract the information Broodryk needs you to have."

The commander looked at Hands. "Intelligence indicates Pentz will be hunting you in particular."

"Hope he brings his game. It's time we settled this."

"Just keep in mind the score is secondary to the mission. Understood?"

"Understood."

"Good. We'll spend some time after this meeting going over satellite images for additional sniper positions."

"Yes, sir."

"Now, Ms. Reese, will you brief us on your thoughts about Broodryk's psychological state and possible game plan?"

Gray sat back and crossed her legs. "I believe all of

this is an elaborate performance in order to reassert his control and dominance. It's important to Broodryk that this show be executed exactly as he has planned it. This is something he needs to have witnessed on an international scale because he must reassure his clients he's untouchable and can strike the US and our allies in ways that they cannot. He is determined not to suffer another embarrassment like high school. As a result, Lexi has become a fixation for lack of a better word. Psychological reports indicate he does not view women as equals and gravitates to those who are submissive or easily manipulated. As Lexi is neither of those, she infuriates him on a primal level."

Hands glanced at me again and I got a feeling he might be in agreement with Broodryk on that.

I tried to make light of it. "Hooray for me."

"Lexi matched wits with him and won," Gray continued. "Now he must reassert his manhood and make an example of her. This obsession with Lexi is his greatest weakness and one we must exploit in order to trip him up. Just so we're clear, it's my opinion he will not harm her in the course of this particular operation. If Pentz is in the vicinity—and I'd say that's almost a certainty—he, and any others, will most likely have been instructed not to harm her. However, that does not stand for the SEAL team. It will likely be open season on them."

Hands leaned back in his chair. "Bring it on."

Gray raised an eyebrow at him. "Anyway, despite the fact I don't believe they will target Lexi, it doesn't mean Broodryk won't try to capture her. Taking her alive would make his game control all the more secure. So, it's my opinion that while he may instruct them not to shoot her, she may be vulnerable to a kidnapping attempt. Everyone needs to be aware of it and take steps to prevent it.

That being said, Broodryk is okay with her getting away with the information and the clues so the game can continue. Bottom line, this operation is a win-win situation for him no matter which way it goes, except if Lexi gets killed. Then it's end game without the impact and dramatic performance he requires, so he will have most likely taken extraordinary efforts to ensure her safety at least in terms of crossfire."

"That's interesting," Hands murmured.

Wills suddenly sat up straight in his chair and wrinkled his nose. "What the hell is that smell?"

We all sniffed.

"It smells like poop," I finally said.

Everyone looked at me, and I lifted my hands. "Well, it does."

Gray nodded. "She's right. It does. Maybe the fox had an accident?"

We looked around but Fennie was nowhere in sight and we didn't have time to go searching for him.

"Maybe, but that's the least of our problems right now," Bischoff said. "Someone shut the door tight and let's get back to the briefing."

Someone closed the door and I turned to Gray. "Do you think Broodryk will be there at the village?"

"Absolutely not." She folded her hands on the table. "He enjoys violence when the other person is weak or incapacitated. Otherwise, he's a coward and fears physical violence. He would certainly not put himself in danger's way and definitely not in the path of a team of highly trained US Navy SEALs. But I guarantee he'll be watching in some manner."

Wills tapped his head. "Odds are he'll outfit at least some of his crew with a real-time camera on a helmet. Probably Pentz for sure."

I thought that interesting. "Well, if he's watching in real-time, we might be able to trace the signal."

Bischoff made a note. "True. I'll pass the info to the team in Washington."

I tried to process all the information. "Okay, once I get to the village—if I survive a fall from twelve thousand feet—then what?"

"We help you find the elder, get the information and get out," Hands said.

"Just like that?"

He frowned. "Not exactly just like that, Keys. But we've got a game plan."

TWENTY-SEVEN

I RUBBED THE back of my neck to work out the knots. "So, what language do they speak in the Central Republic of Africa? What if I can't communicate with this elder?"

"The national languages are French and Sango," Wills said. "I speak French, so I can help out as necessary. However, we'll take a recording device to capture whatever he says, just in case."

"Good idea."

After another intense fifteen minutes of operational planning, the group split up. Hands took the SEAL team members who would be part of tonight's actual operation for a mock run-through of the operation using a couple of empty barracks on the base. Gray and Captain Bischoff went to brief the CIA and NSA. Two SEAL guys, Jimbo and Boots, and a young guy with Naval Intelligence named Jason, stayed behind. Their responsibility was to prepare me for the jump, show me how to use the equipment, and to give me a final intelligence briefing.

Before we got started, we decided to hunt down the source of the bad smell we'd been enduring. Jimbo found it right beneath my chair.

"It looks like the fox took a crap under your chair," he said.

I peered under my chair. "What?"

Boots handed him a plastic bag and Jimbo scooped up the poop, tying the plastic bag at the top. "That's one weird animal."

"Why did he do it under my chair?"

"True love, I guess. Or he's marking you." Jimbo laughed.

"Very funny. Ugh."

After the bag had been disposed of and I put the fox out of my mind, we sat and got down to the serious business of war.

Unfortunately we started with the jump.

"You'll be safely strapped to your partner for the jump," Jimbo said to me. "So, you've really got little to do except hang on. Okay?"

I swallowed. "What if we get separated? I won't have my own parachute, right?"

"You won't get separated. No way. We'll check, double-check and triple-check the lines. You're the asset, so I guarantee you'll be the safest one in the operation. Understood?"

"Intellectually, yes."

"This is how it goes down. The teams will get a six-minute call. That means you have six minutes until jump. The pilot will open the ramp. You'll line up with your partner. When the yellow light goes on, you'll get the order to hang. That means you and your partner must get into position. The best position is with your toes hanging off the ramp so you don't hit your shins on the way out. You will get the green signal to go and you'll jump. That's it. It's a hell of a lot of fun."

I stood up. "I have to use the restroom. I'll be back in a minute."

I found the bathroom and sat on the toilet lid, trying to calm my racing heart. I couldn't do this. I knew myself. I couldn't jump. The plan would be ruined and Elvis would die. All because my heart would stop the second I stepped out into space. I'd be deadweight—literally—

and the plan would have to be aborted. Game over, just like that.

I cradled my face in my hands. I was a geek not Rambo. Yet somehow, some way, I'd have to find the strength to rise to the occasion. After all, history was littered with people who were ordinary until called upon to do something extraordinary. They somehow got past their fears and made a difference. I could do it, too, if only they were asking me to do anything other than jump out of a plane.

After a few minutes, I stood, splashed water on my face and returned to the conference room. Jimbo and Boots had spread out the equipment I was going to use.

"These are the pants you'll wear," Boots said, holding up a pair of dark blue cargo pants with small pockets up and down each leg. "Unlike the SEALs, you'll be carrying only a few items. The pocket on your lower right thigh will have two hundred dollars in cash. Use it as a bribe or for whatever you may need if you become separated from the group. Remember, American dollars will go a long way in Africa."

I nodded, figuring if I got separated from the group I'd be toast, but I appreciated the vote of confidence.

"These other pockets will hold a couple of power bars, energy gels, a tourniquet, a mini recorder and a small medical kit. You'll have a belt to make sure those pants stay on. There will be a few more items that will attach to your belt, but I'll talk about them later."

He set down the pants and picked up something else. "This is your jacket. It's water resistant and warm. On top of that, you'll wear this." He held up a vest. "These are bulletproof plates on a vest. It may be a little large for you, but it's the smallest one we've got. It's surprisingly lightweight and flexible, so it shouldn't hamper your movement too much."

"Will it stop a sniper rifle?"

"A sniper the caliber of Pentz?"

"Yes."

"Unfortunately no. But let's try it on now so we can tighten it and you can get the feel of it. Okay?"

I held out my arms and Jimbo and Boots put it on, adjusting some of the straps until it fit snugly. It was too big for me, but it wasn't as heavy as I expected. After walking around in it, I was confident I could manage it. Especially since the alternative was going without.

We spent a lot of time discussing and playing with the super expensive hi-tech night vision goggles. My stress level went way down as I adjusted them and figured out all of the controls. After that we moved on to the communications gear attached to my helmet until I was confident I understood how to use it and when I was supposed to say something.

"By the way, your call name will be Alpha Star," Jimbo said.

"Alpha *Star*? Really?"

He grinned. "You're the asset, remember?"

"Right." It was a lot of information thrown at me at once, but I didn't have time for a full-fledged SEAL course—not that I would have survived one—so this would have to do.

Boots picked up a gun from the table and held it out to me. "Ever used one of these?"

"Not exactly. My boyfriend gave me a 9mm for Christmas, but I've only had time for a couple of lessons."

"You've got a smart boyfriend."

"You have no idea. Anyway, he says trouble follows

me like a stalker. Given the situation I'm currently in, he has a point."

Jimbo laughed. "I'd say that's the understatement of the century. Well, I'm glad you've at least got some idea of what to do with a gun. That's a start. This is a SIG Sauer pistol. Let's practice going over the procedure for loading and firing it. You're not expected to have to draw or use it during the mission, but we aren't sending you in unarmed."

When we finished the weapons training, Jason, the naval intelligence analyst, had his turn with me. He handed me a small laptop in a special carry case.

"We don't know how Broodryk will play this, but in case you need a keyboard, it's all here. It's got nothing sensitive on it. If you have to, you can leave it behind. We've got a program to wipe it remotely, but if you want to shoot it up, you can do that, too."

I couldn't *ever* imagine shooting a computer, but we do what we have to in the name of national security. He gave me a final rundown of what we might expect Broodryk to do and how they would be tracing any wireless signals coming out of a forty-kilometer radius.

"If he's watching in real-time, we'll find him," Jason said confidently. "We'll lock on the coordinates."

"I can't imagine he'd be that stupid, but never say never."

I looked up as Gray walked into the conference room. "We've been ordered to catch a few hours of sleep before we muster," she said. "You finished here?"

I glanced at Jason, who nodded. "You're good to go unless you have any questions."

"Nope." I shook my head and stood, stretching. My nerves were jangling so much I wasn't sure I'd be able to sleep a wink, but I definitely needed some fresh air and distance from the testosterone.

"They just threw a hell of a lot of information at you," Gray said as we headed back to the barracks. "Are you sure you're going to be okay, Lexi?"

I sighed. "Probably not. There are so many variables to this operation that calculating a success percentage rate is impossible."

She sighed. "Cyber terrorism. The new frontier."

"I wish that's where Broodryk would have kept it. But he wants me out of my element, so here I go. It's so far beyond my comfort zone it's comical, except it's not."

"He wants a show. Cyber terrorism isn't flashy enough. No one would understand a damn thing you two would do. It's too complicated. But guns, death, torture and kidnapping, now those are things every psychopath can get behind."

"Lucky me."

"Just keep in mind that the SEALs are a team—a unit. You have to figure out how to be part of that team and not just the asset if you want to succeed. You guys need each other. Everyone has a vital role. You can't be a loner in this, Lexi. You have to trust them and they have to trust you."

"That's going to be hard when Hands thinks he's baby-sitting me."

"You'll have to change his mind about that."

"How? I'm a total klutz who is afraid of heights and spiders. Even worse, I might be a danger to all of them and myself with a loaded weapon in my hand."

She smiled and patted my arm. "Just be a team player. Don't be afraid to ask for help when you need it and offer assistance when you can. That's what it means to be on a team. Okay?"

"Okay. I'll try."

There wasn't much more she could say, so we grabbed our stuff and hit the showers. When we returned, we stripped down to our T-shirts and undies. It was hotter than hell despite the supposed air conditioning unit. The oversized fan they had put in our room didn't help much either.

Although certain I wouldn't be able to sleep a wink, I passed out the moment my head hit the pillow. Given my anxiety and the overload of information my brain was processing, it was no surprise that I dreamed—and dreamed big.

I stood alone in the middle of the desert. My heart was pounding as if I'd just run a mile at full dash. I turned slowly in a circle, looking for something, all the while knowing that although I couldn't see anything but shimmering sand, *it* was out there stalking me.

I froze in fear. Where the hell was it? The sun was blinding me. I couldn't see a freaking thing. Then I felt it. It swiped my cheek with its hairy, spindly, arachnoid leg.

A desert spider!

I wasn't dreaming anymore. The alarms in my head clanged, waking me with fierce insistence. When I came to full consciousness, it was in panic mode with adrenaline pumping like crazy through my veins.

I pushed the spider off my face and promptly fell out of the bottom bunk, my legs tangled in the sheets. I didn't have far to fall, but the momentum knocked the breath out of me, leaving me unable to scream for help.

I heard something scuttle away, so I groped along the floor for a weapon and found my boot. I threw it in the direction of the noise, but it landed somewhere on my bed with a quiet thump. I debated going for my gun, which was currently next to my backpack on the table, but it was in the opposite direction from the door and I didn't want to shoot Gray by accident.

Whimpering, I crawled to the bedroom door, which was slightly ajar. I pulled it open and stepped into the living room, trying to calm my racing heart so I didn't pass out.

When I heard a clicking sound on the floor behind me, I dashed for the safety of the living room half bath and flung open the door.

Shocked I saw Gray, minus her T-shirt, sitting on the sink with her legs wrapped around Hands's waist as she kissed him. The SEAL was completely naked and braced against her.

Gray saw me first, her eyes opening so wide I thought they might pop out of her head. She pushed at Hands's shoulders. He stepped back, our eyes meeting in a moment of uncomfortable clarity. If certain death in the form of a desert spider wasn't waiting back in my room, I'd have hightailed it back there. Technically, that might have been the better option. As it was, I might well have been facing certain death standing by the bathroom. The murderous expression on Hands's face darkened to purple when Gray buried her face in her hands in mortification.

At that exact moment, something furry brushed against the back of my leg. I gave a gurgled shriek and stumbled forward, promptly tripping over the doorsill. I stretched my hands out to grab something to keep me from hitting the floor.

Too late, I realized what I had seized. Even though I let go quickly, Hands screamed like a girl and went down hard with me.

As we made impact with the bathroom floor, something furry squished beneath my right hip.

The spider had followed me in the bathroom!

"AAAAAAAGH," I screamed at the top of my lungs.

TWENTY-EIGHT

HANDS ROLLED SIDEWAYS, clutching his privates as Wills and Hulk skidded to a stop at the bathroom door, guns drawn.

"What the hell—" Wills said, looking between me, Hands and Gray. "What's going on here?"

Hands staggered to his feet, still holding his package. "Lexi tried to unman me."

I crawled away, coming to my feet next to Gray at the sink who stood covering her bare breasts with her hands. "That's not an accurate description of the situation. It was an accident. I had no idea you and Gray were even in here…together. I would have knocked, but I was just trying to get away from a spider."

"A what?" Hands growled.

I pointed over Hands's shoulder. "Spider. Big. On the floor behind you. I just fell on it."

Wills looked confused. "This is about a spider?"

"Yes. There."

Wills and Hulk crowded into the bathroom next to Hands who turned around. Both men still had their guns at the ready. I couldn't see the spider, but I didn't have to. My imagination filled in any blanks.

There was a moment of complete silence as the men stared at the floor.

"Holy crap," Hands finally said. "Is that what I think it is?"

Wills nodded. "Yep."

I didn't understand why they were standing around looking at it. "I told you it was monstrous. Kill it now. Make sure it's dead."

Hands gave me an incredulous look over his shoulder. "You thought this was a spider?"

"On. My. Face." I pointed to emphasize the significance. "While I was sleeping. It was big enough to potentially suffocate me and possibly poisonous to boot."

Gray tiptoed over to Hands and peered between him and Hulk to see what was on the floor. She turned around to stare at me, her eyes wide.

"Oh, no."

Unfortunately my brain chose that moment to unfreeze from its primal fear lock. I realized, with ill-timed lucidity, the absurdity of the situation. There were five adults smashed into a small bathroom. Hands was stark naked. I was dressed in only a T-shirt and panties. Gray had picked up her T-shirt and slipped it on, but she, like me, wore nothing else but panties. The two other guys were in their boxers only. We hardly knew each other, but here we were up close and personal.

Gray sighed. "Houston, we've got a problem."

Her hair was completely messed up and her cheeks were bright red. It was embarrassingly obvious to all what she and Hands had been doing in the bathroom, especially when she tossed him his underwear.

Hands gingerly pulled on the underwear. He glared at me. "What exactly happened, Keys?"

"I told you. I felt something on my face while I was sleeping." I shuddered. "A spider like the one we saw earlier."

"It wasn't a spider."

"It felt like a spider."

Hands, Wills and Hulk stepped out of the bathroom, and I saw my attacker at last.

Fennie.

The fox lay on its side, stiller than a desert night without a breeze.

"Fennie?" My eyes widened in astonishment. "What's that fox doing here?"

Wills looked up at me. "Not much now. It's dead."

"What?"

Wills put a finger to the fox's throat. "I don't feel a pulse."

Hands smacked a hand to his forehead. "So, on the night before the big mission, the asset attempts to disable the team leader, then kills the captain's beloved fox. There's a couple of operational aspects we didn't anticipate."

I shook my head violently. "No, this is all a mistake. I thought it was a spider."

Hands's glare intensified. "Do I need to remind you that you're on *our* side?"

"This is all a terrible misunderstanding."

"Apparently you fell on Fennie," Wills said. "Squished him flat as a pancake. Maybe that's what was on your face and you just imagined it was a spider."

I started to hyperventilate again. "Oh, God. This can't be happening. I knew that fox had it in for me. It pooped under *my* chair. Why was Fennie in my bedroom in the first place?"

Gray sighed. "I bet it was the beef jerky in our packs. Mine was partially eaten."

"How did he even get in here?"

"Good question," Hulk said. "How *did* it get in?"

Wills walked over to the door. It was ajar. "Who was out last?"

Gray closed her eyes and raised a hand. "Damn it. I'm sorry. It must have been me. I couldn't fall asleep so I went swimming. I was trying to come in quietly but I ran into him." She inclined her head toward Hands. "He had just come in from a debrief on potential sniper locations and we, ah, got distracted and…" She cleared her throat and looked away.

We all knew what came next. Could this situation get any more awkward?

Wills closed the front door while Hands knelt next to the fox.

"So, boss, what are we going to do?" Hulk asked him.

Hands lifted his head and looked pointedly at me. "Protect the asset. It's all about the mission."

Wills whistled. "Dude, you're going to do a run around on the captain?"

"You got a better idea?"

I crossed my arms. "I'm sorry. I had no idea, I swear." I stared at the fox, feeling worse by the minute. I hadn't meant to kill it, but accidents happened. They just happened to me a lot more often than seemed fair by life's standards.

Hands picked the limp fox up by the tail. He was starting toward the door when I scrambled to my feet and grabbed his arm. "Wait. Where are you going?"

"I'm going to dispose of the evidence."

"You can't just dispose of it. You've got to tell the captain."

"We leave in just over one hour for a complex operation. I'd prefer not to have him distracted. Or you, for that matter."

"You can't do this alone. I'm coming with you."

"What?"

"I killed it—Fennie—by accident, of course. But he's

dead because of me. I can't let you just dispose of it. It's not right. Please."

Hands blew out a breath. "You've got fifteen seconds to get a pair of pants on."

"What about you?"

"What you see is what you get. I'm not really feeling like putting on pants at the moment."

I winced, remembering how hard I'd grabbed his privates. "Right. Sorry about that. It looked like a handle in my peripheral vision."

He growled, so I dashed back to the room and grabbed a pair of camouflage pants, shoving my legs in. I would have stopped to put on my boots, but I was afraid he'd leave without me, so I ran back barefoot while zipping my pants. Wills tossed a flashlight to Hands. He caught it one-handed while standing by the door, still in his underwear, holding the fox by the tail.

"Let's go, Keys."

We strode out into the night. There was absolutely no wind, but the moon was bright, lighting our way. The ground heated my bare feet. I tried not to think of the spiders that might be out there waiting to bite my toes. I had to run to keep up with Hands and his long strides, even though at five feet eleven inches I've got pretty long legs.

"Don't we need a shovel?" I asked him.

"I'll find a sandy spot."

"Don't you worry someone will see you in your underwear?"

"Time is of the essence and we're just going here behind the barracks." He slid a sideways glance at me. "Besides, no need to be embarrassed. You've now seen me naked."

I tried to make things right. "Look, Hands, I apologize for interrupting you and Gray, then grabbing your penis. It was an instinctive reflex as I fell. I guess it hurt."

"You think?"

My attempt at smoothing things over was not working. Plus, my feet were hot and I was really concerned about stepping on a spider in the dark. I wished Hands would let me carry the flashlight, but I didn't think it was a good idea to ask him, given that he didn't seem in a very agreeable mood.

Hands stopped at a sandy spot behind the barracks. "So, Keys, you want to know why they really call me Hands?"

"Because you're a good sniper?"

"That's not all I can do with my hands."

"Oh. You're making a reference to your sexual prowess."

"No, I meant I am licensed to kill with these hands."

"Are you threatening me?"

"If we weren't on the eve of one of the most important missions of my career and I weren't so damn mad at you, I'd actually think that was funny. You're a danger to all of us. You have no idea how risky this mission is and the focus we need to have to complete it. This is not a good start. You can't screw us up or we're all dead."

"Look, I know you think I'm incapable. But I *can* complete the mission. You have to believe me."

He stared at me for a long moment, then sighed. "Well, now that I think about it, you single-handedly—pun intended—took me out of action in more ways than one *and* killed the commander's beloved pet at the same time. That's pretty impressive. You might yet make a decent SEAL."

"Sailor?"

Hands spun me around so quickly I nearly fell down. He stood partially behind me, the fox hidden between our bodies.

I stiffened in surprise. "C-Captain Bischoff? How... nice to see you."

TWENTY-NINE

THE CAPTAIN SHONE a flashlight at us, nearly blinding me. "Ms. Carmichael? Hands? What are you doing out here?"

"Ah…" My mind drew a complete blank.

Before I could say anything else, I felt something furry slip up the back of my shirt. I stifled a scream as Hands one-handedly tucked my T-shirt into my pants to hold the fox in place.

"Sir." Hands snapped to attention, moving away from me.

The commander started in surprise. "Are you in your skivvies, sailor?"

"Yes, sir. It appears I am. Out for a breath of air. It was…hot."

The captain looked between us for a long moment, frowning. "This better not be what I think it is."

I was pretty sure I knew what he *thought* it was. But better that than what it *actually* was.

"No, sir. It's not."

Both men fell silent and I realized they were waiting for me to say something. The problem was I couldn't think about anything except the dead fox stuffed up the back of my freaking T-shirt. I was literally seconds from ripping it off and running through the base screaming my head off.

"We were just heading back to the barracks," Hands said, filling the awkward silence. "Right, Lexi?"

"Ah…" Coherent thought had escaped me. I was frozen to the spot, afraid to move and afraid not to.

Captain Bischoff looked at us again and sighed. "I'm out looking for Fennie. He didn't come home. Have either of you seen him?"

The fox twitched and I nearly jumped out of my skin. Several freakish possibilities immediately presented themselves: A.) Fennie was turning into a zombie fox, B.) Fennie was undergoing rigor mortis, or C.) Fennie was still alive. It didn't escape my attention that any of the three meant it was happening while Fennie was trapped beneath my T-shirt.

That fox had to come out *right now*.

"Aaaagh…" I started.

Perhaps sensing my imminent breakdown, Hands put an arm around me. "Captain, permission requested to take Ms. Carmichael back to the barracks. We need to make final preparations for muster."

The captain seemed to be considering saying something, but he waved his hand. "Fine. I don't want to know. Granted."

"Thank you. Sir." Hands hustled me away, his hand firmly on the small of my back ensuring the fox didn't fall out.

"Sailor?"

Hands and I screeched to a stop. "Yes, sir?"

"Good luck tonight."

"Thank you."

As soon as we were out of eyesight of the captain, I ripped off my T-shirt, not even caring I didn't have a bra on and was completely exposed. Hands caught the fox before it hit the ground.

"Are you freaking nuts?" I hissed at him. "You stuck a dead fox up my shirt."

"Better that than the commander finding us with it."

"No, actually it's not. I think it may be still alive."

"What?"

"Check it again. I felt it moving. It might have been rigor mortis setting in, but better make sure."

Hands laid the fox on the ground and knelt next to it, feeling its throat for a pulse. The fox suddenly snapped at his finger. Hands was so startled, he fell backward on his bottom.

"Well, hell," he said. "It's still alive."

The fox was weak, certainly near death, but moving. We had almost buried it alive. My stomach clenched.

"Oh, jeez. We've got to get it to the hospital right now."

Hands stood up, brushing the sand off his rear. "No. We've got to get to the barracks to get our gear for muster."

I snatched the flashlight from him. "We've got plenty of time."

"In what universe is fifty minutes plenty of time when we have to get ready for what could be the most important mission since Bin Laden? I don't have time to explain this to the captain."

I searched around on the ground for my T-shirt with Hands's flashlight. I found it, shook it out several times and pulled it back over my head. It kind of surprised me that at the moment I didn't give a flying crap about Bin Laden or my naked boobs.

"We can't leave Fennie like this. You know we can't. He's going to die if we don't do something."

Hands shifted on his feet, clearly debating. Finally he sighed. "Fine. Let's get it back to our room and let Wills have a look at it again. He's a pretty decent medic."

"How decent a medic *is* Wills? He thought the fox was dead."

"It's possible it was. Maybe all of our shaking it around and holding it upside down revived it."

"True, but if you stick it up my shirt again, I'm *not* playing along."

Hands scooped it up in his hands, being careful to keep his fingers away from the fox's mouth. Without another word, we hightailed it back to the barracks. I flung open the door and we barreled inside.

Gray, Wills and Hulk, all fully dressed now, were sitting in the joint living space.

"What the hell is going on?" Gray said, standing. "Why do you still have it?"

Hands gently laid the fox on the coffee table. "It's a long story. Wills, the fox is still alive."

"What?" Wills jumped into action. As he pressed his hands to the fox's neck. Fennie weakly lifted his head.

"Shit. Someone get me my medical kit."

Hands disappeared and came back with the kit and a pair of pants. As Wills worked on the fox, Hands pulled on his pants. He was still naked from the waist up.

"Hate to put an end to this little party, people," Hulk said. "Time to muster."

Wills gave the fox a shot of something and then stood, cradling it in his arms. "I think it's stable for the moment. I'm going to take it to Jones."

"Who's Jones?" I asked.

"Another SEAL medic. He'll keep it alive until we can take it to the captain. You all better cover for me if I'm late for muster."

Hands nodded. "Do it. And watch out. The captain's out there looking for it."

"Good to know." Wills disappeared out the door with the fox.

Hands pointed at me. "You. Get dressed and get your

gear together. Don't grab any more handles or fight off another spider. Pay attention to what you're doing. Take your time and make sure you have everything. I'll review the contents of your backpack before we muster, just in case."

I swallowed. I'd forgotten all about the jump. "Okay."

I headed back to the bedroom. I still wasn't convinced there wasn't a spider in the room, so I carefully examined every single piece of clothing, my boots and my pack. Thankfully, I found nothing. I had just started pulling on my special blue cargo pants when Gray came in.

She sat on my bunk. "I'm so sorry, Lexi. This is my fault. I left the door ajar."

"No. I'm the one who's sorry. I had no idea you and Hands were engaged in sexual activities in the bathroom."

Her cheeks reddened. "Oh, God. That's it. I'm pretty sure I'm going to have to resign from the CIA. I can't believe I let that happen."

"Why would you have to resign? You're both consenting adults, right?"

"It was stupid. It was unprofessional. We should have been thinking of the mission, not of getting it on."

"Sexual urges can be intensified in trauma situations. You're understandably nervous about this mission, even if you aren't physically going on it. Hands, on the other hand, will be in mortal danger. He's going to be hunted by one of the world's best snipers while trying to protect an incompetent like me. That has to be stressful. So, you both seized the moment in an attempt to release tension and remind yourselves that you are still alive and can enjoy the sensations. It's completely and biologically understandable."

She looked at me in surprise. "Really? You don't think less of me?"

"Why would I? Hands is obviously attracted to you, and I can see how you would be attracted to him, given his excellent physical condition and masculine capabilities."

"He calls me Suit. I kind of like it."

"It must be a SEAL thing. Everyone has to have a nickname."

"I guess so. But it was still a mistake."

I rubbed the back of my neck to ease the tension. "Look, Gray, I've been reading about the effects of stress on human mating preferences. It turns out that psychosocial stress not only heightens our sexual urges and increases our desire to bond, but it also causes us to widen and strengthen our family social group in order to maximize our ability to survive a threat. What you did is perfectly, biologically normal."

She gave me an odd look. "Wait. Why are you reading about stress and relationships? Are you having problems with Slash?"

"Whoa. How did you extrapolate that from what I just said?"

She shrugged. "Never mind. The expression on your face is answer enough. You don't have to talk about it if you don't want to."

I sighed. "We aren't having problems. Not exactly. I mean the sexual urges aren't a problem. He's not happy with me being on this mission. We had a fight about it. Plus I don't know how to integrate him properly into my family's social group. It's been a bit bumpy on both sides. I'm still working on it."

"He's crazy about you."

"Why do you say that?"

"Because I've watched him. I see the way he looks at you. It's a mixture of pride, protectiveness and love. But there's something else. He's afraid and that's why he's holding back."

I stared at her. "No way. You can't see all that from just looking at someone."

"Yes, I can. I'm an excellent observer. CIA analyst and all, you know."

"Well, you're wrong. Slash isn't afraid of anything."

"Yes, he is."

I narrowed my eyes. "Then what's he's afraid of?"

"That, I don't know. You'll have to ask him."

I considered her words. "Gray, I brought that whole stress and sex thing up because I wanted to let you know that it's natural for you to have wanted to engage in sexual activities with Hands given our current precarious situation. Which reminds me, I hope I didn't permanently injure him in terms of penile function."

She giggled. "As mortifying as that entire situation was, I'll never forget the look on his face when you took him down."

"Don't remind me." I winced. "He's never going to forgive me."

She sobered. "So, do you think Hulk and Wills will tell someone about us in the bathroom?"

"What would be the point? Besides, I think SEALs have a code. They've got each other's back. Hands is their team leader, so I can't imagine them gossiping wildly about it. Now, they might rib him in private about doing a CIA analyst in the bathroom, but I don't think they'd use names or do it in front of you. They seem too polite for that. So, I think your secret is safe. I would highly recommend you not resigning. You're obviously a valuable talent for the agency at a time when they are greatly in need."

She blushed, laughed and then stood. "Leave it to you to put it in stark perspective. Thanks, Lexi. I actually feel better. You're right. Time to put it behind me and focus on what's important here."

"No problem. Anytime. Now speaking of important, can you please tell me how in the world I'm going to jump out of a plane at twelve thousand feet?"

I HAD TO admit the two V-22 Ospreys were pretty cool-looking aircraft. They each had two vertical propellers sitting on top of barrel-like cylinders and appeared to be a hybrid of an airplane and a helicopter. According to the information Jason, the naval intelligence officer, had provided, the V-22 Osprey had the functionality of a helicopter with the speed of a turboprop airplane. If I hadn't been so terrified of the impending jump and forthcoming operation, I might have asked to take a peek at the cockpit.

Instead Hands directed me to one of the Ospreys and we climbed inside. He seemed to be walking okay, which made me feel better. The rotors were whirring like a helicopter, beating the air. I glanced at the jump seats that were positioned against the airplane walls in a similar fashion as the military plane on which we'd flown to Djibouti. The other SEALs followed me in. I counted six in all, seven with me. Two teams of three, Captain Bischoff had said. The Alpha and Bravo teams. My call name was Alpha Star when I felt like Alpha Chicken.

The mood was somber. Hands, Wills, Hulk and the other SEALs were completely in the zone. There was no more joking, no more ribbing. It was time for serious business. People could die. People would likely die, maybe even me, despite what Gray had said. I thought about Slash and imagined him in the conference room, watching and listening to the mission over the radio feed. Knowing he was out there somewhere thinking about me and willing the mission to succeed strengthened me. I reached up and touched one of the earrings he'd given me.

Wow. I missed him. A lot.

Before we'd left, Hands checked all of my equipment twice and then had gone through every pocket to make sure I had what I was supposed to have. I'd tested and re-tested the laptop. As a group we'd done a communications check and review. My gun was in a holster on my belt. I'd been told repeatedly to stay close to the team and follow every direction to the letter. We were as ready as we were going to get, whatever that meant.

My helmet felt heavy on my head even without the night goggles. Hands had put those in my backpack, which was now strapped to my stomach. I tried not to be too worried about the fact that Hands had been identified as my jump partner. I'd be harnessed to him for the jump and could only trust he wouldn't unhook me and let me fall to my death. Static and talking played over the helmet radio as the ground team continued to test the communications equipment.

I was the first to sit in the jump seat. My stomach churned madly and I sincerely hoped I didn't throw up. Whereas these guys had been training both physically and mentally for this type of operation, I had neither the confidence nor belief I could actually pull this off, especially the jump.

Captain Bischoff boarded the plane and shook all our hands after giving us a pep talk reminding us of our responsibilities to the mission and each other. My responsibility was to do exactly what Hands and the other

SEALs told me to do and nothing else. It sounded easy, but somehow I didn't think it would be a walk in the park.

Faster than seemed possible, the captain left, the door closed and the engines revved up even louder. I felt the aircraft leave the ground and I closed my eyes.

Elvis, here I come. Hang in there.

When I opened my eyes, Hands knelt in front of me on one knee. "You holding it together, Keys?"

He was almost unrecognizable with his helmet and night goggles. Gray had told me the SEALs would be carrying about sixty pounds of equipment in addition to the tandem drogue parachute, which was about three hundred and sixty square feet in order to support the weight of two people and decrease our terminal velocity as we fell.

I swallowed. I didn't want to think about that yet. I still had no idea if I could do it.

Hands snapped his fingers in front of my face. "Keys, focus here. I need to tell you exactly what's going to happen. We have about three hours until the drop, but I want you to know I've got you. I won't let you fall."

"Actually, I'm not confident on that part."

"Well, get confident. We're on the same team. I won't let you fall. You'll have to trust me on that. So, stay with me. About six minutes before the jump, I'll harness you to me. I've asked the crew to do three checks to assure you the connections are secure. When you see the yellow light and hear the words 'Stand by,' you'll know we have less than thirty seconds before the jump. At that point, we have to walk to the open ramp. When you hear the instruction to hang, it means hang your toes over the edge of the ramp otherwise you may rap your shins on the ramp and that hurts. After that, you'll hear a command 'Green light, go.' That's our signal to jump. I'll give you a thumbs up and we'll jump together, okay?"

I couldn't speak. I just sat there my hands clenched into fists.

"Look, Keys, you cannot fight me. That'll put both of our lives in danger. You must stay calm. Keep in mind that even a few seconds of delay can cause the team to miss our drop point by a significant margin. Because we're jumping at night, I don't even need to pull the ripcord. Our parachute has an automatic activation device that deploys at a specific altitude. All we do is jump and the parachute does the rest."

I licked my lips. "How long...do we free fall?"

"We're going up to about twelve thousand feet, so we'll free fall for about sixty seconds at a speed of one-hundred and twenty miles per hour. When the parachute deploys, you'll feel an initial jerk, but the rush of the wind will slow things down. Unless someone is shooting at us, we should enjoy a quiet flight to the ground that should last about seven to nine minutes. Okay?"

"Okay."

"Good. Then we've got this."

He returned to the jump seat directly across from me, tipped his helmet down over his eyes and went to sleep. I couldn't imagine how he could do that under these circumstances, but I was discovering everyone had different methods of managing stress. I reached up and touched my earring and thought of Slash. And somehow I dozed, too.

THIRTY

"Keys, wake up."

I blinked and then straightened as Hands came into focus. Adrenaline charged through me as I leaped to my feet.

"Where are we? What happened?"

Hands put a hand on my shoulder. "It's the six-minute call. Time to harness."

My eyes widened. "Ah…"

I didn't have time to protest as several guys surrounded me, securing me to Hands and pulling on and adjusting straps. I started to shake as one of them tugged my helmet tighter under my chin.

One of the guys gave me a thumbs-up. "You're good to go."

"Four minutes," someone else called through my helmet.

"Check two." Another SEAL knelt down and rechecked the harness and the straps.

He stood and gave me a thumbs-up, too.

My legs were trembling so badly at this point I could barely stand. Hands mostly held me up. I opened my mouth to protest, but only a croak came out.

A third SEAL did a final examination of the connections. "Check three. Complete. Alpha Star is secure to Alpha One."

"Com check. Alpha Star, do you hear me?"

I swallowed. "Yes. I can hear you in my helmet."

"Good. I hear you, too. Alpha One?"

"Check."

Alpha and Bravo teams all checked in to ensure the radios and mics were all operational.

"Coms are a go. Stand by and good luck."

As I watched in horror, the lights in the interior of the aircraft went out and the ramp at the back of the aircraft opened. I twisted my head and saw Hands adjusting his night vision goggles over his eyes. As my eyes adapted to the dark, I noticed the dim red lighting in the aircraft. It wouldn't be visible from the ground like a white light would. It also wouldn't affect the eyes' ability to see in the dark, which was unfortunate because I knew exactly what was happening.

The aircraft lurched slightly as the ramp cranked completely open. I heard a loud whooshing noise. Air rushing past the aircraft.

Holy crappola. The ramp was freaking *open*. I couldn't see a thing except for the inky blackness outside the plane. I froze in place. I couldn't move. I couldn't speak.

Hands tapped me on the shoulder and gave me a thumbs-up.

I shook my head. Adrenaline, which had been racing around my veins, now gave up and just screamed *no, no, no! Hell no!*

"Yellow light, go."

Hands tried to move, but I was frozen to the spot.

"Keys, move it."

I shook my head more violently now. "No. I can't. Intellectually, I'm trying, but the bottom line is it isn't going to happen."

He gave me a push with his body and we half waddled, half stumbled forward. It wasn't the right way to get into position, and I knew it. But terror clouded my judgment and ability to think properly.

"Hang."

There were three guys in front of us. The voice in my helmet said, "Bravo One, green light, go."

He disappeared silently into the black void. I watched in sheer terror.

"Bravo Two, green light, go."

He jumped.

"Bravo Three, green light, go."

He disappeared and now there was no one between the emptiness of space and me.

"We're next," Hands said calmly through my helmet.

"No!" I shouted.

"Get into position, Keys. Hang your toes over the ramp."

I realized with horrible clarity he would force me to tumble out with him into the blackness if he had to. Panic overwhelmed me. No way in all the depths of all hell was I going anywhere near that ramp. I tried to back up, but Hands didn't budge. I calculated my chances of being able to take him. Given that he was six foot three inches and two hundred and twenty pounds—plus I was harnessed to him—all I got were odds of four billion six hundred and twenty-four to one that I could pull it off.

"P-please, Hands," I stammered. "I changed my mind. I'm sorry. We have to think of another way. I just can't do it."

"Yes, you can. You said you trusted me, right?"

"Yes, but—"

"But" is the last word I said before Hands took advantage of my distraction with the conversation and used his body weight to propel us both out of the plane.

Before I could get mad we hadn't even gotten the official command to "green light, go," we fell. The air rushed past me at a ridiculous speed. Hands and I tumbled once before he stabilized us. We went down, down, down at a breathtaking speed. A weird mixture of terror and confusion swept through me. I couldn't orient myself with a landmark because of the darkness, so it was like plunging into an endless vacuum. Gravity sucked and yanked at me like a greedy child, pulling me to my death.

"Alpha Star. Alpha Star."

The voice seemed to come from a long distance until I realized it was Hands speaking to me through the radio in my helmet.

"Alpha Star. You're okay. However, as we are attempting a stealth approach, it might help if you stop screaming."

I snapped my mouth shut, realizing the air had stolen every ounce of moisture from it. Despite my terror, another part of my brain continued to calculate the fall. The air pressure beneath us was thickening, which meant we were reaching terminal velocity.

Chute time was imminent.

I tried to brace myself, but my disorientation was too great. It seemed as if we'd been plummeting for hours, even if I knew it couldn't have been more than a minute. Suddenly I was jerked backward and upward. My breath lodged in the back of my throat as we swung around and then steadied.

"The chute deployed, Keys. Now comes the easy part."

My teeth chattered and my brain felt completely scrambled.

"Don't try to figure out where we are. It's too dark to see anything, so just imagine you're sitting in a chair in your living room, and I'll handle the rest."

My heart rate decreased as our descent slowed. I wig-

gled my arms and legs to make sure they were still connected to my body. I figured we were now falling at a
speed of about eighteen miles an hour—a huge difference
from the one hundred and twenty miles per hour free fall
we'd just finished. Now it felt as if we were hardly moving at all, more like floating.

I squinted at a couple of blinking lights floating
through the air. After a moment it occurred to me the
SEALs were probably using a small signal light on top of
their chutes so that they didn't run into each other. The
lights would have to be on top of the chute so it didn't
mark them from the ground, but would be visible to each
other from the air.

Ingenious.

We swung to the left and then the right. I couldn't see
it, but I knew Hands was controlling the steering lines.
He deliberately moved us toward a specific location, the
prearranged drop spot. How he saw the lines, let alone
controlled them in the dark, was beyond me. I had to ask
him later what technology he used to determine our drop
spot, but for now I simply trusted the method.

No, I trusted *him*.

Yes. After what we'd just been through, I totally
trusted him.

I started to laugh.

"Keys? You okay?" Hands sounded worried.

"Yes. I'm fine. That jump was…well, it was something else. Holy Batman. I just fell out of an airplane."

"We're not on the ground yet."

"No, but the worst part is over."

"Not by a long shot. You're in much more danger when
we're on the ground."

"Maybe, but if I can survive a fall from an airplane,
I think I can survive anything."

"Don't get cocky."

I laughed again. "Just let me be giddy for a minute because I'm still alive. I can't even believe I did it."

We glided through the darkness. It was strange but, although I was completely blind, I could almost "feel" the darkness of the ground getting closer. I noticed that one of the other jumper's chute lights suddenly swerved around wildly and presumed his chute had just collapsed as he hit the ground ahead of us.

Hands pulled hard to the right on the steering cord and we spiraled downward at a faster rate.

"Ground in about fifteen seconds," he warned. "Get ready for touch down."

Instinctively I began moving my legs as if I were walking. Hands stood taller than me, so his feet hit first and mine followed a second later. He unhooked the parachute and then me. I fell to the ground, laughing and kissing it. It's possible I may have shed a few tears as well.

Hands, however, was all business the moment our feet hit the ground. He detached the chute, deployed an infrared signal light as a marker for the team and then conducted a status check by radio to get an update on the team location.

Thankfully, since the winds were light, the team had all stayed within a short distance of the drop spot. I asked Hands if we had to bury the parachute, but he shook his head.

"No time for that. We're in and out."

It seemed a waste to leave behind an expensive parachute, but we didn't have time to fold it up and I couldn't see how we could carry it, so it would stay behind.

While we waited for the rest of the team, Hands crossed his arms and studied me, still sitting on the ground. "So, how'd you like the jump?"

"Honestly? It was abso-freaking-lutely incredible. But, just so we're clear, I'm never doing that again."

He chuckled. "The first time is always the hardest. Cross it off your bucket list. You're no longer a parachute virgin."

I stood on wobbly legs. "Sorry you had to drag me kicking and screaming. Literally."

"It can be like that the first time. But now you've got a taste of it, I bet you'll change your mind about jumping again."

I pushed the helmet back off my forehead. "Trust me, I won't. But it was still an experience of a lifetime. Whatever lifetime I may have left, that is."

He looked at me for a long moment. "You're a piece of work, Keys. So, this guy you're going to save, is he worth it?"

"Yes. He's my friend."

"Well, just remember, my mission is to keep you alive so you can stop that virus. Understood?"

"I understand the mission, but I have my priorities, too. They aren't necessarily mutually exclusive."

"We'll see. Go get a drink of water. Then get your vest and night goggles out of your pack and put them on."

"Yes, sir."

After I pulled on my vest, Hands tightened it and helped me adjust the night goggles until I could see properly. I almost jumped out of my skin when several SEALs materialized out of nowhere to join us.

Hands held up a hand. "Are all team members accounted for?"

"Affirmative." I recognized Wills's voice.

"Good. We've got a bit of a walk to get to the village," Hands said. He looked at me. "You ready? We need to move quickly and you're going to have to keep up."

My legs were still a bit shaky from the jump, but my resolve was intact. This time when I answered, I not only meant it, I believed it.

"Yes, I'm ready."

It was time to move.

Game on.

THIRTY-ONE

WE FOLLOWED EACH other in a strict formation.

One of the Bravo Team took the lead as point man, followed by Wills, me, Hands and the two other Bravo guys. Hulk brought up the rear. There was no visible road and the ground was flat with no signs of civilization. We kept to what little trees and brush there was to give us some illusion of cover. Sand and dirt clogged my nose and throat. I was perpetually thirsty.

The heat was stifling, made more so by all the equipment and gear I wore. Every drop of sweat that trickled down the middle of my back made me curse Broodryk more.

Clouds obscured the moon, providing an extra layer of darkness and protection. I was still adjusting to the green hue of the night goggles. It was disorienting, especially because it eliminated my peripheral vision. Worse, they were heavy and didn't provide much depth perception. I stumbled a couple of times, but Wills kept close, reassuring me that my brain would adjust to the goggles.

With my luck, it would be the day after tomorrow.

As we approached the location of the village, Hands checked his GPS and guided us so we approached from the correct direction. When the first buildings came into view Hands held up a gloved hand and we all stopped. He quietly deployed Bravo Team, and they peeled off from us, disappearing into the darkness.

I recognized the layout of the village from the satellite pictures we'd seen at the briefing. The meeting building sat at the far end of an open courtyard. Bounding the courtyard on the right were animal corrals made mostly of mud and stone. There were a few clumps of trees near the structure to provide a little shade for the animals during the hot days. I heard the snuffle and shuffling of the animals from where I stood.

To the left of the courtyard stood a garage with a few vehicles parked outside and several old tires and car parts stacked around it. Though I couldn't see it from this vantage, I knew from satellite photos that an eight-foot cinder block wall ran from the back of the garage to the meeting house, creating a border along the full left side of the courtyard. Why in the heck would someone build a wall on only one side of nothing in the middle of nowhere? The best I could come up with was that it must have been yet another unfinished government project.

Directly to the left of the meeting building, and seemingly connected to it, lay a smaller building, which was our target location. Gray and the other intelligence analysts had agreed this was the most probable location of the village elder, so that's where we were going. Well, at least that's where we'd start. If he wasn't there, this was going to be harder…a lot harder.

Most of the village residents lived in small quarters several hundred yards beyond the meeting house. These were mostly shacks, shanties and more tents. However, a few stone structures and a couple of two-story buildings were evident. In the distance, just beyond the residential area, the water tower rose up over the town. I fixated on the tower, looking to see if I could spot any movement and wondering if Abri Pentz was there waiting for us.

Hands was studying it, too. "Bravo Team are you in position?" Hands asked softly via the radio.

"Affirmative."

"Release the drone. We're moving into position."

"Check."

Hands motioned for us to follow him as we crept toward the garage, keeping it between the tower and us. We intended to come upon the elder's home from the garage side. Animals were unpredictable and we couldn't afford the risk of stirring them up and alerting people prematurely to our presence. The only problem I saw was that Broodryk and Pentz would know that, too, and expect us to come from the garage side. That didn't give us that much of an element of surprise in terms of our avenue of attack, but I didn't see an alternative.

I tried not to worry about that as I fell in behind Wills. I had more pressing matters to think about right now, like staying on my feet and out of the way of the SEALs. We ran at a crouch to the near side of the garage, trying not to trip over tires and debris. I felt like I clanked and rattled with every step and was sure that even deep sleepers in the village could hear me.

I replayed the mission briefing in my head as we huddled against the back of the garage. Going in, we were most vulnerable to sniper attack when looping around the garage and running along the cinderblock wall toward the elder's presumed living quarters. Pentz would have at least twenty seconds for a clear shot at us assuming he was on the tower or in the village. For a sniper of his skill at that range, nailing us would be even easier than hacking credit card info from Home Supplies Warehouse. Although Gray had assured us we probably wouldn't be targeted going in, we weren't taking any chances.

I closed my eyes. Even if Pentz didn't go after us on the sprint to the house, the doorway in would be a perfect spot for him to pick us off one by one. We couldn't congregate there. Instead, we'd run past the door, around the corner of the house to a little niche created by the corner of the building, protecting us from the line of sight to the tower. We'd have some protection there from Pentz, if he were indeed on the water tower.

We had a lot riding on Hands's and the analysts' guesses of Pentz's location. If they were right, they each had a nice dinner in their future, assuming I got back to take them out. For now, I knew Bravo Team was planning a distraction to support our sprint to the house. I hoped it lasted long enough to make the subsequent run from the corner through the door. I just hoped to hell there weren't armed men inside waiting to ambush us.

Right now I was breathing so hard, I was sure Wills or Hands would motion for me to shut up. But they were completely in the zone, focused, coiled and ready for action. I squeezed my hands together as tightly as I could and tried to stay calm.

The radio cackled in my helmet. "Alpha Team we have a visual. Confirmed MAM on the tower."

I leaned over to Wills. "What's a MAM?" I whispered.

"Military-aged male," he whispered back.

"Pentz?"

Wills shrugged.

I leaned back against the wall. Oh, God. It was game on.

Right freaking now.

"Stand by Alpha Team."

It seemed like we waited forever behind the garage, but it was probably no more than two minutes tops.

"Alpha Team, you are a go in three, two, one."

Hands suddenly sprinted from behind the garage. We followed him in formation. As I rounded the garage along the cinder block wall, I saw silent plumes of smoke going up around the water tower. Smoke grenades, I presumed, probably dropped by the drone. Silent, but hopefully effective in obscuring the sniper's view of us. I might have marveled more at the ingenuity if I hadn't been so damn scared.

Go, go, go, the voice in my helmet urged.

No one had to tell me twice. I ran like I'd never run before—well at least since the last time I was wearing combat boots, a two-pound helmet with night vision goggles and full body armor. We raced to the small house, past the entryway door, and dashed around the corner. They jammed me into the corner with all three SEALs pressing against me. I couldn't see a thing except for the stone wall. As far as I could tell no one had been shot and we were all still alive.

So far.

My heart was pounding so hard I thought I might keel over.

"Alpha Team in position," Hands said softly.

"Stand by, Alpha Team."

Seconds ticked past.

"Alpha Team, MAM is on the move. Go."

The SEALs instantly acted. Hulk moved into an outer protective stance while Hands gave me a signal to stay put. He went around the corner, got down on his knees and reached up for the door handle. It was unlocked. He held up three gloved fingers and began to countdown silently.

Three, two, one.

He went in low, followed by Wills. Hulk stayed out with me. I realized why they'd moved now. If the sniper was on the move for a reposition, he couldn't shoot us. That made us temporarily safe, relatively speaking. I strained to listen, but heard only faint sounds from inside the house. Adrenaline coursed through my body and it seemed like each of my senses strained and stretched on overload. After about a minute and a half I heard a noise and the radio cackled.

"House clear. Target acquired. Do we have a location on the MAM?"

"MAM is still moving."

"Alpha Star, enter the house."

Hulk moved in front of me as I rounded the corner and pushed open the door. I slipped inside while Hulk remained outside and disappeared back around the corner.

Wills took my arm. We stood in a lit room partitioned by sheets. I caught the faint scent of onions and garlic. Hands had pulled aside all of the curtains and left them open. A glance to my right showed a young woman and two small children, probably no more than three or four years old huddled together on a mattress. To the right of me, a man, perhaps the father of the children, sat backward on a chair, his hands bound behind him. Hands had his weapon trained on a gray-haired, bearded man wearing a long gray gown, probably his nightclothes. He stood in what looked like the kitchen. Hands motioned to him with his rifle and the man moved toward me.

"I am Abdou Ngobogo. Who are you?"

I pulled off my helmet. My ponytail was plastered to my head. "I'm Lexi Carmichael. Do you speak English?"

"Yes."

"Are you the village elder?"

"Yes. I am expecting you. You look like your picture."

"That's a miracle. I've looked a lot better."

He smiled a bit at that. "However, I must confirm it is you."

"How do you propose to do that?"

"I have a device. You will press your index finger to it and it will confirm your identity."

Hands listened to something and I assumed there was chatter on the radio. I no longer wore my helmet, so I couldn't hear it.

"Where is this device?" I asked.

"In that top drawer." He pointed to a dresser.

"Get the woman in here," Hands said to Wills. "Have her retrieve it."

Wills came back with the woman. She was clearly terrified. I wanted to tell her it would be all right, but I didn't know if that were true. I said nothing.

Abdou murmured something to her, then she walked to the dresser on trembling legs. The kids stood nearby crying for her. If it were possible, I hated Broodryk even more for dragging children into this. He would have known the elder's family lived with him and that children would be put in danger.

The woman carefully reached into the drawer while Wills kept his gun trained on her. She pulled out a small device about the size of my palm. She tried to hand it to Wills, but he motioned to me with his gun, so she walked back to me and handed it over. Tears were pooled in her big brown eyes. I took the device gently. She ran back to the children and hugged them to her breast. I flipped the device opened.

"It's a biometric reader," I said, examining it.

"Are you sure?" Hands asked. "Can you work it?"

"Probably. Give me a minute."

It was easier to figure out than I'd expected. "Got it. I press my finger here. Confirmation of my identity should be instantaneous. Broodryk's probably already got my fingerprint in here, so it will just be a matter of confirming the match."

"Are you sure it's safe?"

"I think so. That's the best answer I can give you."

"Do it," Hands said. "The clock is ticking."

I pressed my finger to the spot and waited. Two seconds later a green outline appeared around my finger with a word in French. I angled it at Wills, who read it. "Accepted. You're confirmed, Lexi Carmichael."

I took the device over to Abdou and showed him. "I'm me, so let's deal."

"Not yet. There is one more test."

"Test?"

"Yes. Here." He started to reach into his pocket, then paused when Hands pressed the gun against his neck.

"Take it slow, buddy."

Abdou carefully pulled out a crumpled piece of paper from his pocket. He handed it to me.

I took it and unfolded it.

"What does it say?" Hands asked.

"I don't know yet. It's in code."

"We don't have time to play games."

I looked up from the paper. "It's not a game. It's a test, just like he said."

Abdou nodded. "You must solve it, Lexi Carmichael. If you do not, than I am unable to provide the information you seek. He said you would be able to solve it."

"I will."

His hands shook. "Please. If you do not, he will return and kill my family."

I met his gaze. "I will provide the answer. I promise. Just give me a minute."

"We don't have much more than a minute," Hands warned. "So make it snappy."

I dug in my cargo pants for a pen. I found it and moved over to the table, starting the calculations.

It was a standard ASCII code, which was good because I was really nervous and that made it hard to think straight. Plus my fingers were sweaty. They kept sliding off the pen, making it hard to form the numbers I needed to make. Regardless, it only took me about three minutes to break the code.

"I did it," I said.

"Great," said Wills. "Tell him the answer and let's go."

"It's not that simple."

Hands sighed. "I had a feeling you were going to say that."

"I broke the code, but it's a riddle."

"A what?" Hands let out a stream of curse words. "You've got to be kidding."

"I'm not. This is what it says. 'I exist for the young, but the old can use me, too. I'm a thief, but I'm a welcome guest to those who don't wish to pay. I capture sound, although I make none. What am I?'"

Hands lifted a hand. "What the hell does that mean?"

I shook my head. "I don't know."

"Well, you'd better a get an idea soon or we're going to need a new plan of action."

I closed my eyes to think. But instead of trying to solve the riddle, I thought about its purpose. Broodryk had used a biometric scanner to ensure my presence. But biometric readers could be fooled, if we had come prepared and considered that possibility. So, just in case, he'd want to have a backup plan, another way to ensure I'd truly come on the mission and not sent someone else in my place. Therefore, it was logical to assume a code and subsequent riddle would be one only I could solve. The code was the initial layer, but the answer to the riddle would have to prove to him I was indeed Lexi Carmichael.

That was actually a positive development because that

meant by necessity, the riddle would have to be born of our shared experience. That narrowed the field of possibility and variables considerably. Now would be the time to put my photographic memory into play.

I started reviewing our contact from the moment I'd first seen Broodryk's face on the computer screen at the high school. The riddle answer came to me faster than I expected.

I opened my eyes. "I have it."

"Hallelujah," Hands said with enthusiasm. "Tell him and let's get a move on."

Abdou shook his head. "No. She does not tell me. She has to enter the letters on a box. It is the code to open it and retrieve the information you seek."

Hands frowned. "Where's this box?"

"No. I will not tell you yet. You must first give me the information on the Kwabano. It was the deal."

Hands looked like he was about to argue, but I held up a hand. "Fine. I'll go first. I'll pull up the information on the Kwabano on my laptop and show it to you, so you can be assured I have it. You'll then give me the box. When I'm convinced I have what I need, I'll write down the coordinates for you, so you don't have to rely on your memory, which can become impaired under extreme duress. When we are both satisfied we have the information we need, we will leave so you can resume your regularly scheduled life. Okay?"

Abdou thought for a moment and then nodded. "That is fair. I will not trick you."

"Right back at you. We don't have a beef with you."

I'm not sure he got the colloquial phrase, but he didn't protest when I unzipped my backpack, pulled out the laptop and sat on the floor as I booted it up. I pulled up the information he had requested and turned the screen toward him.

"Here you go. These are the most recent coordinates we could find on the militia leader who kidnapped the members of your village." I tapped the keyboard, pulling up a satellite image of the first coordinate. "I think you should start here. The leader of the Kwabano was spotted in this village just over twenty-four hours ago. Satellite images also indicate a large number of children in this location, too."

I swallowed, sickened by the thought that young boys and girls had been kidnapped and used as pawns in some kind of local power struggle.

"I sincerely hope you find them and get them back. This kind of thing, kidnapping and hurting children, makes me sick. I wish you the very best."

He looked surprised, then nodded. "Thank you. We were desperate, which is why I agreed to do this."

"I understand completely. It's okay. Good luck, and I mean that. Now it's your turn. Where's the box?"

"I must retrieve it from under my bed."

Hands moved closer, pressing his gun against Abdou's neck. "Nice and easy."

Abdou and Hands shuffled to his bed and reached underneath. He felt around and pulled out a small rectangular box. He held it up and I took it from him.

I put the box on the table and examined it. The top had a small screen and a keypad. It was live and blinking, so it was probably working off of a battery.

"You must not try and take the box from my house." Abdou spoke softly. "He says it will explode. You must open it while in the house in order to deactivate it and obtain the information inside."

"What if I plug in a wrong answer?"

"I do not know."

I glanced over at Hands. "What do you want me to do?"

"You know the answer to that riddle?"

"I think so."

"You think so?"

"Yes. I'm going with a 96.4 percentage rate of certainty that the answer is Phantomonics."

"What the hell is that?"

"It's a music pirating software used mostly by teens that Elvis planted in the school's computer system during Broodryk's terrorist operation. It didn't stop him, but it pissed him off. He needed a student to shut it down, so I volunteered. By doing that, it permitted me a front row seat at the show and the opportunity to put a crimp in his plan."

"Which you did."

"Yes."

"Well, stop him again. Do it."

Nodding, I leaned over the keypad and typed in the letters. My finger trembled as it hovered over the enter button. "Okay, here we go."

I held my breath as I pressed the button. There was a beep and the box popped open. A flash drive was nestled inside.

I grabbed the flash drive. "It worked."

"Good." I could hear the relief in Hands's voice. "Bravo One, package secure."

I quickly plugged the flash drive in to the laptop and data scrolled across my screen. I downloaded the information and then pulled the flash drive out, giving it to Hands. After that I asked Abdou to get me a piece of paper. He handed me an old piece of newspaper on which I jotted the coordinates he needed.

I handed it to him. "We're good now. Thank you."

I knelt and returned my laptop to the pack, hoisting it on my back. I retrieved my helmet and secured it under my arm.

"Time for this party to be over," Hands said. "Alpha Three, how are things out there?"

"Quiet," Hulk replied. "Cobra 1 has been notified and has begun the tactical descent on schedule."

"Bravo Team, any sight of the MAM?"

"Negative. We lost him."

"Shit."

"I bet it was part of the plan," I offered. "Broodryk gave me a simple, but time-consuming code and riddle to stretch out our operation. He had to make it easy enough for me to solve fairly quickly, but long enough to give him precious minutes to do whatever he is planning to complicate our exit strategy. I would venture a supposition that Broodryk did that so Pentz could have time to reposition if we were able to interfere with his initial line of fire, which we were. Seeing as how our planned escape via an exit within this hut is no longer viable, we're going to have to go back out the front door, where I believe Pentz is all lined up and ready to play target practice."

The room fell silent with all the men staring at me, including Abdou.

Hands spoke into his helmet. "Bravo Team, we have a problem."

"Alpha Team, report."

"Time to move to Plan B. Intended egress is a no go. Our assumption that this structure has an interior door to the meeting house is incorrect. We have to go back out through the door we came in. We're going to be sitting ducks. Check those two-story buildings for him. He'd want the height."

"Already checked, Alpha One. No visual and no thermal signatures sighted there."

"Damn. We don't have time to wait. Drop the smoke grenades near all of the tall buildings and we'll move."

"Negative. We're out of smoke. Flash grenades only."

Hands shifted the gun and grimaced. "Great. When they go off, everyone within ten miles of the village will wake up and all hell will break loose. Time until Cobra 1 arrives?"

"Four minutes."

I looked between Hands and Wills. We had four minutes to live…if we were lucky.

THIRTY-TWO

"THE VILLAGERS WILL kill you if they find you here," Abdou said. "They are not friendly to Americans and we are quite well armed. Even more so now that we are prepared to launch an attack to get our children back."

"Tell me something I don't know." Hands motioned for Abdou to sit at the kitchen table, then quickly cuffed his hands behind his back. "We're out of time, people. We've got to move no matter what."

"Wait." I held up a hand. "Isn't Bravo Team going to use the flash grenades?"

"Yes, but their effectiveness at a distance is limited. Worse, just one of those babies will wake up the entire town. This all goes south really fast as soon as we wake everyone up. If Pentz isn't in close enough proximity to a grenade to be temporarily blinded, he'll still be able to shoot us. If we don't know where he is, we can't target him effectively. But we'll give it an educated guess and set off random grenades, hoping for the best."

Hoping for the best didn't seem like a militarily sound maneuver, but we were running out of time.

My brain raced. "Pentz would use a laser designator on his night scope to shoot, right?"

Hands frowned. "Yes."

"Can we use that to pinpoint his location?"

"Maybe, but only if we could watch how the target pip moves on a rotating subject. Even then it would only provide a general location. It wouldn't pinpoint him exactly."

"But close enough for a flash grenade to be effective, right?"

"Possibly. What are you getting at, Keys?"

"I just want to make sure I understand properly. So, in order to get a decent fix on Pentz we have to get him to lock on to a slowly moving target for long enough to estimate his position."

"Negative. He won't linger on any target because once he has it, he shoots."

"Then we have to give him a target he won't kill."

"What target?"

"Me."

His eyes narrowed. "Oh, hell no."

"Why not? It makes perfect sense. I go out there without my helmet so there's no mistaking it's me. If it's Pentz, he won't shoot right away. You know he won't. He *has* to make sure it's not me. I'm not a sniper, but I believe his instinct will be to lock on to the first thing out that door. He won't expect it to be me. Tell me I'm not right. Then all you have to do is estimate his position, relay it to Bravo and they can position the drone to set off the flash grenades to cover your exit."

Hands took a slow step toward me, holding out a hand. I could see he was calculating how to grab me before I bolted. Right now, nothing stood between the door and me. In my peripheral vision, I saw Wills start to inch sideways.

"I appreciate the thought, but we can't risk you, Keys." His voice was soft and soothing. "We don't know for certain he won't shoot you. We, on the other hand, get paid to take these risks all the time. We've survived much worse. Look, it's only one guy with a rifle."

It wasn't just *any* guy or *any* sniper. Next to Hands,

Abri Pentz was one of the most decorated snipers in the world. He wouldn't miss and we all knew it.

I set my jaw. "You're right, Hands. I don't know for sure he won't shoot me. However, I *do* know he'll shoot you or any of the other guys, and he *won't* miss. We don't have time to take this to a committee."

Before either of them could stop me, I dashed for the door, yanking it open and stepping outside. I tensed as Keys and Wills shouted something, but I couldn't make it out.

Then I saw it. The red dot on my chest.

I turned sideways so I was half-looking into the house where Hands and Wills had screeched to a stop just inside the doorway, their arms flung out as if they could still catch me. Hands saw the red dot, too. I watched the recognition flash across his face.

Everything after that seemed to happen in slow motion. I squeezed my eyes shut, bracing for a shot that didn't happen. Slowly, I held my arms out and turned in the direction I thought Pentz might be. Summoning a bravado I didn't feel, I made a deep bow. I sure hoped Hands, Hulk and the entire Bravo Team were paying attention and figuring out exactly where Pentz was located.

After what I hoped was sufficient time, but was probably less than ten seconds, I turned and scampered around the house toward the safety of the far side of the garage. The back of my neck itched. I worried Pentz might change his mind and blow my head off just to spite me, but the shot never came.

Loud chatter sounded from the helmet under my arm, so just before I reached the edge of the garage, I stopped and raised it near my ear so I could hear what was going on. I had no time to put it on properly and fuss with the night vision goggles.

"Three, two, one. Go!"

The rapid bursts of two flash grenades in the distance startled me, followed a second later by the concussive thump. Moments after that Hulk, Wills and Hands came barreling around the building in full sprint, not even bothering to crouch. I stood frozen watching them. Hands stumbled once, but miraculously regained his footing and kept running.

I watched, mesmerized by the action, until I jolted back to reality. Hulk thundered directly toward me, sweeping me under his arm without breaking stride, and hauled me around the garage.

Pausing momentarily to regroup and plan our next actions, I pressed back against the wall next to Hands.

I couldn't see his face clearly, but I could hear the anger in his voice. "I would so kill you if it wasn't my mission to protect you. What the hell were you doing?"

"Hopefully saving us."

"Damn it. You didn't follow orders."

"Not this time. I followed logic."

He growled and then held up a hand, quieting me. "Bravo Team. Give me a status report on the MAM, Cobra 1 and the locals."

"This is Bravo One. MAM is hightailing it out of the village to the south. I suspect he doesn't want to be mistaken for one of us. He also appears to be suffering from a loss of his night vision, as he just raced into some barbed wire surrounding a corral. Ouch, that's got to hurt. Okay…hello. We have locals with guns emerging from the tents south of the corrals and signs of activity in the village itself as well. The bangs got their attention. ETA on Cobra 1 is sixty seconds. I would suggest you hurry. They won't want to wait around long."

I'd started to put my helmet back on when Hands

grabbed my arm and rasped, "We don't have time for that now. Just follow me."

He took off, practically dragging me with him. I staggered along off balance, holding my helmet beneath my other arm. Though I had complained about wearing the night vision goggles, I realized how much of an advantage they provided in the dark. Fortunately, given Hands's support, I was able to remain upright.

As we approached the positions that Bravo Team had established, I heard the thunderous whopping of the dual rotors of the Osprey landing. I could also hear the crackle of what must be small arms fire, though I couldn't tell if it was friendly fire or from the village. It didn't sound nearby, so I suspected the latter. My helmet was a cacophony of noise, and I could understand none of it.

We ran past a Bravo Team SEAL hunkered down in a firing position just as the Osprey landed. To my surprise, Hands didn't take me directly to the aircraft, but left me near a tree.

He released me and pointed me at the aircraft. He leaned in close and shouted. "Wait here for fifteen seconds and then hightail it to the plane. I'm going to do a sweep to make sure the area is clear of anyone wanting to pick us off as we board. Charlie Team will get you on board."

"Okay," I shouted back.

"So, count to fifteen and run like hell for the plane, Keys. Oh, and close your eyes on the way."

"What?" I shouted after him as he disappeared into the darkness. "What was the last part?"

He didn't answer, so I assumed he didn't hear me over the rotors. I bent over, bracing myself with one hand against the tree, trying to catch my breath. I had a stitch in my side and it hurt. I pressed my hand against my side and started counting. Suddenly gunfire erupted around me and I crouched down. Fifteen seconds had passed, but I wasn't sure if it was safe to run. I was considering my options when the world around me erupted in light and concussion, throwing me a good distance sideways and to my knees.

Holy flash grenade. Bravo Team must have set up a perimeter of flash grenades around the landing site to keep the locals away. I'd probably been steps away from one of them. Why hadn't I just dashed for the plane? Hands was really going to kill me now. I was *so* not going to be voted into the SEALs' Hall of Fame anytime soon.

Now I had no idea where I was or in which direction I faced. I couldn't see a thing and my ears were ringing. I was really going to regret not having put my helmet back on. Oh, God, speaking of my helmet—where was it? It had to have been knocked from grasp when I fell following the blast.

I felt around on the ground for it. No luck. I stopped, trying not to panic. No sense worrying about my helmet now. I had to get on that plane. Though I still couldn't see well, I got to my feet, hoping someone would see me and lead me to the plane. Just as I rose, there was a burst of gunfire nearby and someone shouted, *"Down!"*

I dropped to the ground again, hugging the dirt and deciding I would never, ever complain again about how cold they always keep the server rooms.

The shooting was getting closer. Fortunately I was beginning to regain limited vision. A SEAL shouted, "We've got hostiles all over the place. Fall back, now!"

Feet thudded to my right.

"Wait!" I screamed, but I wasn't sure anyone heard me over the rotor noise. The Osprey's rotors increased speed, spinning up.

Oh, God. They were leaving.

Without me!

I decided to risk the small arms fire and stood. Although barely able to see, I staggered toward the sound of the aircraft, hoping those who might be shooting at me couldn't see much better.

The engines revved louder and I vaguely saw the large mass start to lift. Staggering toward the airplane and waving my arms, I thought I heard the engines change again. Just as I was trying to decide if it were my imagination or not, I tripped over something and fell face-first to the ground, getting sand and dirt in my mouth and eyes.

I was now spitting sand and crying uncontrollably. Not a great way to meet whatever fate the villagers had in store for me.

As I crawled to my knees, a strong hand slid under my elbow, helping me up. "Alpha Star?"

It was a calm, assured and very American voice.

"Who are you?" I could barely see a dark shape.

"A member of the Charlie Team. I've got you. We need to leave now. The plane is holding for you."

"Oh my God. Thank you. Thank you so much. I thought you were going to leave without me."

"We almost did. I was doing a final area check as we were lifting off when Hands started shouting you were missing. Then I saw you stand up and run for the plane. With all the small arms fire, when I saw you fall, I thought you'd been shot. Had my worst moment of the mission right then. If I'd have lost you, Hands would have chewed my ass to the end of time. Not a good thing to lose the asset."

I was so thankful the best I could choke out was, "You came back. Oh, God, I thought you were going to leave me."

"No, ma'am. Not on this mission. Or any mission, for that matter. It's the SEALs' code. No man—or woman—left behind."

THIRTY-THREE

MY VISION HAD partially returned as we made our way to the plane. Several guys hopped off the plane, running out to meet us. Two of them got on either side of me and actually lifted me off my feet and kept running, while two others offered cover, facing outward and running backward with their rifles drawn. When we got to the plane, they hoisted me up into Hulk's waiting hands. Then the guys on the ground hopped in and the plane took off. Hulk deposited me in a jump seat and then lurched as the plane swerved. We were taking fire from below. I could hear the plinking of the bullets against the plane and prayed none of them would find the gas tank. After a moment, the engines revved louder and we climbed too high for the villagers to reach.

I closed my eyes and hoped it was too dark for anyone to see my dirt, sand and tear-streaked face. A thump sounded in front of me. I opened my eyes. Hands stood there, his hands on his hips, glaring at me.

"Why the hell didn't you count to fifteen and run to the plane like I told you?"

"I stopped to catch my breath. Then there was gunfire. I got scared and I wasn't sure it was safe to run. The flash grenades went off. Things were moving a bit too fast for me. I'm sorry. Apparently I need more training."

"You're joking right now?"

"It seemed appropriate, given your dark mood."

"Don't ever do that again."

"Fine. I'm not that good at jokes anyway."

"Not that. Risk your life by playing target."

I stared at him. Green dots still danced around my eyes. "That just makes no sense whatsoever. We're all risking our lives here."

"Pentz could have killed you."

"He could have, yes. But he didn't. It was the right call."

"It wasn't yours to make."

"I know. I'm sorry for that. I understand the military culture and the importance of following orders. I also understand that my actions may have inadvertently undercut your authority as a team leader. That was not my intention. But the alternative was having all of you get killed for nothing."

Even with impaired eyesight, it was impossible to miss his fierce scowl. "Damn it, Keys, it wouldn't have been for nothing. It would have been for the mission."

"While that's an admirable thought, it's also highly illogical. Your deaths would have been completely unnecessary and tragic. Everyone on this plane, back at the base in Djibouti, and in the control center in Washington knows full well that Pentz would have picked you off one by one going out that door if we hadn't pinpointed his location. You can yell at me all you want, but the facts speak for themselves. It was the right call."

Hands opened his mouth to say something, but instead made a strange noise in his throat and stomped across the aircraft toward the cockpit. He opened the cockpit door and slammed it shut. I suspected he had more to say but that he'd moved away before he strangled me.

I glanced around. The entire aircraft was silent except for the hum of the engine. I didn't know what else to do, so I shrugged out of my pack and put it between my legs. I leaned back, closed my eyes and thanked all the stars above I was still alive. After a few minutes, I felt a hand on my shoulder and looked to my left. Hulk sat there, his long legs sprawled out.

"I've never seen Hands so mad," he said in his deep voice. "It took a lot of guts to stand up to him like that just now, kid. Leave it to a woman to make him lose his cool."

I wasn't certain of the appropriate response, so I said nothing.

Hulk tried again. "He's pissed because he never had a chance to engage Pentz and then you took the risk instead of him. Give him time to cool off."

"I will. But this was about the mission, not his beef with Pentz."

"Yeah, which pisses him off even more."

"So, I guess I screwed up."

He punched me lightly on the arm. "No, you didn't. I'm saying you did dayum good, kid. Cool head under pressure. Hooyah." Then, he laughed in his deep baritone voice.

Others in the cockpit started laughing and cheering. I was glad they hadn't seen me blubbering like a baby when I thought they had taken off without me.

It was as if all the tension of the mission suddenly released. I wasn't sure what I felt. Relief mixed with worry and sheer exhaustion as the high of adrenaline faded. My fingers itched to take a closer look at the data on the computer. I wanted to examine it right then and there, but my eyes were still wonky from the flash grenades and they needed a rest, along with my brain and the rest of my body.

Someone from Charlie Team walked through the cabin, throwing us bottles of water and energy bars. I took a bar and downed it in three bites. I was ravenous, so they tossed me another one. Who knew mortal danger made a person so hungry?

I drank the entire bottle of water, gulp after gulp, until it was gone, not caring that water dribbled down my cheeks and chin. Water had never ever tasted so good.

After that I leaned back in my seat and closed my eyes. Despite the noise and bumpy ride, I dozed. Except for that following-orders thing, maybe I was becoming a decent SEAL after all.

THIRTY-FOUR

GRAY WAS WAITING for us when we got off the plane. She shook her head as Hands stalked past her without a greeting or a look, a huge scowl on his face.

Then she saw me. To my surprise, she ran over enveloping me in a big hug.

"Oh my God. I'm so glad you're okay, Lexi. You gave all of us heart failure when you stepped out of the house to face Pentz. Seriously, Captain Bischoff had to sit down and I heard audible gasps from the brass in Washington. What a brave thing to do."

"Why would that give any of you heart failure? It was a completely logical action. You said Pentz wouldn't shoot me."

"Well, yes, but I'm just an analyst—a junior one, at that. It was a best guess, not a certainty."

"Wow. *Now* you tell me. Oh well, a best guess is all we had time for. Thanks, Gray. I owe you dinner. Looks like your work was solid."

She slung an arm around my shoulders. "God, after that performance I need a serious drink. Come on. I'll walk you back to the barracks. How are you feeling?"

"Exhausted, grimy and hungry. I need a shower and some fuel. I'm pretty sure I suck at being a SEAL. But just the fact that I survived tells you volumes about *their* skills."

She laughed. "Oh, God, that's funny. Hands looked

seriously pissed. Let me guess, he's furious because you played target without his consent."

"That would be the winning scenario, although the fact that I paused to catch my breath and almost missed the plane home would be the second strike. I got disoriented and couldn't see where I was going. Jeez, I was totally the weak link in the operation."

She laughed. "I don't even know why I think that's hilarious, but I do. We must all be wound too tightly."

"No kidding."

Captain Bischoff spotted me and walked over, pumping my hand. "Good work, Ms. Carmichael. Hell of a thing you did." He thumped me on the back, knocking me forward a few steps. "Not sure what else I can say."

I shrugged out of my backpack and handed my laptop to him. "I downloaded all the information. Hands has the flash drive."

He took the laptop from me. "Great. I'll transmit the data immediately to Washington. We have a team standing by to receive it."

I knew exactly who was at the head of that team, and I missed him more than ever at that moment. I wondered what Slash had thought of the mission.

"Did you get a signal from Pentz?" I asked. "Was he broadcasting to Broodryk as expected?"

Bischoff nodded. "Yes, he was. Just as Ms. Grayson anticipated. We got a lock on the coordinates."

A smile spread across my face. "Oh, man, that's the best news I've heard all day. You trace it?"

"He jammed us with some pretty sophisticated stuff. But we were expecting it, so they're working on it in Washington now. I'll give you an update at the briefing in an hour. Go hit the showers, sailor." He paused and then coughed. "I mean... Ms. Carmichael."

I chuckled. "Yes, sir."

He started to walk away when I called out to him. "Wait. Ah, Captain, did you ever find Fennie?"

He nodded. "Yes. Apparently he ran off and got into some trouble. He met up with someone or something that beat him up pretty badly."

I winced. "Maybe it was just an accident."

"I don't think so. He suffered a few broken bones and some internal injuries, but thankfully he was found and rescued. Fennie is resting now and should make a full recovery."

"Wow, that's great news. About the recovery, I mean."

"It certainly is. It's turning out to be a good day. Or night, I should say."

"Certainly can't argue with that."

I'D JUST LEFT the shower and was headed back to the barracks when Gray ran out to meet me.

"Lexi, hurry."

I had no idea what was happening, but I ran after her without question, my wet hair plastered to my T-shirt. I dashed into the barracks and saw Gray had set up her laptop on the coffee table.

"Sit," she said.

I sat and she angled the screen toward me. She pushed a button and, with a pat on my shoulder, left. I watched until a beep sounded and then I saw his face.

Slash.

I grinned like an idiot, and for a moment he just stared at me. We reached out and pressed our hands against the screen at the same time.

"Cara."

"Slash. Oh, God. It's so good to see you. I... I miss you so much."

He smiled. "I miss you, too."

"Were you following the activities of the mission?"

He nodded. He had a five o'clock shadow on his cheeks and chin and black circles under his eyes. He looked exhausted and clearly hadn't been sleeping much.

"You look so tired."

"I'm fine. How are you?"

I ran my fingers through my wet hair. "Scared, exhausted, exhilarated. It all happened so fast, Slash. I jumped out of a freaking airplane! Sort of. I still can't believe I did it. We got the next clue. Have you seen it yet?"

"Not directly. Captain Bischoff just sent it. The team is reviewing the data as we speak. Good work."

"You, too. I heard we got a lock on the coordinates from Pentz's helmet cam."

"Yes. We've already broke through and analyzed them. They put Broodryk in a mysterious compound in Gabon. We're checking it out. It could be him. Just in case, Bischoff is mustering a SEAL unit there at Camp Lemonnier as we speak."

"That's excellent news. I'm headed to the debrief soon, so I hope to get more info then."

"I've been working on some things of my own. I'm following a system's trail regarding Pruxrat. There are some things about this situation that don't add up for me. I'm chasing those anomalies. I'll update you as time permits."

"Okay." I was intrigued, but we didn't have time right now for that kind of detail.

He fell silent, staring at me.

"Slash, what's wrong?"

He shook his head. "Nothing. I just want to look at you and thank God you're safe." He slipped his small gold crucifix out from beneath his shirt and kissed it.

"You know what I did. Stepping out in the line of fire so the team could get a fix on Pentz."

He closed his eyes. "I know."

"You don't approve."

"No. I don't approve of you putting yourself in harm's way."

"It was the right thing to do, Slash. I wasn't going to stand by and let Pentz pick off the SEAL team one by one."

"It was dangerous, reckless and risky. It was also quick thinking. If anyone else had done it, I'd have approved. But not you. Never you."

"At least you're speaking to me. Hands isn't."

"I'm not surprised."

"I have to figure a way to make it right with him before the next mission. Doing that kind of thing is not my strong suit. Any advice?"

"Let him come to you. As a leader, it's his responsibility to make sure his team is right. Give him time to work it out. He will."

"Okay." I felt relieved that I wouldn't have to make the first move. "Can you update me on Xavier?"

"Of course. His condition has been upgraded. He came through the latest surgery on his spleen with flying colors. He's still in serious condition, but he's stabilized."

"Wow. That's great news. Have you contacted Basia?"

He smiled. "She calls me about every two hours to make sure I stay on top of the situation."

"Thanks. That's really nice of you."

"I'm fielding calls from your brother Beau, as well. He's keeping your parents updated. They know nothing except you're hard at work on the case and are currently unavailable for visits. I've told them you're fine."

I rubbed my temples. "I appreciate that more than you

know. I don't want them to worry. It's hard to think about them and the mission at the same time. I don't know how service men and women do this. But it's important. Family is important."

"*Si*, family is everything. It's time for the briefing, *cara*. Go now. We'll talk again soon."

"Okay. Hey, Slash?"

"*Si?*"

"Thanks again for sticking with me."

"You won't get rid of me that easily."

I smiled. "I can't tell you how much of a relief it is to hear that."

THIRTY-FIVE

GRAY AND I were headed toward Bischoff's conference room when Hands intercepted us.

"Can you give us a minute?" he asked Gray.

"Sure." She raised her eyebrow at me as she walked past.

Hands had showered, shaved and dressed in a fresh T-shirt and camouflage pants. He seemed struggling with something he wanted to say. He stuck his hands in his pockets and shifted on his feet.

I waited.

"Damn it," he finally said. "I'm really pissed at you."

"Really? I hadn't gotten the memo on that."

He kicked at the sand. "Okay, that didn't come out the way I'd intended. Look, I'm pissed about a lot of things, but mostly at myself. The mission didn't go like I thought it would."

"We all came home alive. We got what we went for—the clue. We're another step closer to Broodryk, with a boatload of new data. I'm not a military analyst, but I'd call that a successful mission."

"Everything is carefully planned for a reason."

"I know, but part of being a good leader is being adaptable. You brought us home safely, Hands. That's on you, no matter what any of us did or didn't do. I guarantee you there isn't one member of the team who isn't thankful to you for that."

"You deserved the dressing-down, but I was out of line on the plane. I lost my cool."

"It's okay. I appear to be a master at pissing off people lately."

He frowned. "What the hell did you do to this Broodryk guy?"

"What didn't I do? I put a big crimp in his illegal cyber operations. Possibly cost him hundreds of millions of dollars in the process. Guess that was enough to cause him to blow his top."

"Yeah, I guess that would do it." He rubbed his forehead. "Look, just for future reference, I need you to follow my orders, okay? We have to act as a seamless unit and I can't do that if you don't obey me."

"I understand, but do you?"

"What?" He narrowed his eyes. "Wait. That wasn't an answer."

"No, it wasn't. Look, Hands, I trust you with my life, which is why I'm still here. But I'm not going to let you or anyone else sacrifice their lives needlessly if there is another logical option. I know Broodryk, the way he thinks, the way he does things. You need to trust me on that. I understand you have to protect me, but I don't want to be a burden on this team. I want to be a valued team member, which means my opinion has to count, too."

His mouth dropped open. "You want to be a member of the team?"

"Of course, I do. You just said we had to act as a seamless unit. So, technically, that makes me a part of this team. I realize I'm a liability in the sense that I'm not properly trained and have a few—okay, *a lot*—of drawbacks, but I'm not just deadweight. I'm more than an asset. I occasionally have ideas, too."

He considered my words and then nodded. "Fair enough. But from now on, final decision rests with me."

"I'll agree to that as much as I can without knowing the exact parameters of each situation."

He studied me, then narrowed his eyes. "You didn't agree to anything, did you?"

"Not really."

"Hell, I figured as much."

I smiled. "But I will defer to you most of the time. Just so you know, I think you're a good leader and I'm glad you're on my side. Plus, after that tandem jump, I feel much more comfortable with you. Especially since you didn't unhook me and let me plunge to my death."

He grinned. "It crossed my mind."

I grinned back. Thankfully it seemed as if we were making a bit of progress in terms of a working relationship. "So, are we cool, Hands? At least for the time being?"

He sighed. "Yeah, we're cool, Keys."

We walked the rest of the way to headquarters and filed into the conference room. Hands and I were the last to arrive. I sat at the table in that last empty chair next to Gray while Hands leaned back against the wall next to Wills.

Bischoff stood. "We're all here. I want to congratulate everyone on a successful mission. We got what we went for and more. The analysts in Washington were able to isolate the coordinates from Pentz's helmet camera to a military-style compound in Gabon. Initial satellite imaging indicates that it's a secure location—guarded, isolated and wired to the max. It would fit the parameters of the set-up required by Broodryk."

"You really think it's him?" Hands asked.

"It looks promising. That's all I can say at this point.

We're mustering another SEAL team for the Gabon compound from here. Meet Echo Team."

I twisted around in my chair and saw several new guys leaning against the wall.

Gray flipped through her papers. "Broodryk has used Gabon as a launching ground before, but not this particular compound. What if he leaves before we get there?"

"We're now monitoring all comings and goings from the compound. If he leaves, we'll know it."

I didn't think it would be that easy, but I wanted to know where they were going with this. "So, what's the plan?"

"The plan is, we send in Echo Team to Gabon to extract Broodryk while you're keeping him busy and distracted at the shack."

I raised an eyebrow. "Extract him?"

"If possible. We'd like to question him on certain things."

I didn't want to know what those things were or how exactly they would question him. "What if it's not Broodryk there?"

"We'll handle that when and if we have to."

I didn't ask how they would handle it. No one else did either.

Hands pushed off the wall. "So, what was on that flash drive we got from the village elder?"

"A location where Broodryk wants to meet Lexi next."

"What? Where?" I asked.

Bischoff exhaled. "Somalia."

There was audible murmuring in the room.

Hands shook his head. "Somalia. Goddamn bastard."

"It fits." Gray closed her file, rested her hands on top of the papers. "It's dramatic, over the top, and summons images of the horrific situation that went down in the book and movie *Black Hawk Down*. Plus the SEALs have been hitting extremists and pirates along the coast lately. It's so him. He probably amused himself thinking it up. It wouldn't be hard to recruit local help against Americans. It's cagey, but let's not forget he's a raving lunatic."

Wills set his water on the table with a frustrated thump. "So, we have to keep playing this stupid game?"

"We do," said Gray. "If we don't play, or he thinks we're not following his directions, he'll set the virus loose."

"He's going to set it loose no matter what," I clarified. "But the key is to distract him into thinking we don't know that so we can take him down before he actually *does* it."

It all seemed impossibly complicated. I wished more than anything I could wake up in my own bed and realize this had been nothing more than a nightmare. The comfort and anonymity of cyberspace called to me and I ached to respond. But I couldn't help either one of the twins if I escaped into fantasyland. There was much more at stake than a mythical kingdom of Xenath. I had to stay focused in the here and now—the brutal cold reality.

"What do we know about the location of the shack in Somalia?" I asked.

Bischoff had Jason pull up a map and narrow in on the coordinates. "Not much without a current satellite photo. We have a lower resolution Google Earth photo while we await the next satellite fly over. Won't have anything for another two hours at the earliest and even then we won't get the best sun angle."

"What about the geography and the politics?" Hands asked.

"Well, the geography around the site is semi-arid. Sandy soil, scrub brush, low acacia-type trees. Few mountains, but the terrain is somewhat rough and broken. Few roads except near the coast and they aren't in good condition or are probably mined. This area shot was taken about four days ago. Politically, no one owns this area. It is a site of dozens of excursions by the Kenyans trying to keep the Arab extremists from setting up camps near the border. As the Kenyans have been pushed back behind their border this week, I can tell you upfront, this is no friendly zone. Still, there's good news and bad news. The good news is the target location is close to the border with Kenya and they are willing to assist us."

I waited, but no one else asked, so I made myself do it. "If that's all we get for good news, I'm afraid to ask what's the bad news."

"The bad news is since the Kenyans are back on their side of the border, the brutal extremist group, *al-Shabaab*, has probably returned to the other side, right where you are heading."

Wills shook his head. "Great. So, what's the latest on *al-Shabaab*, beyond the usual beheadings, torture, suicide bombers and mass murder?"

Bischoff sighed. "Well, the Kenyans are noticing less activity than usual from them. They are more silent now on the intercepts. In the past, that has indicated a big operation was afoot. As a result, everyone is on high alert across the region. Something big is happening. I just hope it is you guys and not something else we don't know about."

I pressed my hand against my forehead and looked at Gray. She had dark circles under her eyes and her hair had fallen loose from her usual tight bun. We all looked like we'd crawled out from under a rock, and we were tired of Broodryk's sick games.

Bischoff walked with his hands behind his back as

he spoke. "I'm not understating the political situation when I say the situation in Somalia is about as bad as it can get. There is no US presence in terms of an embassy or consulate. The situation, particularly in the southern part of the country where you are headed, is highly volatile and unstable. Terrorists and armed gangs roam sections of the country unchecked. There is fighting among clans, factions and families, not to mention political and regional organizations. It would not have been difficult for Broodryk to find allies to support his efforts, especially if he's willing to throw money or weapons around."

"Or," Wills noted, "if he offered them a bunch of Americans as a present, all tied up and packaged with a ribbon."

I swallowed hard. "Jeez."

Hands leaned forward, seemingly undisturbed by what Bischoff had just said. "What do we know about his intentions?"

"The game is we have forty-eight hours to stop this madness or it's over. He gave us coordinates and an exact time to show."

Hands jerked his head toward me. "What about her?"

"What about her? She's what Broodryk wants. We have to get her to that shack in the next forty-eight hours."

"What about me?"

"Nothing about you this time, Hands. You're off the hook."

"Pentz is going to be there. I guarantee you."

"We don't know that."

"He missed me and he went out of that mission without a single kill. He's pissed. He won't be absent from this opportunity, I promise you." Hands glanced over at Gray. "What's your take, Suit?"

Gray considered for a moment. "It's possible he'll be

there, but I can't be sure. Somalia is a pretty unpredict-able and dangerous place right now for Westerners, even bad guys. Pentz himself might not want to risk it despite the prize. As this is supposedly end game, Broodryk might not want him there either. I assure you, Broodryk already has every single little detail planned out for the final denouement. He's likely had it planned out for days. He may have ordered Pentz to stay out of it."

Wills spoke up. "So, how do we go in?"

"Our plan has to be two-pronged attack," Bischoff said. "One mission in Somalia and one mission in Gabon. Hopefully that's where Broodryk is sitting and master-minding the operation."

"How do we do that?" Gray asked.

Bischoff sat down. "The first question is *who* we do it with. Washington thinks we should swap out the SEAL teams. We've got enough men here in Djibouti for fresh teams."

"What?" Hands said, his face incredulous.

"We need clear-headed boots on the ground, Hands. Like the last mission, Washington wants two small in-sertion teams on this operation. Small groups—fast in and fast out."

Hands stiffened. "Permission to speak candidly, sir."

"Granted."

"If there is even the slightest chance Pentz will be there, I should be on that team. I know him and his meth-ods. If anyone could take him out, it's me."

Bischoff shook his head. "You just heard Ms. Reese. We don't know that he'll be there. In fact, it's highly unlikely he will. At this point Lexi is the only required player in the game." He softened his voice. "Besides, even if you were there, Hands, you wouldn't be able to engage Pentz on that level. Here, just like last time, the mission is about the asset, not your long-standing feud. You'd need to be light and mobile instead of carrying a heavy rifle and scope. Plus we won't have enough men on the ground to spare you for the hunt."

"Yes, sir, I understand that. But it's not always about the rifle. It's a mind game, too. It's about how he will think, how he will act. No one knows that better than me. No one knows *him* better than me. Besides, the asset has just gotten comfortable with me, with all of Alpha Team. Bringing in a new team creates an unnecessary and untried dynamic that we don't have time to work out at this point in the game."

All heads in the room swiveled toward me.

"Ms. Carmichael?" Bischoff said. "What do you think?"

I looked between Hands, Gray, Wills and Hulk. Hands was the only one not looking at me. He stared straight ahead, so stiff I thought it would be possible to bounce a basketball off his chest and he wouldn't move an iota.

I nodded. "Hands is right. I'm comfortable around the Alpha Team. If they are willing to risk their necks again, have time to get a decent rest, and are up for another shot at Broodryk, I'd like to stick with them. They're my unit. I trust them with my life…and this mission."

The room was silent for a full minute before Bischoff said, "Alpha Team. Are the rest of you in agreement with this?"

Wills gave a thumbs-up. "I'm in."

Hulk nodded. "Me, too."

I saw a slight smile touch Hands's mouth, but he said nothing. He didn't have to. His gaze met mine and I knew we had an understanding.

Bischoff sighed. "Fine. I'll run it past Washington,

but there's no guarantee they'll green light it. But, for the time being, let's move on."

Hands relaxed his shoulders, visibly relieved, as Bischoff continued. "Here are the ground rules. The reason Washington is authorizing a small insertion team is because that's the way Kenyan officials want it, and we need their cooperation to pull this off. Also, it helps Washington save face if this turns out to be a disaster. Loss of life will be minimal."

It didn't seem minimal when it was *my* life they were talking about, but I understood the reasoning. Tactically it would be hard to move a large force across the border unnoticed, which is what we wanted to do.

Bischoff looked over at Hands. "Team leader, you have any thoughts on how we proceed under these restrictions?"

"Yes, sir. Jason, let's start with Google Earth so that I can get a feel for the surrounding area."

Jason found it and broadcast it onto the big screen. It was a bit fuzzy, but I could make out what looked like a single white shack with a road leading up to it. No vehicles or signs of life.

Hands studied the image for a few minutes and we remained silent while he thought. "Back it out a bit," he instructed. When the picture was where he wanted it, he walked over to the table and picked up the pointer from where Bischoff had left it.

"The shack is situated in a spot easily visible from multiple vantage points. It's located in a bit of a depression with small hills on either side. Either hill could be a good place for opposing forces to muster. Both have a lot of waist-high thorny scrub brush, and rocks for concealment. If we venture into that stuff, we need to be careful. The thorns are long and nasty and will make quick movements difficult. We also have to remember that this is the dry season, so if we decide to use fire, we have to do it very carefully, because those bushes will burn quickly and produce a lot of smoke. The door to the shack opens here to the southwest. From this perspective, I don't see any windows or other egress, but there might be some on the backside that we just can't see. But I doubt it, as he wouldn't want us to be able to reconnoiter the building through a window."

He tapped the screen with his pointer. "A sniper would have to stay on the door. If I were Pentz, I'd take this jar-shaped hill to the southwest for my preferred position. Either end of the hill could provide cover for anyone, terrorist or otherwise, wanting to monitor the comings and goings from the shack.

"Focus here and enlarge." Hands pointed to the opposite side of the screen and paused until it popped up. "This side has an even bigger hill and we've got trees here. More cover, but it's farther from the shack and no direct view to the door."

"But aren't trees better for snipers?" Gray asked. "The height advantage and all."

"Yeah, but whether it's Pentz or anyone else, it's all about entrance and egress. Climbing a tree limits your mobility and therefore your options. The risks outweigh the benefits unless that is your only vantage point. One way or the other, we have to assume that snipers will be covering that door. It's a guarantee. No one comes or goes without their permission."

I considered. "That also means as soon as I'm in the shack, Pentz, or whatever thugs Broodryk has hired, are free to start shooting at you, right?"

He didn't sugarcoat the truth. "Yes."

"There's another message here, right? Broodryk

doesn't intend to let me or Elvis walk away even if I play the game to the end and win. He wants to be sure that even if we somehow win...we lose."

No one said anything.

I glanced at Gray and she nodded.

"I'm sorry, Lexi. Despite all his talk, I'm afraid it's game end only when either you or Broodryk is dead. We've never been closer to putting him out of business than right now. It's still a long shot, but we still have a chance if we can get the final information we need. We can stop the virus, if we can pinpoint Broodryk. That means you have to keep playing his game all the way to the end, even knowing the likely outcome."

Bischoff's face was serious, strained. "Hands and his guys will do their best, but I'll be honest. The odds aren't great for you or Elvis...actually any of you. Nevertheless, we can't do this without you. We can't force you to risk your life. We have some other options, but they are all a lot worse.

I tried to imagine worse options than what was staring me in the face.

Bischoff continued, looking me squarely in the eyes, "If we don't get him now, he will do a lot of damage and a lot of people will get hurt. In addition, he'll never stop hunting you and the people you love. Regardless, we won't stop until we bring him down with or without you."

A heavy silence fell over the room. Everyone watched me intently.

To my surprise, Gray reached out and lightly touched the top of my hand with her fingers. "I'm glad I don't have to make this decision. It's a brutal one. The bottom line is that everyone in this room, and the people at the highest levels in Washington, are offering you a chance to be the key part of making Broodryk old news. But we want you to fully understand what you are committing to. The final mission all comes down to this, a less than fifty-fifty chance you'll make it. So the question is—despite those odds are you still in?"

THIRTY-SIX

I'D KNOWN FROM the beginning that Broodryk would never let me or Elvis go even if I played and won his little game. He was a liar, cheat and a first-class sociopath. This was an ugly business, whichever way you looked at it. But I was not a scared little girl. I knew the risks when I'd signed up, and I'd see it through.

"I've already signed all the paperwork, but if it's required for me to state it for the record, then let it be known that I'm agreeing to this operation of my own free will."

Gray looked at Bischoff. He pressed his lips together and nodded. "Understood."

Now it was settled, I felt calmer. "Let's move on. Do you think Broodryk will have the shack wired to blow whenever he wants?"

Hands considered. "Probably. But he won't blow it right away. Not until he has time to play."

"I agree," Gray said. "Broodryk needs to have the perfect performance first. A big show for the world. This means he's got to either be taping or recording what happens. As a result, it's extremely likely he'll have electronic equipment of some kind in the room set up to provide a Skype-like connection between Lexi and him. He has to be able to test and taunt her, and then record the game for a much wider audience later."

Hands noted, "On the imagery, it looks like a line of telephone poles running along the road. I can see a set of wires going to the shack. What do you think? Power, phone and network?"

My brain raced through the possibilities. "He'll need a good and highly reliable connection for his interaction with us. Too much of his satisfaction rides on being able to see and manipulate what will go on once we arrive. He'll avoid using a landline, as the local infrastructure and network would be way too unreliable. So we are looking at a satellite feed. I am sure he expects us to try and monitor it, but it will be encrypted on transmission and he won't give us enough time to crack it."

"Yes," Gray added. "I agree that approach is almost a certainty."

"One advantage is that the satellite feed will limit his bandwidth, and the encryption will hurt his performance even more. That won't allow him to monitor everything simultaneously. We should be able to take advantage of that."

"Good. What systems would you expect him to deploy to monitor the actions?"

I considered the ways he might do it. How *I* would do it.

"Well, there isn't going to be much available to him in the middle of a hellhole like Somalia, so he'll know we'll finger him on whatever he intends to use. I'm guessing some autonomous systems, like door alarms that are low bandwidth, with at least one video/audio connection so he can watch our expected futile attempts and goad us on. That's a given. I also expect at least one camera, potentially several so he can monitor Elvis, the inside of the shack, and probably the outside approach to the door."

"Will he need a satellite phone or antenna?"

"Absolutely. I had forgotten about that. We could stop him from seeing us by taking that out, but we can't shut him down, especially if he has stuff on timers, so we have to play the game first. It does mean, however, we're going to need first-rate communications of our own in place. They'd better be impenetrable or Broodryk will be all over them."

Jason nodded. "Nothing but the best for you. We'll have both local comms for you all to talk on the ground, and a full service, encrypted satellite link to 'Mother' for real-time observation of approaching hostiles and any special deliveries. All should be in place in a few hours. We'll make it airtight."

"Good. That's a must."

Hands studied the map. "Let's talk the plan of engagement. From what I can see, we've got a single story shack in the middle of No Man's Land. One door and no apparent windows. One road in and out. The bad guys know where we are coming from, can engage us both coming and going, and unfortunately know exactly when we are expected to arrive. So we don't have the element of surprise. There are firing positions for opposing forces on either side of the shack with which we'll have to contend, and no natural high ground from which we can defend the building while Lexi's inside. Still, we've got something in our favor."

I didn't see anything, but I didn't want to be the black cloud of gloom, so I kept my mouth shut.

"First, we know that *they* know we are coming, so we can plan for that. As a result, we'll have airpower."

"We will?"

"Yes." Hands looked at Bischoff. "That's helpful. But how do we get to the site? Do we have a ship in the area?"

Bischoff nodded. "We do. It's making its way closer to provide even more air support if things really go south."

"That's very good news."

"The plan is to helicopter you out to the ship, refuel and proceed to the rendezvous point with our Kenyan friends at the border who are delivering your transportation. From there it's about an hour's drive to the site."

I perked up. "Drive?"

Not that the thought of driving through extremely hostile territory in the middle of Somalia didn't terrify me, but oddly it seemed a better alternative than jumping from twelve thousand feet again.

"Broodryk has scheduled it so we have to go in during the day," Hands continued. "Jumping makes us sitting targets for anyone waiting for us. Helicopters are likely to attract too much attention and bring too many people to the party early. So, driving it is."

"Tanks?" I said hopefully.

Hands rolled his eyes. "Land Rovers."

Land Rovers seemed pathetically small against whatever evil forces we might be facing, but I guess the operation's transportation budget could only afford the economy model.

I unscrewed the top of my water bottle and took a slug. "Then what?"

"Then we go in small and tight. Two teams—Alpha and Bravo. We drive off-road to minimize the chance of meeting hostiles and IEDs."

"IEDs?" I asked.

"Improvised explosive devices," Wills explained. "A nice little one will create a crater six feet across and toss what is left of the shell of the vehicle more than a hundred feet. We generally try and avoid them."

"Right. Jeez."

"Anyway, when we get to the shack, we'll use the Land Rovers as initial cover," Hands added. "Alpha Team will position here." He tapped at a location about forty yards from the front door."

I cocked my head to get a better view.

"We angle the jeep so it provides initial cover to the door against whomever may be positioned on Jar Hill. Although it won't stop a decent sniper, it's the best we have. Bravo Team drives over here to the other side of the building and across the road and sets up a holding perimeter against the mango-shaped hill. We will have to rely on the Predator drone overhead to warn us if any unexpected guests are coming to crash our party. Air extraction from the carrier is available if escape routes are sealed off or if there is no enemy presence at mission completion."

I liked the idea of leaving, even if we had to do it on a helicopter.

"So, while Lexi has to deal with the electronic complexities of the situation, our mission is a basically a hold, snatch and run. We get Lexi in, she figures out how to finger Broodryk's location and free the hostage while we hold off the bad guys and get them both out safely. We should all be sipping Mai Tais on the beach in Kenya by sunrise."

At first I wondered who Hands was trying to fool with his bravado. But looking closer at him, I realized he really believed what he was saying. He had full confidence in our abilities to do this, and especially in *mine*.

Jason tapped a pen on the table. "Here's my thought. Broodryk has to have brought locals in on this. He wouldn't risk his own neck in Somalia by setting up the game room himself."

"Yes." Gray spread her hands on the table. "He'll pull in a favor from someone in the area who owes him, most likely a representative of *al-Shabaab*."

"Great," Wills said. "This scenario just gets better and better."

I held up a hand. "Okay. Let's say Broodryk has got an *al-Shabaab* guy doing the set-up at the shack for him. That actually works in our favor."

I couldn't believe I'd actually come up with something positive about all this.

"Because...?" Gray asked.

"Because it means he didn't do it himself. From a technical point of view, working remotely with amateurs leaves me a lot more hopeful about finding a weakness in his set-up. Broodryk will be limited to what he can manage and what they're able to provide for him. That's a plus for me."

Hands turned his attention to me. "So, what do you see in this game room, Keys? What's the set-up?"

I closed my eyes, imagined myself as Broodryk. What would I need? What would I want?

After a few seconds of reflection, I mused, "That's real conjecture right now as we don't know what end game looks like to him other than all of us dead and the virus released. That would be easily achieved by having the shack blow up upon entry and hordes of *al-Shabaab* coming over the hills to take care of the rest. But I don't think that will happen, at least not immediately, because there is no satisfaction for him in that."

"Agreed," Gray said.

"So, I think that means he has to let us in, or at least me. I have to communicate with him and see Elvis alive. Hopefully he's there. If so, he'll almost certainly be restrained."

"It would heighten the dramatic effect," Gray added.

I continued to visualize the set up. "A shack that size can't have more than one or two rooms or maybe even one big room, partitioned with sheets like at the elder's house. To talk with me he will need a camera, or cameras, and a laptop or TV. He'd use the speakers on either one of those to talk to me and hear my response. I'm actually leaning toward thinking he'd use a television screen or monitor, probably hung from the wall and connected to a laptop. It's big, grandiose. He'd have to have the laptop networked to at least two cameras, one for the room and one for outside so that he could watch all the fun. Without a doubt everything we say in that room will be heard, seen and recorded by Broodryk."

Hands bent over, rested his palms on the table. "Will he be able to pick up our comms?"

"He may hear noise if things are quiet, but he shouldn't be able to discern what's going over the comms in our helmets. So, we'll have a small edge there. It does mean there may have to be a lot of one-way conversation going on in terms of what's happening in that room. I'll have to choose every word I say very carefully."

"What's he going to want you to do?" Wills asked.

I shrugged. "Anything that he can think of to first humiliate me and then assert his dominance intellectually. After having proved I am not worthy, he'll dispose of me. Pretty simple. Truthfully, I have no idea. I believe Elvis will have to be there since that's been part of his plan from the start and he'll want me to have a visible reminder of my failure to save my friend. He wants me shaken, upset and at his mercy. I'm certain that wherever, or however, Broodryk positions Elvis, he'll be in some kind of precarious situation. Like Gray said, it will make for good drama and television."

I heard a growl and looked down the table see Hulk frowning. "Psychopath," he muttered.

I nodded. "That's who we're dealing with."

"So, what do we need to get you ready, Keys?" Hands asked.

"I don't know exactly what yet. Something is bugging me about the compound in Gabon, but I can't put my finger on it. I need to talk to Slash. I have a thought, but I need his input."

Bischoff nodded. "No problem. I'll see it happens pronto."

THIRTY-SEVEN

TO MY RELIEF, Slash had the same concerns about the coordinates of the compound in Gabon as I did. Luckily for me, he was already one step ahead and had already started down the road I was about to propose. I was so thankful we were on the same page I had to take a moment to compose myself. Then we got to work, hammering out technical details and bouncing ideas off one another until we had a solid plan in play.

It was damn risky, but it could work.

When all was said and done, I wished we had another three weeks to test and retest our theory. Unfortunately we didn't have near enough time to perfect our strategy, but the more we worked it, the more I liked it. So did Slash.

We ran our alternate plan by Woodward, Gray and the SEALs, filling in as many details as we had come up with, expecting them to flesh out the rest. I expected a lot more push back, but it didn't take us as long as I expected to get everyone onboard. The reality was, as we had discovered, that even if they had truly understood what we were talking about, no one had any better options. They simply had to trust us. Not knowing as much as we did in terms of the structure of Pruxrat, they couldn't fully comprehend the cyber intricacies of the plan we had created.

I had a heady moment when I realized Slash and I were on the forefront of a new style of warfare that combined cyber, special operations and traditional military forces. Code Man would have been proud.

We barely had time for an updated intelligence briefing, a look at the just-received satellite imagery, and another attempt by the best military fashionistas to fit me into the latest military version of body armor topped by the always popular Kevlar combat headgear. As always, trying on new clothes wore me out, so I was able to get a decent night's sleep, minus spiders or foxes, before my initial part of the plan's execution. I had to be rested and at my best if I had any chance of pulling this off.

I wasn't crazy about flying in a helicopter, but it seemed safer than jumping out of an airplane, so I sucked it up. Rotors on the helicopter were thumping as Hands, Wills, Hulk and I climbed on with the members of Bravo Team. I couldn't hear anything over the noise. I found the rapid beat of the rotors matched the stress-induced palpitations from my heart. I scrunched as far in the back of the helicopter as I could. For some unfathomable reason, Even though there were doors on the helicopter, the SEALs left them wide open. I kept waiting for someone to close them, but like dogs out a car window, the SEALs kept leaning out to see whatever was hundreds of feet below us. The fact that they could fall out at any time didn't seem to bother them.

The helicopter pitched forward alarmingly as we transitioned from vertical to forward flight, and the Bravo SEAL in front of me almost caught my breakfast down the back of his neck. I swallowed hard and closed my eyes. Soon, the tight quarters, the rhythmic thumping of the rotors and keeping my eyes shut shortened the trip considerably as I unexpectedly dozed off.

As we approached the carrier, Hands nudged me awake.

"Get up, Keys. You know, you've got the makings of a

real SEAL, sleeping soundly while riding into battle and
crammed body-to-body with a bunch of oversized men."

"I actually think it's a defensive mechanism. If I'm
asleep or unconscious, I have no idea what's going on
around me."

He laughed. "Well, keep your eyes open. We're about
to land."

I did keep my eyes open as we landed on the aircraft
carrier. I figured—well, I sincerely hoped—it would be
the last time I ever had to do something like this, so cu-
riosity won out over queasiness.

The seas were a little rough as we approached, and the
carrier's deck was slowly pitching up and down several
feet as we landed. The reverse pitching motion began
again, slowing our forward movement in order to go vertical. It reminded me how much I preferred the simple
pleasures of riding in my Miata over some of the other
modes of transportation I had experienced lately. Still, I
was proud of being able to restrain myself from screaming, *"We are going to crash,"* at the last moment.

As the crew cut the engines I reminded myself grimly
I was one step closer to Elvis. I could do this. All I had
to do was keep my head in the game.

The SEALs hopped out of the helicopter. Hands
reached out to help me. I half jumped, half fell into his
arms. He pulled me underneath the slowing rotors toward
a couple of men who were standing by an open door. I
staggered a bit on the rolling deck, not used to the sway
of the ship, and trying *not* to remember what happened
the last time I was on the water, which involved a sudden re-acquaintance with parts of my lunch that were
better left forgotten.

We followed one of the men. He held the door open
as I entered a conference room filled with odd items like

large bells, wooden plaques of unit patches, and a large model of an older carrier behind the seat at the end of the table. A map was spread out across the table. The three men already sitting there leaped to attention when we entered.

"At ease," the man behind me said.

I pulled off my helmet and turned around. The man had short, graying hair and twinkling brown eyes. He held out a hand.

"Pleasure to meet you, ma'am. I'm Admiral Grimble and this is Captain Quick." The captain stepped out from behind the admiral. I shook both of their hands.

The admiral motioned me to a seat and took the one next to me. The captain took the seat on my other side and the rest of the SEALs crowded in and leaned against the wall.

My stomach lurched with a rolling motion that seemed to have gone undetected by everyone else in the room. I eyed the gray Navy trashcan in the corner. I might be getting up close and personal with it soon.

"Welcome aboard, men and ma'am," the admiral said. "The captain and I have been briefed on the mission and the support we have been asked to provide. While we are refueling your chopper for the next leg, I have heard the latest intelligence. It isn't much, but we do have a Predator drone on station providing video. From the initial Predator video, there appears to be no activity at the site or along your planned route of travel. That being said, intelligence analysts still recommend you avoid the roads as much as possible. We'll have air rescue units available for extraction, if necessary, and are repositioning another Predator. That way we can have one unit providing real-time awareness and limited air support, and the other to monitor other avenues of approach. Captain Quick was just in contact with the Kenyan military and they confirmed two fully fueled Land Rovers are in position and awaiting your arrival. Who's the team leader?"

Hands stepped forward. "Here, sir."

Pointing at a sailor just outside the door, the admiral said "Chief Petty Officer Watson will take you to where you can take a load off your feet and check your equipment. If you need anything, just ask him and he has my orders to provide you with anything you want."

"Yes, sir."

I wished Chief Petty Officer Watson would ask *me* what I wanted. Because right now what I wanted was to be at home snuggled on my couch with my comfy bathrobe and slippers on and all of my friends and family safe and sound. Although if I were really keeping it real, I also wanted to be about two steps closer to that wastebasket.

The admiral smiled at me. "Good luck, Ms. Carmichael. I understand a lot is riding on your shoulders."

I swallowed hard. "Sure. No pressure."

He chuckled and patted me on the shoulder. "Well I can assure you that if you had to risk your life with anyone, this group of professional scoundrels is just who I'd pick. The reports I've heard of you are most impressive. It seems you fit right in with the team. I'm confident we are in good hands."

"Thank you, sir. I appreciate the vote of confidence."

After the SEALs and the Admiral left, I swung around the table to sit next to my new best friend, Mr. Wastebasket. I stared at the map, wondering what Elvis was doing…if he were still alive. Did he know I was coming? If the situation were reversed, I wouldn't have wanted him to come for me. He would have anyway. Still, I worried that despite all the hoops I had jumped through, I wouldn't be able to save him.

After a few minutes, I had time to go the bathroom, where I kept a close eye on Mr. Wastebasket's identical twin. But as I am a woman of only one formal relationship at a time, I left him unrequited. I couldn't believe it, but I was actually looking forward to getting on the helicopter and off the ship.

Before I knew it, we loaded back into the helicopter and headed straight into my worst nightmare. My stomach churned as we lifted off, but I think I was getting a little bit used to it. Either that or my stomach was planning to defect to someone else and was too busy typing me an email of resignation to notice we were flying again. It helped to imagine I was sitting in front of my computer eating cornflakes and playing an online fantasy game. But then I remembered Elvis and Xavier wouldn't be there to play with me and suddenly it didn't seem so attractive as an alternative.

I opened my eyes and Hands flashed me a thumbs-up. I couldn't see how he was so cheerful going into a situation where the odds of him coming out alive were significantly less than even. It occurred to me at that instant that despite the danger, he loved his job, the danger, the feeling of a mission and all of that. No, he *thrived* on it. I thought it similar to the feeling I got when I started a hack. He probably got the same rush. To each their own, I guess.

It took us about thirty minutes from the ship until someone in their best ancient mariner accent called, "Land Ho," over the radio. Despite the very cramped quarters, one by one, each of the SEALs carefully pulled out their gear, inspected everything very carefully, and then returned it to its place. The process was the same for each of them and not a word was spoken. They were very deliberate and thorough—leaving nothing to chance. I wondered if I should pull out my laptop, cell phone, flashlight and ballpoint pen so that they knew I was ready, too.

Once we crossed the coast, we angled to the south, heading inland toward the rendezvous point. The ground underneath us contained a few scattered trees, patches of open rocks, thickets of a yellow-greenish bush and a lot of low scrub. It reminded me of Texas without the cacti and a lot more brush. The pilot circled the spot where the vehicles awaited and then landed us in the middle of a low scrub clearing.

The guys were moving even before the helicopter touched down, flowing effortlessly from the aircraft. I was the last one out. This time Hulk helped me down. As we gathered our stuff and Hands headed off to talk with our contacts, I watched the helicopter lift off amidst a cloud of sand and dust.

How had I so rapidly evolved from a girl who liked crossword puzzles and gaming to one dressed in battle armor and accompanied Navy SEALs on a mission in Kenya? Jeez, I hadn't even had to show anyone my passport.

Sighing, I followed Hulk and the other guys to the Land Rovers that were parked about fifty yards from where we had touched down. A couple of Kenyans were already there and handed Hands and a guy from Bravo the keys. As Hulk waved at me to hustle, members of each team were giving the vehicles a thorough once over. They were inspecting the vehicles with the same interest and intensity as they did with their gear in air. Clearly, when the mission and their lives rested on it, the SEALs left nothing to chance.

As I reached them, Hands pointed to the black Land Rover. "Back seat, passenger's side."

"What about my pack?" I noticed none of the SEALs had put their gear in the spacious rear cargo area.

"Hold it in front of you."

I did as he requested and the other guys finished the vehicle inspection. Wills drove with Hands in the front seat while Hulk and I squeezed in the back. It was uncomfortable, especially as Hands had run the seat all the way back to give him room to hold and operate his weapon. Hulk was so squished his knees went up to his chest and his head pressed against the ceiling. Forty miles like this would seem like an eternity.

Will had smashed his pack and gear on his lap. How he was going to drive like that was beyond me.

Hands turned around in the front seat, eyeing me seriously. "So, you ready, Keys? Mission on."

THIRTY-EIGHT

I RAISED MY CHIN, my resolve firm. "I'm ready."

Hands raised an eyebrow. "You know, I'm impressed. You've got a lot of guts for a civilian. But now that the mission is officially underway, you're going to have to go in under our terms."

"I already told you I'll do my very best to follow directions this time."

"Not *those* terms."

"I don't understand. What terms?"

"The terms that state you're no longer just the asset." He gave me a salute. "We're making you an honorary SEAL."

Confused, I leaned forward, resting my hand on the back of Wills's headrest. "Wait—what? I'm a SEAL?"

"Yep. It was Hulk's idea, but everyone seconded it. You're an official part of the team now. A full member."

He tossed me a gold pin of an eagle clutching a pistol, anchor and trident. "Pin it on, Keys. Congratulations."

I was so touched that it took me several seconds to collect myself in order to respond.

"Really? You want me even though I didn't want to jump out of a plane, I'm a major klutz and I don't like spiders? Are you sure those are acceptable characteristics for an honorary SEAL?"

Hands nodded. "Of course, because you're also willing to face your greatest fears and take a sniper's shot for the team."

A lump formed in my throat. "Well, in that case, thank you so much, guys. I'm honored. I don't know what to say, other than I will try and hold the screaming down to a minimum as I now have the SEAL reputation to protect."

They all laughed. As I pinned the eagle to the collar of my jacket, it occurred to me that these men were willing to die in order to help me complete the mission, and this time, I might not be able to keep that from happening.

"How long will it take us to get to the shack?" Hands asked Wills.

"About an hour assuming no interference or detours," replied Wills. "We're going to loop in, avoiding the roads, and enter from the south, as far off-road as we can. I'm guessing the hostiles have instructions not to be overly active until Lexi is safely in the house. But we have to assume if they can limit it so only Lexi gets in, they will. It means they'll take a shot at anyone who tries to accompany her, meaning yours truly. This will be a tightly controlled operation on many levels, mostly because it could quickly become messy if too many locals get word they've got Americans on the ground nearby. Broodryk likely paid a lot of money to keep the group small and tight."

"Ha. The more the merrier I always say," Hulk grumbled.

Hands adjusted his pack. "Just get in and keep to the script, Lexi. Make contact. Distract Broodryk. Plug in and pass the location info to the team. The virus is our number one priority here. If possible, grab Elvis and get the hell out. We've got to remember the ultimate mission will be delivering Broodryk a special welcome-to-the-neighborhood gift."

I thought of the SEAL team headed toward the compound in Gabon. I worked through a mental checklist of all the things that had to happen for Slash's and my alternate plan to work. We all had our missions. Right now, *my* mission was at the shack. I had to stop the virus and save Elvis. Elvis took priority in my heart, but millions of lives were at stake with the virus. If it came down to a push of a button, I wasn't sure what I'd do.

That scared me. What if Broodryk won after all? What would that mean?

Logic said it would mean life was a risk however we lived it, and in the end I supposed the greatness of a person wasn't defined by what they had, but by what they were willing to risk for others. Besides, no matter what happened, even if I went down, Broodryk wouldn't leave me defeated.

As planned, we drove off-road to the shack. After about five minutes en route, I made a mental note to find and beat to death with a heavy keyboard the intelligence analyst who called this area gently rolling. While Land Rovers were built for this type of off-roading with heavy-duty shock absorbers, the combination of a heavy load, the relentless speed Wills was maintaining, and the uneven ground was punishing. I kept my teeth tightly clenched to protect my tongue from getting bitten.

If Hands and Hulk were bothered by the terrain, you couldn't tell by looking at them. They were on high alert, their heads were swiveling non-stop, looking for hostiles. The windows were rolled down to allow freedom of fire and prevent flying glass if we became targets. As much as I longed for a smoother ride, this was the way to go. The roads were likely peppered with IEDs or heavily patrolled by *al-Shabaab* militants, the same group responsible for the vicious attack on a shopping mall in Nairobi.

I wasn't anxious to encounter them anytime soon and I suspected the guys weren't either. But it was highly likely that at least a few guys from this group were poised to engage us at some point at the shack. I couldn't see how Broodryk could have pulled it off otherwise.

Somalia had a rugged sort of beauty, but it was hard to appreciate the scenery while jammed into my seat with my pack on my lap and my head flopping around with every jolt. Body armor plates I couldn't reach to adjust were attempting to relocate my spleen. I found it impossible to do anything else but stare at the back of Hands's head, so I mentally rehearsed the lessons from our last mission.

A.) Avoid embarrassing face plants; B.) No hysterical screaming; and C.) Under no circumstances should I take my helmet off. That last one almost got me left behind and I had no intention of spending the rest of my life in Somalia.

Finally Wills announced over our helmet comm link that we were approximately ten minutes out from the shack. I had no idea how he could possibly know where he was going or how Bravo team even managed to keep up. Still, given that notification, Hands and Hulk somehow completed yet another equipment check while barely taking their eyes off our surroundings.

We abruptly hit a moment of surprising calm as the ground smoothed out. Apparently it was the eye before the storm, maybe my last one ever. I scanned the three guys, looking for any sign of anxiety or concern. Here we were at the last minutes before a fight we might not walk away from, yet they seemed completely at ease.

I struggled to understand it. Their peace couldn't just be due to experience. It was something more.

Hulk looked over at me and gave me that infectious smile of his. "We've got this, kid. It's going to turn out good."

Suddenly I understood. It was faith. Not necessarily the religious type, although they may have that as well. I had never asked. But this was faith in themselves, in each other as a team, the mission, everything. They knew that each of them would do the best they could do and together that would be enough, no matter who or what they faced. It wasn't rational, but they shared it, and now I was a part of it and I felt calmer, too.

Our planning would pay off, the bad guys would fail and we'd come out alive. I refused to let myself calculate the odds. For the first time in my life, I didn't want to know.

Hands asked over his shoulder, "You're awfully quiet. Everything okay, Keys?"

"It is now."

I thought of Slash, and somehow that calmed me further. *Be smart, be careful, but more than anything,* don't let anyone manipulate you.

Don't let anyone manipulate you. Easier said than done. Being able to outwit Broodryk in the middle of Somalia on his terms wasn't looking like such an attractive option. But we are who we are and we can only do the best with what we've got.

Hands spoke softly to someone on a separate radio—possibly to Bravo or maybe Mother. He wasn't speaking through his unit comm.

"One mile," Wills called. "Last weapons check."

Everyone gave their weapons a final check even though I had no doubt they were in perfect working order. I swallowed hard, my heart starting to beat faster. I braced my hands on the hand rest and the back of Hands's seat where I sat waiting for the next bump. The telephone poles in the distance pointed the way to our destination.

Surprisingly, Hands turned around and handed me an automatic handgun. "I heard you can use this and may find it useful. We have no idea what you may find in that house and if Wills is incapacitated, I want you to be able to take care of yourself."

Without a word of protest, I took the gun. That's how I rolled these days. I didn't have a holster, so I made sure the safety was on and jammed it into my backpack.

"Target in sight. Alpha Star, get down." Hands's voice came through my helmet. I instantly dropped to the seat, my head nearly in Hulk's lap.

"We have a visual on the house," Hands broadcast on the radio to Mother. "Are the overhead assets on station?"

"Affirmative. You are a go and we have detected no additional activity at the target. The winds are kicking up out of the southwest, so drop your grenades early and expect it to dissipate much quicker than usual."

"Roger that." Over the helmet comm Hands asked, "Wills did you get that smoke report?"

"Sure did. Alpha Star and I will make it quick."

"You'd better. If you don't you may find yourself with more holes than a Congressman's alibi."

I rolled my eyes and Wills snorted as Hands ordered, "Bravo, report."

"Ready and at your six o'clock."

"Good. We release two smoke grenades from each vehicle as we round the south end of Jar Hill. Toss the grenades out the left side and as far as you can. Delay the release of the right-hand grenades for a count of three and then throw them over the car. The wind should carry everything up hill and give a few extra moments. Bravo, then continue to your positions. Release another set of smoke grenades as soon as you take your positions. Alpha Star, you stay put in the vehicle until I say so."

"Okay," I answered.

Wills abruptly yanked on the wheel, spinning the vehicle as we came around the end of the hill. I thought for a breathtaking moment he had miscalculated the speed and we would topple over. But he righted it at the last moment just as Hulk and Hands tossed the smoke grenades out the window. Then he slammed on the brakes and we skidded to a whiplash halt. There was so much noise and action, I had no idea if we were under attack or not.

"Out! Out! Out!"

I couldn't tell if the voice was coming from my helmet or not. "Alpha Star, be prepared to move once we have secured the area. Alpha Two, check the shack entrance. Let's get a move on, team."

I clenched my fists in a death grip. What were the three things I was supposed to remember? No screaming, keep my helmet on no matter what and…what the heck was the last one?

"Alpha Star, exit the vehicle now." Hands's voice came through commanding and calm. "The site is secure, but the smoke isn't lasting as long as we expected. You need to get inside quickly."

I threw open the car door. There was an awkward moment when I struggled with my pack, which had become wedged between the front seat and me. I yanked it free and leaped out of the Land Rover.

Unfortunately, I forgot how much higher a Land Rover is than a normal vehicle and I hooked my foot on the sill. As my momentum carried me to the ground, I executed a perfect face plant in the dirt.

THIRTY-NINE

I HEARD SOMEONE swearing via my helmet comm. It seemed like I lay there with sand in my face for an endless minute, trying to process what had just happened.

Wills's voice sounded in my helmet, "Alpha Star, get a move on. Now."

I rolled onto my side to get my knees under me and grabbed my pack, slinging it on my back. I glanced over my shoulder at the telephone pole standing near the shack, with its power transformer hanging just under the crosspiece. I was struck by how normal it looked. It could have been one of any thousand such poles in Maryland, and yet here it was in rural Somalia.

"Alpha Star, the smoke is starting to thin." Wills's voice was pleasant, but urgent.

I scrambled toward the door where Wills was waiting. I glanced around. The vehicle was sitting there with all four doors open. I could see Hulk's feet, but the rest of him was hunkered down. I couldn't see Hands so he was probably beyond the SUV. Beyond the vehicle and through the smoke I could just make out the dark bulk of Jar Hill rising about fifteen to twenty feet above our position. At the left end of it, large clumps of the thorny thicket provided cover to anyone hiding there. It was absolutely silent except for my harsh breathing. Looking up, I saw a camera mounted on the roof, facing to the southwest. Broodryk wanted an outside view, too.

"We've got a camera on the roof," I said. "Pointed southwest."

"Roger that." Hands's voice came through my helmet, sure and steady. "Just like we planned, Alpha Star. You've got this."

I didn't trust myself to answer, so I nodded at Wills. I stood directly behind him to protect his back and hide what we were doing in case anyone was watching through the smoke. He bent down on one knee to the side of the door, then pulled something out of his pocket about the size of a cell phone, opened the door a crack and stuck his hand inside. As the door opened, an alarm inside began to sound insistently. It took about three seconds before he withdrew his hand and gave the device to me. He left the door ajar.

According to the plan, he'd snapped a few photographs in a panorama of the room. I glanced quickly through the pictures getting familiar with the layout. The room was pretty dark, without windows and lit by a single bare overhead bulb. A large television screen hung on the wall opposite the door. Beneath it, a small table held a laptop with cords running to the screen. There was a door to the right that probably led to another room based upon the dimensions of the shack. The rest of the room was empty except for a camera mounted high on the back left wall and positioned so that it covered the entrance door, the laptop, the television screen and the mystery door to the right. Assuming there wasn't another camera above our heads over the entrance door, it was good news because it meant Broodryk would only have one fixed view.

Elvis wasn't in sight, but behind the door to the right was probably where we would find him. On the phone screen it looked like there was some device on the door handle, but I had only a dim, partial view. I handed Wills the camera and nodded again.

I glanced over my shoulder and could see parts of the hill emerging from the smoke.

"Now," I said, tapping Wills on the shoulder. "Remember, whatever we say inside will probably be monitored, so be discreet."

He nodded and withdrew something from his pants pocket, opened the door a bit wider, then tossed in another smoke grenade. I heard a thump and a hiss. The alarm was still sounding inside.

"Time to party," Wills said.

He rose from his knee and entered the room in a half crouch. I couldn't see a thing, but I followed him in until I felt the wall. The door banged shut behind me. I felt along the wall to the left until I was under where I estimated the camera hung. I knelt down, shrugging out of my pack and unzipping it.

"Well, how nice that you've finally arrived," Broodryk voice said from the smoke, startling me until I realized it came from the television screen I couldn't see. The alarm cut off and it was eerily quiet.

"Well, well. What's this? A smoke grenade? Really? How crude. I assure you there are no hostiles in the house. However, now that you are here I would suggest you don't try to leave. I have an expert marksman, whom I believe you know, covering the door with instructions to shoot anyone who attempts to leave."

Pentz. Oh my God. He had come and now he was out there hunting SEALs. The sound of gunfire from outside made me jump. Broodryk's game of life and death was officially underway. I felt sick to my stomach knowing that Hands, Hulk and the others were out there exposed so we could complete our mission inside.

Have faith, Lexi. Everyone is doing their job. Just do yours and it will be all right.

"Crude or not, I don't trust you, Broodryk," I said. "Tell your guard dogs outside to stand down. This is between you and me."

He laughed. "True, but I did promise them some fun. Ah, it's so nice to hear your voice again. I've missed you, you know. But I'm afraid you aren't in charge here, my dear."

With the thick smoke swirling around me, I spread my arms and walked around trying to locate Wills to give me a boost to reach the camera. In the meantime, I had to keep Broodryk busy.

"Where's Elvis?"

"He's fine and in the other room," Broodryk answered. "But first, I want to see you. Open the front door and clear out the smoke or I'll kill him right now."

I really needed to find Wills. Just then someone or something grabbed the top of my right shoulder. The combination of the dark, the smoke, and jittery nerves made me scream.

"It's just me." I heard Wills's comforting voice in my helmet.

My scream amused Broodryk. "Screaming already, are we? I am most disappointed. I assumed that you had a little more fortitude than that."

I pressed my lips together and tugged Wills in position beneath the camera. First it was the face plant and now the scream. I wasn't an honorary SEAL. I was a freaking basket case.

"You wanted me here, so I'm here. Let's get down to business, Broodryk. Why did you bring me all the way to Africa? Afraid to meet me on my own soil?" I spoke loudly to try and hide my position and buy myself a few more moments.

"Why not? It's my show. Why should I suffer from jet lag?"

I knelt, groped for my pack until I found it. Unzipping it, I pulled out my laptop. I opened it, took the side cord already attached to my computer in one hand and then stood. Holding the cord in my teeth, I fashioned Wills's hands into a step and then stuck my foot there. He caught on and helped boost me up. I used my hands to feel for the line leading from the laptop to the camera.

I took the cord from my mouth and tried to stabilize myself against the wall. "Just so we're clear, not everything is on your terms. Still, I'll play. Might as well, seeing as how I'm already here. But I'm not your puppet. I'm not going to do what you want for the sake of your show. My participation will be on my terms."

My voice sounded confident, but my hands were trembling as I unscrewed the jack on the back of the camera. I nearly wept when it came loose and I was able to slip my intercept device in between the connections and secure the connection again. I wiggled my foot and Wills helped me down. I knelt down next to my laptop and felt around for the return button. When my fingers found it, I pushed it activating the pre-loaded application.

Now the next time he accessed that camera *our* game began.

"I'm warning you, Lexi. Clear the room or suffer the consequences."

I pushed my laptop back against the wall under the camera where it wouldn't be visible from either of the cameras on the wall or the laptop.

"Fine. But I need some reassurance first. I need to know Elvis is alive."

Outside the shooting intensified slightly. I could hear Hands on the unit comms shouting for Alpha Team to reposition and talking to Mother on the radio about assisting with identifying the location of the hostiles shooting at them.

"You are operating on limited time," Broodryk said. I could hear the growing anger in his voice. He didn't like my little stunt with the smoke grenades. The audience wouldn't tune in if they couldn't see. "Every minute you waste is one minute you don't have to try and save your friend. Tick tock. From this moment forward, you have thirty minutes. The countdown has started."

Thirty minutes to live.

"We have a confirmation on the Snake," Hands's voice came through my helmet. "Repeat, the Snake is in the grass. I recognize the crack of his gun. Alpha Three is down. Status unknown."

I covered my mouth in horror. Hulk was down. Pentz had shot him.

"Bravo Team, hold your position," Hands said. How he managed to keep his voice steady was beyond me. "The Predator feed shows we have no newcomers to the party yet. It looks like most of the hostiles are facing Bravo. Beware of them trying to flank your position. Mother also reports that we have weather moving in that may impact their ability to provide video. We need to take care of Snake or no one will be able to leave the shack. I'm going to coordinate with Mother while we still have options to see if we can make him move so I can go after him. It won't be easy for him to reposition in that brush with his large rifle."

My helmet radio fell silent. I steeled myself. Time to focus on the here and now.

"Where is Elvis, Broodryk? I need that or I don't play."

He sighed. "He's in the side room. Since you can't see, you'll have to feel your way there. Do not try and open the door. It is wired. Simply knock on it and yell to him. He's drugged but he might respond to your voice."

He didn't have to tell me twice. I stumbled across the room to the door and banged on it.

"Elvis," I shouted. "Elvis, are you in there?"

There was silence and then, "Lexi?" The voice was faint but unmistakably Elvis's.

I nearly burst into tears as I pressed a hand against the door. "Hang on, Elvis. I'm right out here. Okay?" I could hear some noise on the other side.

"How do I know it's not just a recording or something?" I said to Broodryk. "That you aren't tricking me."

"Go ahead and ask him a question and see what he says. But you are wasting valuable time. It's him, I assure you."

I turned to the door again. "Elvis. It's me, Lexi. Look, I need to make sure that it's really you. Can you hear me?"

His voice was weak, but I heard him. "Yes. I hear you."

"What's your mother's first name?"

There was silence and then he said, "Ottilie."

"It's him. Open the front door, but don't get in the line of fire," I ordered Wills.

I heard Wills's footsteps cross the room. The door swung and the smoke began to drift out. With the additional light from the door I was able to take a closer look at the device on the handle. It looked like an oversized cell phone with a numeric pad on the front. Wires ran from the back of it through the crack in the door and snaked inside the room. The device was firmly secured to the handle and couldn't be easily removed. I carefully examined the back as best I could. I'd never seen anything like it.

"Ah, that's better."

I could see the TV and laptop now. Broodryk was on the television screen watching me. He was masked again, probably to keep his identity as secret as possible from whomever else might be watching the show. But his eyes… I knew his eyes. Ice Eyes, I'd called him, and it fit. Pale blue and devoid of any feeling or remorse.

He chuckled. "So what do you think of my little setup?"

I straightened and crossed my arms against my chest. "You really don't want to know what I think."

He studied me for a moment. "Why, look at you. You're dressed for the part—playing soldier. How delightful. You amuse me."

"The feeling isn't mutual."

"Actually, I didn't think you'd make it this far. Even with the help of the entire US government behind you. You've got spirit, my dear."

"I'm not your dear. But yes, I'm resourceful."

"Indeed, you are. But that's not all you are. You're my destiny. We were fated to meet at that high school. I see that now. It was all leading to this glorious moment in time."

Wills shot me a glance across the room. I didn't have to be a psychologist to understand the meaning behind it. Broodryk was completely certifiable. It chilled me to the bone, but I had to act unaffected. I remembered Gray's words about being a worthy opponent. That was important to him. Do not show fear.

"Whatever. I'm here now. What do you want?"

"Well, in the next twenty-six minutes, one of two things is going to happen. Either you will save your friend

or you will save your country. It's your choice. I love giving my adversaries options."

"What?" I frowned. "What do you mean I have to save
my friend or my country?" I had to repeat Broodryk's
words for the benefit of the team listening in, but it also
gave me extra time to process.

"It means you have a choice to make. You can spend
time working on the device on that door to break the
code in time to save your friend. It's not difficult and
shouldn't take you too long. All you have to do is to come
up with the right four digit number sequence. Once you
plug in the code, it neutralizes the wires running to him
and he is saved. However, if you take longer than your
allotted minutes or try to force open the door, he will be
electrocuted."

"Electrocuted?"

"Yes."

I opened my mouth to reply when the lights in the
house suddenly flickered off and the television screen
went dark.

I stood frozen to the spot. "Broodryk?" I whispered.

FORTY

BEFORE I COULD figure out what had happened, the lights turned back on. Broodryk's face on the television screen wavered back to life.

I looked around the room. Wills had his gun out, pointed at the door. I shook my head and he lowered the gun, leaning back against the wall.

"What happened?" I asked Broodryk.

He studied something to the right of him, probably his monitoring equipment. "A storm is coming. A bad one. There was a surge. I'd suggest you hurry. A similar surge might just kill your friend earlier than planned. Oops."

My hands shook, so I clasped them behind my back. "You said something about a choice. What's the other one—the country choice? I presume we're talking about Pruxrat."

"Ah, so you know about my baby. Resourceful, indeed. Yes, you are correct. See the laptop underneath the television? There's another challenge there. Crack that program and you'll have access to the source code for Pruxrat. You can then take the program and delete it, copy it, or do whatever the hell you want with it. Once you have it, it's useless to me because you'll be able to figure a way to counter it. That means I'll have to start from scratch and create a new virus. As you know, that takes time. Therefore, your country will be safe…at least for the time being. So which will you choose, Lexi? Friendship or country?"

My brain raced. There had to be another option.

"What if I do nothing? What if I don't choose between friendship or country?"

He laughed. "Then the virus is released and your friend dies, along with all of your soldier friends outside."

"And me?"

"Well, I still have hope for you, my dear. However, I will have to think about the worth of your life based on your choices and performance today. Right now, I am not impressed."

Determined, I headed for Broodryk's computer. I quickly pulled up the program and the code that protected it. I recognized it. It was a relatively simple code challenge given to second-year students to introduce them to critical security concepts, but it was complex enough that it would take me a full twenty minutes or more to solve—unless he had left any additional traps, and I couldn't rule that out. He could easily have set this up so I failed on both fronts.

I returned to the door with the device on the handle and studied it. Broodryk had made this challenge easier. Much easier. But I still didn't have time to do both.

In the background I could hear Hands requesting that Mother target the Predator's Hellfire missile to the upwind side of Jar Hill. There was something about a fire to smoke him out but I lost the rest to static.

So what choice could I make? Would I make?

The unit comms were silent. Even the firing had stopped for some inexplicable reason. It was as if the entire world was waiting for me to say something, do something. When neither option was acceptable, what was the right answer?

Think, Lexi. Think.

Thoughts flashed through my brain so fast it made me dizzy. Some part of my brain knew something, but where was it? I could see Broodryk sitting there on the television watching intently, smirking. He knew I had only unacceptable choices.

Suddenly the phrase "unacceptable choices" jogged a memory of a class I'd had at Georgetown called Red Teaming and Deception Analysis. What had the professor asked us?

When surrounded by only unacceptable choices, what should you do?

I'd raised my hand and answered logically that a decision should be made as a result of the calculations of the consequences, thereby making the best decision based on the least amount of adverse reaction.

My professor had slammed his hand down on the desk, startling all of us, as he was normally a pretty unassuming guy.

"Wrong! When all the choices are unacceptable, you must create a new choice. There is always another choice somewhere. That's the correct answer."

Of course. That *was* the correct answer. I had to create another option. But what?

I stared at the wires running from the device on the door and disappearing into Elvis's room. If I didn't think of something fast, he would be electrocuted mere steps away from me.

Electrocuted!

Just like that, I had it. The third option.

Hands's voice sounded in my helmet. "This is Alpha One. I need that fire started now. We're running out of time and can't get a visual on the Snake. He is too well hidden. I need to force him to move so I have a chance.

Have the second Predator ready if the first one doesn't start the fire."

"Affirmative. Stand by Alpha One. Your firing pass is in progress."

I glanced up at the television and saw Broodryk watching me, an amused look on his face. He had no idea what was going on in my head. He was simply enjoying my pain, indecision and stress, reaping the rewards of his meticulous planning. Hulk had been shot, probably dead, Elvis was possibly minutes from electrocution, and Hands was going to have to expose himself to hunt a well-hidden sniper. A strange powerful force surged through me. I didn't like it, but I was sure going to use it.

Hate.

I'd never imagined hating anyone as much as I hated Broodryk at this exact moment. This was new emotional territory for me. While popular literature says that hate is the first step down the road to the dark side, I needed it now to get through this. It helped steady my nerves and gave me a newfound determination. I'd have to worry about the consequences later, if I lived that long.

I stalked across the room to Wills. "Do you have a piece of paper and a pen? I need to make calculations."

He looked startled, but gamely fumbled around in his pockets. A bit sheepishly, he handed me a candy bar wrapper and a pen. It would have to do.

I walked back to Broodryk's laptop on the table. I turned slightly so that my body shielded my writing from the wall camera and the angle from the laptop was bad. While the laptop camera and keylogger would monitor every keystroke, it didn't matter to my plan now.

"Ah, so she is going for country over friendship," Broodryk said. "Interesting. Didn't expect that of you, but I understand. You do owe them for bringing you here. Hooray for the red, white and blue."

"Shut up," I said curtly. "You're interfering with my concentration."

I scribbled a message to Wills. *Take out electrical transponder on telephone pole. Shoot for the ceramic insulator on the top. Break that and it will short the transformer. Be quick and use the distraction of the approaching firebomb. It should keep Pentz busy long enough for you to get off a shot.*

I pretended to shake the pen. "Damn, it's not working." I walked back over to Wills. Keeping my back to the television monitor, I pressed the wrapper in his hand. He read it and our eyes met. He nodded slightly.

"Do you have another pen?" I asked him.

He shook his head and I gave a loud sigh. "Never mind. I'll just do the calculations in my head."

I returned to the computer and started working. I knew Broodryk would not keep his word even if I broke the code, but I had to make it look like I was making a good faith effort. Time was of the essence. I had to give Echo Team time to respond to the house in Gabon.

The electricity surged again, wiping out my last set of calculations. I stood, glared at Broodryk. "Hey, what happened? I just had my work cleared."

He laughed. "It's the cost of working in a hellhole. The storm is closer. You may have mere minutes left."

"It's not a fair game if you cut my time," I warned.

"Since when has life been fair? Hasn't anyone told you that yet? Nonetheless, you'll have your full thirty minutes. I am a man of my word, after all."

I sat down and had just started to redo the calculations when I heard a voice in my helmet. "Missile away. Alpha One, impact in five seconds."

"Standing by," Hands said. His words were followed almost immediately with a ground-shaking *boom*.

I looked over at Wills and then he was out the door. I was alone with the monster.

"What was that?" I asked Broodryk.

He was looking at something off screen, most likely the outside monitor. He swiveled his head back to me. "Apparently the US government is trying to make a show of force. It's a mistake. It will do nothing but draw unfriendly persons to you. I have made arrangements to keep this gathering small, but I cannot stop others from crashing the party if you insist on attracting attention. Unfortunately, it's out of my hands at this point. So, where did your protector go? I see we're all alone now."

"I don't know where he went. He doesn't ask my permission to do his job."

"I like it this way. Just you and me."

A voice spoke in my ear and I stiffened. "This is Alpha Two. I'm out of the shack and in cover. Alpha Star has requested I take out the electrical transformer. I'll need to be exposed momentarily to do it."

"Negative." Hands sounded emphatic. "Do not attempt at this time. I still do not have a visual on the Snake. The smoke from the fire is progressing up the hill, but it may not have affected his position yet."

"Alpha Star needs that electricity off now. I believe I can get a shot off before the Snake could hit me. I don't think he knows where I am. Besides, if he shoots me, he reveals his position to you. It's a win-win situation. Request permission to proceed, sir."

I froze. Wills would take a bullet *on purpose* to knock the transponder out and get Pentz to reveal himself?

Oh, God. Had I just sent a man to his death?

There was radio silence and I stared blindly at the code

on the laptop. At this rate, I wouldn't get one fourth of the code unraveled, but I had to make a show of trying.

Tick tock.

Time stood still for no one. I wanted to know if Elvis was okay in the next room. I wanted to make sure Wills would be safe. I wanted an update on the SEAL team in Gabon. I wanted to go home.

Keep the faith, Lexi. Keep the faith.

The radio cackled. "Alpha Two, proceed."

I closed my eyes. Move and countermove. Kill or be killed. My hands clenched into fists.

Please be safe, Wills. Please.

"Alpha Two is in position. Stand by."

I stood, then planted myself in front of the television. I needed to keep Broodryk focused on me so he couldn't monitor what was happening outside. I'd have a better chance of things working if he thought the electricity went down as a result of the storm rather than a deliberate act by the man I'd just sent out of the shack.

"Look, Broodryk, I can't work under these conditions." I tried to sound demanding, bossy. Like I wanted his attention and I wanted it now. "If you wanted a true test of my ability, you should have chosen a place with consistent electricity."

His icy eyes met mine and I had to suppress a shudder. "I keep getting these surges that are messing up my work and—"

Kaboom. The television screen and the lights blanked out at the same time.

Score one for Wills.

I made my move.

FORTY-ONE

I RAN TO my backpack to retrieve my gun and then to Elvis's door.

My helmet radio exploded with noise. "Alpha Two hit the target. Alpha Star, can you hear me?"

"Alpha One, I hear you. The electricity is out. How's Alpha Two?"

"Alpha Two's status is unknown, but I have a bead on Snake's position. I'm moving."

I staggered sideways. "Unknown? Was Alpha Two hit?"

"Alpha Star. Please proceed with mission."

I wanted to know, but I had to hold it together. If I fell apart, Wills's efforts would be in vain.

"Understood. I'm going to rescue the hostage. Stand by."

There was more noise and the crack of small firearms outside. The battle had begun again in earnest.

I drew my gun and aimed it at the device. It was no longer lit up. I double-checked, but I could see no battery connection. Still, I could be wrong. I could blow us all sky-high. But we were out of time for any more options, even if I were able to think them up. I tried to focus my aim. My arm shook so badly I had to support my elbow with my other hand. Tears blurred my eyes. I was about to save Elvis or kill him. It was hard to tell.

I offset myself so I wouldn't catch a ricochet, turned my head and squeezed the trigger.

Crack.

The device was split open but still hanging on the door. I hit it with the only thing I could think of, the butt of the gun. It fell to the floor with a thump. I paused a beat, then slammed the door open with my shoulder.

The room was dark and the dim light from the main room revealed little of what was beyond. I snatched the flashlight from my belt and turned it on. A man sat in a chair, his back to the door. Wires ran from the door to the chair. A quick sweep of the room indicated no other furniture or items present. I walked slowly toward his front and lifted the flashlight to his face.

Elvis!

I dropped to my knees in front of him sobbing. "Elvis. Oh, God, Elvis, are you okay?

"You...came? I told you not to." His head rested on his chest and his face was a mess of bruises and cuts. His words were slurred, but he was alive...for now. I had to get him out of there quick.

I took an inventory of the wires that bound him. I used a small knife to cut his bindings, but my helmet prevented me from reaching far enough behind him to cut the final one.

Great, there went the helmet rule. I quickly slipped it off and placed it on the floor at his feet, then put my gun in the helmet so I wouldn't lose it. I couldn't stop crying. Tears dripped off my cheeks and chin. When I finished, I grasped him under his arms and helped him stand.

He swayed and fell into my arms. I had to brace myself to hold him up, but for the moment, I wrapped my arms around him and savored the fact that he was here and we were alive. I could feel his body shake, his heart beating, and it made me cry harder.

"Lexi," he breathed against my neck.

"Yes, it's me, Elvis. We're going home."

"Broodryk…"

"Isn't going to win this time. Come on."

I heard a noise in the outer room. Wills? I suppressed the urge to scream out and leaned Elvis up against the chair.

"Wait here," I whispered.

I approached the door cautiously and saw a man framed in the light of the doorway aiming a gun at me. My appearance in the doorway must have surprised him. I'd never seen him before, but he was clearly a native. He was yelling something at me in a language I didn't understand, and I had no idea how he'd gotten in unless he'd come from the Alpha Team side. Now that Hulk and Wills were down and Hands was busy hunting Pentz, we were apparently vulnerable to approach from that side.

My heart pounded. I didn't know if this guy had any friends with him, but I held my hands up slowly, assessing the situation. I calculated one positive to my current situation. It was dark in the room behind me, which meant he couldn't see Elvis from his vantage point. I didn't think he knew Elvis was there.

However, I had two bigger problems. Both my helmet and gun were now out of my reach. That meant I had no protection and no way to reach the team. I also had no idea what to do next.

FORTY-TWO

"Don't shoot," I yelled. It wasn't for his benefit, but for Elvis's. I didn't know if he was alert enough to understand that we had a situation out here, but it was worth a shot. Actually, it was probably my only shot. I had run out of scenario-altering ideas.

The man motioned with his gun for me to enter the main room, so I kept my arms up and walked toward the laptop. Panic swept through me. Time was ticking. I had to start up that computer and make contact or Broodryk was going to send the virus and/or blow the shack.

Lucky for me, the man didn't shoot me on the spot. He probably knew who I was and wasn't sure if it were safe to kill me yet. The fact that I was female, wasn't armed and was apparently alone definitely worked in my favor, too.

I pointed to the television. "Broodryk," I said, hoping he'd understand that. "I have to get him back."

I made typing movements with my fingers and pointed towards my pack with my laptop. At first the man said something, but he didn't try to stop me or shoot me. Keeping his gun trained on me he picked up and checked out my pack and then handed me my laptop. I knelt, swapped out the cables with Broodryk's laptop and started typing. He came up behind me and pressed the gun to my neck. I swallowed hard. At least his back was to the room with Elvis.

I glanced up at him. "Broodryk," I repeated and

pointed again to the television screen. He grunted, which I took to signal approval.

Thank God, my computer was working. My fingers flew across the keyboard as I sought access to Broodryk. The gun against my neck loosened.

Twenty seconds passed. Thirty.

Broodryk could blow the shack whenever he wanted. Or maybe he was busy releasing the virus. I momentarily wondered about the search team in Gabon. It was all slipping out of my control. It was probably an illusion that I had any to begin with, but still it had been comforting. If this was going to work, we needed some sort of break.

Crack!

My captor lurched and fell sideways to the floor, his gun skittering out of his hands. Gasping, I scooted back and looked at the dark room. Elvis stood in the doorway with my gun. While I watched in surprise, he staggered across the room and shot the guy two more times.

I blinked and looked up at Elvis. "Are…are you okay?"

"I'm perfectly fine."

I looked down at the guy and then nodded. I don't know what had happened to me. I felt nothing. No sadness, no regret, no nothing. This was war, and it was changing me. I wasn't sure it was for the best. It had definitely changed Elvis. He'd been kidnapped and tortured. The man at my feet was the second person he'd shot in just the past two months. What did that do to a person, especially one who hadn't trained mentally or physically for such things?

I pushed the emotions away. "Thanks, Elvis." It seemed inadequate, but it was heartfelt.

Elvis positioned himself by the door, still holding the gun. "Where are we?"

"Somalia."

"Seriously?"

"Seriously."

"Sorry I asked. I realize we're in a dire situation. Do what you need to do. I've got your back."

"I know. Thanks. Just don't open that door. There's a sniper positioned on it. Okay?"

"Okay."

I ran back into the room and grabbed my helmet and smashed it on my head.

I quickly updated the team. "Alpha Star here. We're okay in here. Both of us. Repeat, the hostage is free and alive. Bravo Team, we had a local visitor who probably came in through Alpha's position. He's down now, but we might need support from that direction if you can provide it. Do not enter the shack. It could blow at any moment."

I switched to the radio link with Mother. "Update, please. Status of Drop Team?"

"ETA is approximately six minutes."

"What about the virus? Has it been released?"

"Not as far as we can see. Proceed as planned, Alpha Star."

"How much time has passed since the Hellfire impact?"

"Six minutes."

That meant the power blackout had happened about five minutes ago. It seemed like hours. I was surprised Broodryk hadn't released the virus yet. That could only mean he wasn't sure what had happened to the electricity and was trying to reestablish contact with me. If he weren't able to get me back soon, he'd release the virus and blow the shack.

I had to ask. "What's the status of Alpha Two?"

There was a pause and this time it was Hands who spoke. "Still unknown. I've got a fix on the Snake and am closing in. He's on the move, which puts us on equal footing. He's probably unhappy about that. Cobra 1 is approximately ten minutes out. Broodryk's thirty minutes runs out in seven minutes, so I would be out of the shack by then just in case."

I closed my eyes. Wills was down. Hulk was down. Elvis and I were trapped in the shack. Had any of this been worth it?

Almost as if he had been listening to my thoughts, Hands said, "Close it out Alpha Star. Have faith."

I glanced over at Elvis. He seemed steadier now, more alert. He held two guns—the dead guy's and mine. There was a determined expression on his face. Yes, it had been worth it if we had saved Elvis and could bring Broodryk down for good. Otherwise he'd be at it again, playing his sick games with me or someone else.

Elvis saw me staring and a smile touched his lips. "I'm okay." He nodded at the keyboard. "Go get him."

"Okay, I'm on it. Stay there and be quiet for the moment."

"Yes, ma'am."

I smiled as my fingers flew over the keyboard. I had to get Broodryk back, and fast.

I re-launched the backtracking program I had executed earlier. I hoped that the broadcast results of its scans were helping the searchers close the noose in time.

After a few halts and starts I suddenly had a view of him. It was a side view, probably from a laptop camera. He'd removed the mask and was working on another computer, typing furiously.

I steadied myself. "Hey, Broodryk."

He turned to face me and blinked a few times, staring into the monitor.

"Well, I admit I'm surprised. How did you do it?"

"You could probably figure it out if I gave you some time. Let's say, thirty minutes."

He smiled. "Clever. You plugged in a laptop of your own and ran a reverse location search on me. So, here we are. What next?"

"It's your game, Broodryk. You tell me."

"Did the electricity come back on?"

"No. I'm working off the battery."

"I do realize that you're now tracing my location. Don't worry. I'll be long gone before anyone gets here. From what I can see you haven't broken the code. Only four minutes left. What a pity. I expected you to at least have one success."

Elvis came over, peering at the screen over my shoulder. He put one hand on my shoulder and with the other he gave Broodryk the bird.

Broodryk laughed. "You think you won because you released him? You can't possibly think you can bring me down. A novice like you? You do realize that you are in a shack in the middle of Somalia with just a few pathetic soldiers between you and the most horrible death a woman could endure? I didn't even need to rig the shack with explosives. It would have been a waste of valuable powder. Once you arrived, you were never going anywhere else again."

"I'm not running scared." I looked him in the eye as I said it, because I meant it. "But you should be."

He leaned forward. "Now *you* listen to *me*. Your country is moments from having its most valuable infrastructure being orchestrated into beautiful chaos by me." He jabbed a finger in his chest. "Billions and billions of dollars are at stake and it's just one *fokken* keystroke away."

I had to keep him engaged. "You're brilliant, Broodryk, I'll give you that. But you are also pathetic, twisted, psychotic and blinded by conceit. You underestimated me, something you never should have done."

He frowned, his eyes cold and hard. "No, you underestimated me. You and your pitiful little plans. You think I don't know about your strike team only moments away from the location in Gabon that I so helpfully provided? You witless, stupid girl. It was all a set-up. Do you think I didn't know? I knew *exactly* what you would do, which is why I *gave* you those coordinates. Your completely incompetent and pathetic cyber teams are no match for me. Cyberspace is *my* domain."

His lips curved into a smile. "Let it be known to all who are watching that this is what happens to those who try to cross me. You will not win. You will be eviscerated. I have taken on the most powerful nation in the world and won. Watch and learn."

There it was, his staged speech for his clients or potential clients, almost word-for-word as Gray had predicted. No question, game end was nearing. But Broodryk wasn't quite finished with me yet.

"Just so you know, Lexi Carmichael, your precious SEAL team is moments from capturing and taking down my biggest commercial threat and former partner, Gregor Muller. For that, I sincerely thank you."

Grinning, he picked up a laptop and angled it toward me. "Shall we watch it together? Shall we all watch the fumbling actions of the United States? God, this turned out far better than I ever envisioned."

Although it was distorted, over the next several minutes I watched grainy security camera images of a SEAL team breaking down the door of a structure and disappearing inside while Broodryk gloated and commented on their lack of stealth. Elvis's hand tightened on my shoulder.

The radio in my helmet crackled. "Drop Team is in. One minute."

I held my breath.

"So, I guess this is game over, my dear. It was a magnificent performance, one that far exceeded my expectations. I shall think of you quite fondly."

"Don't worry, Broodryk. I won't think of you at all."

"No, you won't. You'll be dead." He set down the laptop. "But I'm not without compassion, you know. Seeing as how you helped me get this far, I'll let you watch as I release the virus. Actually, you should thank me, you know. You won't be around to deal with the messy fallout and it will keep your replacement hacks fully employed trying to deal with the consequences."

The gunfire outside intensified and I looked toward the door. So far the teams were holding position and the hostiles weren't pressing too hard, probably on the instructions of Broodryk. He couldn't have his grand finale interrupted.

"Well, this is it, my dear." He swept his finger up in a grandiose movement and let it hover over the enter key, taunting me.

I stretched out a hand toward the monitor as if I could physically stop him from pressing the key. "Wait. No, don't do it, Broodryk. Please. I… I beg you."

He laughed. "Oh my God, how wonderful. My last glimpse of your face will be one of desperation and fear. Things simply couldn't be better."

Suddenly a surprised look crossed his face. He slumped onto the keyboard and lay still. Elvis gasped as a familiar face came into focus on the monitor.

"Very nicely timed, if I do say so myself," Slash said. "Now get the hell out of that shack."

FORTY-THREE

A SHOUT OF joy sounded in my helmet. "This is Mother. Drop Team mission complete. Echo mission in Gabon complete. Alpha Star, what's your status?"

I couldn't stop staring at Slash's face. "Oh my God. It worked."

"It worked," Slash said gently. "Go, *cara*. Come home to me."

I bolted to my feet and spoke into my helmet. "We're okay in here. What's the plan?"

I suddenly realized that during the final moments with Broodryk, I had been unaware of the approaching sound of a helicopter—one that was clearly landing nearby.

Hands's voice came over my helmet. "Alpha Star, time to wrap up this party. Head directly for the chopper. Bravo Team, give your playmates a final goodbye and retreat to the bird. Charlie will cover you."

"Let's go," I shouted to Elvis. We could hardly hear each other over the loud whooping of the helicopter's rotors. The entire shack shuddered. I yelled directly in his ear. "Head straight for the copter. Okay?"

"Okay," he shouted back.

I took his hand, gripping it hard. I finally had him back and I wasn't going to lose him now. I reached up from a crouched position and flung open the door. No sense in offering a clear target to anyone with a scope on the door. I waited to see if anyone would shoot and when nothing happened, I grabbed Elvis's hand.

"Now," I shouted and pulled him out of the shack behind me.

I almost collided with Hands, who seized me by the arm.

"Go, go, go," he shouted at me. "I've got him."

He put an arm around Elvis and steadied him. We fell in line to board behind two guys dragging someone between them. A few other guys formed a protective ring around Elvis and me as we loaded.

I saw who the guys in front of me were carrying as they lifted him onto the helicopter.

"Hulk," I shouted.

One guy on the helicopter helped pull Hulk's form on board and then grabbed Elvis's hand, hauling him in as easily as lifting a grocery bag.

"Up you go, Keys." Hands lifted me off my feet and into the waiting hands of another SEAL. "I'm not leaving this time without you."

Once on the copter, I threaded my way back to Hulk, kneeling down beside him as a medic ripped the wrapping off of some kind of needle and jammed it in his neck.

"Is he okay?" I shouted. "Is he alive?"

The medic didn't pay any attention to me and kept working on Hulk. I turned around and saw Hands helping more guys onto the helicopter. There was a sudden ping over my head as a bullet penetrated the skin of the aircraft and bounced around reminding me that we were far from safe still.

"Where's Wills?" I shouted at him.

He pointed to the back of the helicopter where two people were knelt over a body. I staggered that way and dropped to my knees.

Stricken I looked up at one of the guys. "Is he dead?"

"Not yet," he yelled over the rotors. "But he's close.

He's lost a lot of blood. They've got a surgical team standing by for him if we can stabilize him en route."

Two more guys jumped on. We were taking heavy fire and one of the SEALs using a mounted gun got hit in the arm. To my amazement, he shifted to firing with one arm without even pausing.

"Lift off," I heard someone shout and we were airborne at last.

Hostiles were firing up at the helicopter, but it was too late for them to reach us now. I watched the shack below as a squad of militants swarmed it. My stomach heaved and I had to swallow the bile before I hurled. Where was Mr. Wastebasket when I needed him?

A soldier closed the helicopter doors as I crawled next to Elvis and linked fingers with him. Someone had handed him a blanket, which he'd thrown around his shoulders. He squeezed my hand and I took a good look at him. His face was a swollen mess of bruises and cuts, and his nose looked crooked.

"Hey, bud, you feeling okay?"

"I feel nothing short of euphoric to be alive. You came for me."

"Of course I did. Was there really any doubt?"

"I told you not to come. Or maybe you didn't hear that part."

"Oh, I heard it. But you should have known I'd come anyway. Wouldn't you have come for me?"

"Yes." He answered without hesitation.

"Well, there you go, then. Pretty simple."

He sighed. "If something would have happened to you—"

"It would have totally been worth it."

"No, it wouldn't have been, but there's no sense in arguing that now."

"There's not."

Elvis swallowed and I could see he was struggling to say something. "Lexi, is Xavier...okay? I don't remember a lot about the attack except he was screaming..."

"He's alive, Elvis. He's okay. He's in a hospital in Greece and has stabilized enough that he's going to be transferred back to the States soon. He'll probably get home before you. Slash arranged for private transportation from the Greek hospital he's been in to George Washington University hospital in DC, where he'll stay until he's ready to be discharged."

Elvis closed his eyes. His hands trembled. "I don't know what to say or how to thank you or Slash for everything you've done."

I put my head on his shoulder and he slid his arm out from beneath the blanket and put it around me. "Friends don't have to thank friends."

As soon as I said it, for the first time in my life, I truly, deeply understood it. Even more, I *appreciated* it.

Relationships, like the deep ones I had forged with Elvis, Slash, Xavier and Basia, were special. Despite the messiness, complexity and illogicality of them, I suddenly understood that I wouldn't have traded those relationships for anything. Not even my computer. I finally grasped that people, not my virtual reality, my IQ, or my skills at the keyboard, gave my life meaning. Relationships were by no means safer, logical or comfortable, but they *were* more profound and satisfying, which is perhaps the point of living after all.

Hands wedged in next to us. "Well done, Keys. Mother reported that Drop Team got Broodryk. Just like you planned."

"I heard. He didn't even know it was coming. It never crossed his mind that a girl could best him."

"You're not just a girl. You're a SEAL."

I appreciated his words more than he knew. "Right. I just haven't had time to savor the victory yet. But Slash was correct. Broodryk was in South Africa all along."

"So, the cyber team was able to trace his coordinates?"

"Yes, from the moment I plugged in to his IP-based camera. Our plan worked perfectly. Slash was able to follow a reverse ping that led directly back to Broodryk. Additional teams were on stand-by in several cities throughout South Africa. Slash and Gray always thought Broodryk wouldn't go far from home, and they were right. Since Slash's team was the one who actually got him, it means Broodryk was in Cape Town all along. He never even left his hometown."

"So, who'd they get in Gabon?"

"Gregor Muller, Broodryk's former partner. He's bad news, too, involved in assassinations, money laundering and all kinds of cybercrime. So, we got two for the price of one today."

"Impressive."

"More like lucky. It wouldn't have happened if the Washington bigwigs hadn't agreed to let Slash travel to South Africa. No one wanted to agree to it at first, but it was the only way. Other than me, Slash was the only one with the knowledge and capability to implement the technology to track Broodryk. Honestly, I don't think they would have agreed to let Slash go, but most members of the team didn't believe Broodryk was in South Africa. They thought Slash would be safe. That's why they let him go. But we knew better."

Elvis glanced at me. "Seriously? They let Slash in on a SEAL operation?"

"They sure did. Me, too." I shifted my body so he could see the SEAL pin on my collar. "I'm an honorary

SEAL. Elvis, meet Hands, our team leader. Hands, this is Elvis Zimmerman."

Hands reached across me and the two men shook hands.

"Looks like I owe a lot of people my life," Elvis said. "Thank you."

"Don't thank me." Hands jerked his thumb at me. "Thank her. It was all about you from the get go. She's the actual brains of the operation. I just shot at stuff."

I shook my head. "He did a lot more than that. They all did."

My heart clutched as I glanced over at Hulk and then Wills. The medics had placed blankets over both men and they were receiving fluids from handheld IV bags. I couldn't even begin to examine my role in their injuries. But seeing them lying there reminded me I still had an unanswered question for Hands.

"What happened with Pentz?"

Hands leaned back against the wall of the copter. "Once Wills took the bullet I was able to get a bead on him. I used the smoke and constant movement to keep him from settling. As soon as he started moving, I knew his big gun became a liability instead of an asset. It was touch and go at the end. Pentz ditched the gun and back-tracked, trying to ambush me with a pistol. Luckily a thorn bush snagged his shirt and made just enough noise to let me know his position. Before he could free himself, I reintroduced myself."

"He's dead?"

"Let me tell you something. True snipers plan to die with a rifle in their hand after they have expended every bit of ammunition. I didn't let Pentz have the satisfaction. He went to hell with a five-inch barrel and a fully loaded magazine."

I considered a moment and said the only thing I could think of that was appropriate. "Hooyah."

He nodded, his eyes somber. "Now you're getting it. You know, Keys, you did pretty good for a rookie SEAL. I'd be proud to serve with you again."

"No offense, but I think the Navy SEALs will operate far smoother without me."

"Possibly, but we wouldn't have near as much fun." He bumped my elbow. "By the way, did you know you have sand in your eyebrows?"

FORTY-FOUR

THERE WAS A medical unit standing by when the helicopter landed on the ship. Elvis didn't want me to leave his sight, so I stayed in the room on a chair next to his gurney while a medic worked on him. A medic attached an IV drip to his arm and gave him several shots. As his injuries were not as life threatening as the others', the medic told me his job would be to stabilize Elvis for the flight back to Camp Lemonnier. At this point, most of the medical team on the ship was involved in a desperate fight to save Wills and Hulk.

I could barely keep it together looking at the two men as the staff worked frantically to keep them alive. The smell of harsh antiseptic mingled with blood and sweat nauseated me, and the rush of the adrenaline had passed, leaving me shaky and exhausted. At some point, someone pressed a bottle of water in my hands and told me to drink it. I sipped it, keeping one hand touching Elvis at all times.

At some point the medic left Elvis and went to help the others. Elvis had been given some pain medication and apparently was feeling better.

He rolled his head sideways where he lay and looked at me. "Lexi, are you okay?"

I glanced over at the gurneys where Wills and Hulk were still being treated. "Not really. I want them to pull through and I'm terrified they won't. They're really great guys. I'm struggling with guilt. I sent Wills out to shoot the transponder. He got shot doing it on my orders. If he dies…that's on me."

Elvis held out a hand and I took it. "You can't blame yourself. This is all on Broodryk."

"Intellectually, I know. Really, I do. But I'm not good with it yet. I might never be. It's too hard to say at this point."

Elvis fell silent for a moment. "So, how did you do it? How did you bring down Broodryk?"

I released his hand and took a sip of my water. "It's a long and complicated story. The short version is that Broodryk was stringing us along the entire time. Apparently he thought he could pull off a double coup of teaching us, meaning you and me, a very public lesson about what happens to those who cross him while, at the same time, having us wipe out his competition. He sent us on a crazy clue hunt that required us to run around Africa trying to track him down."

"Really?"

"Really. Most of the team thought we had him after we ran a trace on a signal from a helmet camera perched atop of a sniper who was sent by Broodryk to hunt us in the Central African Republic. We were there looking for clues to your whereabouts. Anyway, those coordinates put Broodryk in a military-style compound in Gabon, which was well fortified and electronically wired to the max. It looked like a perfect hideout for him. But I didn't like the feel of it and neither did Slash. It seemed too directed, too easy.

"So, Slash, our CIA analyst Grayson Reese and I worked through it. We decided based on the information we'd pulled together that Broodryk was far more likely to be in South Africa in order to effectively manage an operation of this magnitude, especially Pruxrat, a network penetration virus he'd created and was threatening to release. Based on that hunch, Washington dispatched several SEAL teams around South Africa. Slash and another SEAL team flew to Broodryk's hometown of Cape Town yesterday and were standing by. It was a risky assumption, but it was based on the best intelligence, both human and cyber, we'd gathered.

"Then Slash and I came up with a plan to co-opt the camera feed as soon as I got into the shack. When we arrived, the SEALs threw a smoke grenade into the shack. While Broodryk's view was impaired, I put an interceptor on his IP-camera and plugged it into my laptop instead of his. Slash ran a reverse ping and, surprise, we had a real-time location on Broodryk just like that. As we suspected, Broodryk wasn't in Gabon. I found out later he'd helpfully provided us with the coordinates of his former partner and competitor in hopes that we would wipe him out and save him the trouble."

"So, Broodryk was in South Africa all along."

"Yes, right in downtown Cape Town. Slash and the team made it to his place with just moments to spare. I didn't think they would be in time to stop him from releasing the virus."

"Wow. Just wow. I'm going to need a lot more details later."

"You've got it."

I put my hand on Elvis's arm. "I need to tell you something else. I met your mom. I didn't mean to snoop in your private life, but I thought your family needed to be informed about what was happening to you and Xavier."

He blinked. "My mom?"

"I'm sorry. I tried to find info on your parents online, but I came up empty. So, I went to your house. Basia told me where the spare key was hidden and gave me the alarm code. I apologize…but I had to go through some of your papers until I found a trail to your mother. I really feel bad about it. It's just that under the circumstances, I thought your parents should know what was going on. I went to visit her, but in the end, I didn't tell her anything. I didn't want to upset her. I—I didn't know."

"It's okay, Lexi. She's not well. She hasn't been well for a long time."

"Actually, I liked her. Honestly, Elvis, I think she and I could be friends. Especially since she'd be one of the few people with whom I wouldn't have to worry about my conversation skills. We kind of understood each other in that way."

He smiled. "True."

"She asked me to bring you to her the next time I visited. I promised her I would. So, can I go with you the next time you go to see her? I also owe her some flowers and a book to make up for my grievous omission last time."

He studied my face. "Are you sure, Lexi?"

"Of course. I have no ambiguous feelings on this topic."

He smiled. "Then it's settled, I guess."

"I guess so. By the way, I also kept Bonnie apprised of your situation as much as I could. She was very worried. She really likes you."

"Thanks."

I paused, struggled with what I wanted to say, but knowing I had to say it. "Elvis, can I ask you something?"

"Always."

"Well, this whole dating thing…me with Slash and you with Bonnie. I think it's changing things between us. I suppose that's natural, but I'm afraid of losing your friendship. I don't know how to adapt to the situation, how I'm supposed to act, or whether you even want to be the same kind of friends we've always been. This is all new territory to me. The old Lexi would have just ignored it and gone back to my safety zone of gaming and programming. But that might mean I'd lose your friendship, and I've realized I don't want that to happen. The bottom line is I'm really struggling because I'm not sure what to do next. Do you want to stay friends? More importantly, *can* we stay friends?"

"Wow." He pressed his hand to his forehead. "Do I want that? Of course, I want that. You're the best friend I've ever had. You came halfway around the world for me. As to whether we can stay friends, I think that's up to you."

"Me?"

"Yes. I know it's a lot for you to juggle a boyfriend and a best friend who happens to be a guy. But I'm in if you are."

The breath I'd been holding rushed out. "Of course, I'm in. That's really great, Elvis. Let's make a deal that if we ever worry about the appropriateness of anything related to our friendship, we just ask each other straight up. No guessing, no games. Especially because we're both smarter than that."

"Truth."

"Then it's settled. It will be kind of like the blind leading the blind. Could be fun."

He grinned. "Could be. So, Lexi…this thing with Slash, it's serious?"

"Yeah, it's serious. He's pretty amazing."

Elvis reached out and linked fingers with me. "Then I'm happy for you. He's a good guy. Even better, he's good for you."

"He really is." I leaned down and gave him a quick,

careful hug. "Oh, Elvis, I'm so glad you're back. I couldn't imagine my life without you."

"Ditto." He reached up and touched my cheek. "I believe it was Helen Keller who said, 'Walking with a friend in the dark is better than walking alone in the light.' I can't imagine anyone else with whom I'd rather walk in the dark."

I smiled. "You've got that right."

FORTY-FIVE

CAPTAIN BISCHOFF, GRAY, Jason and the others were on hand to greet us when we landed at Camp Lemonnier. An ambulance was waiting and whisked Hulk, Wills, Elvis and a couple other SEALs who had received minor wounds away to the base hospital. Gray practically jumped in my arms, she was so happy to see me.

"You did it." She spun me around. "It worked. I can't believe you got Broodryk."

"*We* got Broodryk. Your assistance was invaluable. We got Muller, too. It was a good day's work, but we took some serious hits. I hope Wills and Hulk will be okay."

"I hope so, too. They've got a good medical staff here, Lexi. They'll do everything they can to save them."

"I know." We started to walk to the barracks. I desperately wanted a shower, food and six years of sleep.

"I can't believe how calm and focused you were. So cool under pressure. You never cracked."

"If you only knew how much that wasn't true. But thank you anyway."

She put an arm around my shoulder. "You're welcome. We did a lot of people a favor today."

THE FLIGHT BACK to Washington was uneventful, most likely due to the fact that I slept through a lot of it. Wills and Hulk were left at Camp Lemonnier until their injuries permitted them a medical evacuation to Germany and then finally back to the US. The good news was that while both men had suffered serious wounds, they were expected to fully recover. I was beyond relieved.

I'd been told Elvis had significant injuries, too. He suffered from severe dehydration, three broken ribs, a broken nose and cheekbone, a fractured elbow and some internal bruising. Broodryk hadn't wanted to damage his prize too badly, so Elvis had been spared worse. Of course, I had no idea of the psychological damage he'd suffered and how that would all play out.

Right now, I was simply thankful he was alive. We could work out anything else later.

The medical team at the base wanted to keep him for observation, but Elvis was adamant that he travel back to the States with me. Since he was medically stable enough to do so, the suits in Washington agreed to it.

I sat next to Elvis on the military plane home and introduced him to Gray and all the SEALs. Although Elvis seemed a bit overwhelmed by the attention, he listened intently to Hands's unabashed embellishment of the actions that led to his release. Even I couldn't help but laugh in certain places and be charmed by his story, though it had me single-handedly fighting off a group of bloodthirsty militants with my bare hands.

I was coming back from the bathroom at some point during the flight when Hands pulled me down into an empty seat next to him.

"I'd like to ask you something, Keys, before we go our separate ways."

"Sure. What's up?"

He bobbed his head toward Gray, who slept with her head back against the headrest, her mouth open. I was pretty sure she was snoring, possibly drooling.

"What do you think about a girl like her and a guy like me?"

"Wait—what? You're asking for relationship advice from me?"

"Well, you got to know her on the mission. I know she's way out of my league, but I hoped maybe we'd made some sort of connection."

For a moment I simply marveled. Hands was asking *me* for relationship advice. I tried to think how to answer appropriately. Instead I asked a question of my own.

"There are leagues?"

He snorted. "Yeah, like classy women and guys like me."

"Like you?"

"You know, working stiffs."

"I think you're classy."

He raised an eyebrow. "You do?"

"Sure. You are a decorated sniper and quite capable in your job. I'd probably go as far to say you exceed expectations in your work. Plus, you are honest and hardworking. All of those things are classy to me."

A smile crossed his face. "So, you think I have a chance with her?"

"Does that mean you intend to pursue her?"

"I'm thinking about it."

I glanced at Gray again. Her head had lolled sideways and she was definitely drooling. "That may be difficult. She hasn't had many successful relationships in the past."

"Well, it's not like I'm batting a thousand in that department either."

I looked between the two of them. "You know, and it's really odd for me to say this and even odder that I even *thought* about it in the first place, but I think you two might be good together."

"Really?"

"Really."

"Hey, would you put in a good word for me? That is, if you have any good words to say."

I considered. "I've never put in a good word for anyone before. Until now, that's been completely outside my area of expertise. I'm willing to give it a try, though. And yes, I've got at least a few good words to say."

"Thanks. I'd appreciate it."

We fell into a comfortable silence. There was something I'd been meaning to ask him, but the time had never been right. Now the timing was right, but I struggled to find the right words. Finally I just decided to ask.

"Hands, can I ask you something? You don't have to answer if you don't want to."

"Ask away."

"How do you do it? Day after day."

He didn't need me to clarify. He knew what I wanted to know. "Someone has to do it. Better that it's the good guys. We try to do it right."

"But how do you keep your sense of self intact? Your humanity? Your faith?"

"Those are a lot of weighty questions, Keys. You worried about me?"

"Yes, and if I'm being honest, I'm worried about me, too."

He shifted in his seat to face me. "Then let me say it this way: I'm okay with myself when I go to sleep at night. What I do isn't pretty and it isn't for the faint of heart. But someone has to be on the front lines doing what is right. If I didn't believe that, I wouldn't be here. So, this is how I see it. God, or whatever you believe is a higher moral authority, has an eye on the big picture— the greater good. For me, it's all in the details. Have I done right by that person, that situation? Hard to say, but so far, my conscience is clear."

I studied him. "You surprise me, Hands. There's a thoughtful man beneath that outward bravado."

He grinned. "Look, Keys, I want you to know that anytime you need my assistance, I'm at your service."

"Thanks. That's good to know. Likewise, I wish you the best of luck with all your future missions. I had no idea of how much danger you and your fellow SEALs put yourselves in day after day. I can only say I stand in awe of you and the others who serve so selflessly in the armed services. You have my sincere gratitude and respect."

He held out a fist. "Keep in touch. And for God's sake, stay out of trouble."

I bumped my knuckles to his, quoting the SEAL motto. "The only easy day was yesterday."

FORTY-SIX

UPON ARRIVING AT Andrews Air Force Base, we were met by the Assistant Director of the NSA and the Director of the Department of Homeland Security's Cybersecurity Center. They shook our hands, gave a little speech, and invited us to a reception to be held in our honor in one week. I wanted to attend the reception about as much as I wanted to jump from an airplane again, so I smiled and didn't commit to anything.

Some official had started speaking to me when I noticed a man nearby, leaning against the wall and watching me. Right in mid-conversation, without even excusing myself, I stepped away and broke into a run.

"Slash. You're here."

I jumped into his arms at full force. He held me tight, kissing my hair and cheeks and murmuring things to me in Italian.

"Nowhere else I'd rather be, *cara*."

"Oh, it's so good to see you. I'm glad you came."

"Why wouldn't I?" He pulled away and cupped my cheeks. "Hey, you're crying."

"Tears of happiness, I guess."

He flicked away the tears with the pads of his thumbs and then pulled me into another hug, resting his chin on the top of my head. "*Mio dio.* You have no idea how good it is to see you, to hold you again."

"Likewise. You were great, Slash. Brilliant. We saved Elvis. We shut down Broodryk. We did it."

"*Si*, we did."

"I wasn't sure our plan would work. What if Broodryk hadn't been in South Africa? What if you and the team hadn't made it to his compound in time? What if I'd misjudged the electronic set-up in the shack? There were so many variables that could have gone wrong that it's mindboggling."

"Sometimes, *cara*, things line up and the good guys win. It doesn't happen all the time. In fact, it doesn't happen as often as it should. But this time it did."

"I heard that Washington gave orders to try and take Broodryk alive."

Slash shrugged. "*Try* being the operative word. There wasn't time for a vote, so I did what I thought best. He was nanoseconds from releasing the virus."

I considered his words. "You did the right thing. Were you able to secure all his computer equipment?"

"It's already at the NSA."

"Oh, Slash, I'm so glad you're okay."

"I am now that you're here with me. That's all that matters. That's all that ever mattered."

"No, that's not all. You matter. You matter to me."

I studied his face. He'd gotten some sleep. He looked tired, but the exhaustion and intense stress I'd seen before I'd left was gone. He was freshly shaved and smelled wonderful, as always. The strains of worry around his eyes had eased, and a smile settled on his lips. He looked at me and I saw love there. He'd *said* he'd loved me before, but how was it that until now I'd never really *seen* it?

"You love me."

He raised an eyebrow. "*Si*. I love you."

"I like hearing that. At first it scared me because I wasn't sure what you meant by it. But here's the deal. I get it now. And I think I love you, too. I'm not sure what all that entails or where it's headed, but when you came to the airport to see me off—when you made your decision to stay with me—*that's* what mattered.

He stared at me as if he couldn't believe my words.

"You...love me?"

When I smiled, his expression and posture relaxed. His brown eyes warmed as he lowered his mouth to mine for a long kiss.

I wound my arms around his neck and held on tight. After a bit, he pulled away and gently cupped my cheek with his hand.

"Now what?" he asked.

"Now I want you come to dinner again. Let's go back to my parents' house, not because they're making me ask you, but because I want to integrate you into that part of my life. There is a high statistical probability they'll do exactly the same annoying stuff they did before, but I still want us to go. Because we're a team, and I know what that means now. It means we'll always stand together, even when my parents are watching."

His face softened as he looked at me. "I'd be honored. But first, right now, I want to have you all to myself. So, what do you say, *cara*? Are we done here?"

I glanced over my shoulder where Hands, Gray and the other SEALs were talking with dignitaries. Elvis was being transferred to a stretcher. Our eyes met across the room. He gave me a smile and a thumbs-up. I gave him one back.

My world had righted.

Turning, I leaned into the warmth that was Slash. "Absolutely. Let's go home. Mission out."

* * * * *

REQUEST YOUR FREE BOOKS!
2 FREE NOVELS PLUS 2 FREE GIFTS!

HARLEQUIN®

I N T R I G U E

BREATHTAKING ROMANTIC SUSPENSE

YES! Please send me 2 FREE Harlequin® Intrigue novels and my 2 FREE gifts (gifts are worth about $10). After receiving them, if I don't wish to receive any more books, I can return the shipping statement marked "cancel." If I don't cancel, I will receive 6 brand-new novels every month and be billed just $4.74 per book in the U.S. or $5.49 per book in Canada. That's a savings of at least 12% off the cover price! It's quite a bargain! Shipping and handling is just 50¢ per book in the U.S. and 75¢ per book in Canada.* I understand that accepting the 2 free books and gifts places me under no obligation to buy anything. I can always return a shipment and cancel at any time. Even if I never buy another book, the two free books and gifts are mine to keep forever.

182/382 HDN GH3D

Name _____ (PLEASE PRINT)

Address _____ Apt. #

City _____ State/Prov. _____ Zip/Postal Code

Signature (if under 18, a parent or guardian must sign)

Mail to the **Reader Service:**
IN U.S.A.: P.O. Box 1867, Buffalo, NY 14240-1867
IN CANADA: P.O. Box 609, Fort Erie, Ontario L2A 5X3
**Are you a subscriber to Harlequin® Intrigue books
and want to receive the larger-print edition?
Call 1-800-873-8635 or visit www.ReaderService.com.**

* Terms and prices subject to change without notice. Prices do not include applicable taxes. Sales tax applicable in N.Y. Canadian residents will be charged applicable taxes. Offer not valid in Quebec. This offer is limited to one order per household. Not valid for current subscribers to Harlequin Intrigue books. All orders subject to credit approval. Credit or debit balances in a customer's account(s) may be offset by any other outstanding balance owed by or to the customer. Please allow 4 to 6 weeks for delivery. Offer available while quantities last.

Your Privacy—The Reader Service is committed to protecting your privacy. Our Privacy Policy is available online at www.ReaderService.com or upon request from the Reader Service.

We make a portion of our mailing list available to reputable third parties that offer products we believe may interest you. If you prefer that we not exchange your name with third parties, or if you wish to clarify or modify your communication preferences, please visit us at www.ReaderService.com/consumerchoice or write to us at Reader Service Preference Service, P.O. Box 9062, Buffalo, NY 14240-9062. Include your complete name and address.

HI15

REQUEST YOUR FREE BOOKS!
2 FREE NOVELS PLUS 2 FREE GIFTS!

ⓗ HARLEQUIN®

ROMANTIC suspense

Sparked by danger, fueled by passion

YES! Please send me 2 FREE Harlequin® Romantic Suspense novels and my 2 FREE gifts (gifts are worth about $10). After receiving them, if I don't wish to receive any more books, I can return the shipping statement marked "cancel." If I don't cancel, I will receive 4 brand-new novels every month and be billed just $4.74 per book in the U.S. or $5.49 per book in Canada. That's a savings of at least 12% off the cover price! It's quite a bargain! Shipping and handling is just 50¢ per book in the U.S. and 75¢ per book in Canada.* I understand that accepting the 2 free books and gifts places me under no obligation to buy anything. I can always return a shipment and cancel at any time. Even if I never buy another book, the two free books and gifts are mine to keep forever.

240/340 HDN GH3P

Name	(PLEASE PRINT)	
Address		Apt. #
City	State/Prov.	Zip/Postal Code

Signature (if under 18, a parent or guardian must sign)

Mail to the **Reader Service:**
IN U.S.A.: P.O. Box 1867, Buffalo, NY 14240-1867
IN CANADA: P.O. Box 609, Fort Erie, Ontario L2A 5X3

Want to try two free books from another line?
Call 1-800-873-8635 or visit www.ReaderService.com.

* Terms and prices subject to change without notice. Prices do not include applicable taxes. Sales tax applicable in N.Y. Canadian residents will be charged applicable taxes. Offer not valid in Quebec. This offer is limited to one order per household. Not valid for current subscribers to Harlequin Romantic Suspense books. All orders subject to credit approval. Credit or debit balances in a customer's account(s) may be offset by any other outstanding balance owed by or to the customer. Please allow 4 to 6 weeks for delivery. Offer available while quantities last.

Your Privacy—The Reader Service is committed to protecting your privacy. Our Privacy Policy is available online at www.ReaderService.com or upon request from the Reader Service.

We make a portion of our mailing list available to reputable third parties that offer products we believe may interest you. If you prefer that we not exchange your name with third parties, or if you wish to clarify or modify your communication preferences, please visit us at www.ReaderService.com/consumerchoice or write to us at Reader Service Preference Service, P.O. Box 9062, Buffalo, NY 14240-9062. Include your complete name and address.

HRS15

REQUEST YOUR FREE BOOKS!

2 FREE NOVELS
FROM THE SUSPENSE COLLECTION
PLUS 2 FREE GIFTS!

YES! Please send me 2 FREE novels from the Suspense Collection and my 2 FREE gifts (gifts are worth about $10). After receiving them, if I don't wish to receive any more books, I can return the shipping statement marked "cancel." If I don't cancel, I will receive 4 brand-new novels every month and be billed just $6.49 per book in the U.S. or $6.99 per book in Canada. That's a savings of at least 19% off the cover price. It's quite a bargain! Shipping and handling is just 50¢ per book in the U.S. and 75¢ per book in Canada.* I understand that accepting the 2 free books and gifts places me under no obligation to buy anything. I can always return a shipment and cancel at any time. Even if I never buy another book, the two free books and gifts are mine to keep forever.

191/391 MDN GH4Z

Name	(PLEASE PRINT)

Address	Apt. #

City	State/Prov.	Zip/Postal Code

Signature (if under 18, a parent or guardian must sign)

Mail to the **Reader Service**:
IN U.S.A.: P.O. Box 1867, Buffalo, NY 14240-1867
IN CANADA: P.O. Box 609, Fort Erie, Ontario L2A 5X3

Want to try two free books from another line?
Call 1-800-873-8635 or visit www.ReaderService.com.